THREE

CAL ROGAN MYSTERIES BOOK 4

ROBERT P. FRENCH

FOREWORD

Thank you for purchasing *Three* the fourth Cal Rogan Mystery. At the end of the book there is additional information and contact details.

ACKNOWLEDGMENTS

So many people go into the writing of a book and I would like to thank those who helped me with *Three*.

A big thank you goes to Sergeant Lyndsay Irwin of the Royal Canadian Mounted Police, that wonderful Canadian organization which helps to make this one of the safest countries in the world. She filled me in on some details of police procedure that were really helpful. Any mistakes I made in that area are 100% mine. Thanks too to my good friend Don Siemens for his advice in an area which I won't mention here because it might be a spoiler.

Most of all, a thousand thanks to every single member of my Launch Team for your support. You guy's rock!! I would like especially to thank the following members of the team who helped me hone the plot and whose eagle eyes found errors missed in the proofread. I made some significant changes based on your feedback. You all made this a better book. Alphabetically: Alice Campbell, Andrew Tucker, Beverley Canuel, Cindy Warrick, Connie Charron, Eleanor Andersen, Eva Beaton, Francine Bloom, Gina Hines, Helen Heald, Janet Cline, Jeffrey Benham, Kathy Lindback, Larry Branson, Linda Dimezza, Linda Harbour, Lisa Mauk, Lorraine Garant, Mel Calaby, Reg Allen, Roz Wood, Sheryl Korljan, Sue Ann Kelly, Susan Brauner, Susan Sullivan and Terry Cochran. I apologize if I missed anyone.

As always, I would also like to thank the Vancouver Public Library for providing the perfect working location for any writer. Every word of *Three* was written here.

Dedication

To my wonderful wife Penny who believed in me when I had stopped believing in myself.

ALSO BY ROBERT P. FRENCH

Junkie (Cal Rogan Mysteries Book 1)

Oboe (Cal Rogan Mysteries Book 2)

Lockstep (Cal Rogan Mysteries Book 3)

Cabal (Cal Rogan Mysteries Book 5)

Captive (Cal Rogan Mysteries Book 6)

Jailed (Cal Rogan Mysteries Book 7)

All are available in large print paperback from Amazon.

1

TOMÁS

MONDAY

I have some strange news *Patrón*." He has difficulty with the last word. For him *Patrón* was always my father. He will learn. My father was quite clear that I would be the one to succeed him if anything happened but these people need more than my father's instructions. They will need to respect and fear me as they did him. Javier, as the number two man in the Santiago organization, is the key. I look at him and give an almost imperceptible nod.

"Our lawyer says that a man was arrested and charged with the murder of your father, the politician and the Bookman," he says.

I avoid showing any surprise. "That's not possible. You and I were both on the boat that night. We killed the assassin. Both of us saw his boat explode and sink." He must be dead. Except for one small thing: our lawyer has always been completely reliable.

"I told the lawyer that. But..." he shrugs.

A wave of uncertainty passes through me but he doesn't see it; I have too much control. We killed the man trying to escape. I'm sure of that but maybe there was more than one assassin.

"Did the lawyer tell you the man's name?"

"Yes *Patrón*. It's a strange name: California Rogan."

"Get back to the lawyer. Tell him I want to know everything there is to know about Mr. California Rogan. Get our own people on it too. If he was involved in the killing of my father, he's going to repay the debt with a very high rate of interest."

"Yes *Patrón*, immediately." The word came more easily to his lips this time. He's starting to learn I am a worthy successor to head the Santiago empire, perhaps even better than my father.

He leaves. Now to get back to the task of rebuilding that empire following the loss of our headquarters on Samuel Island. Sadly, we can never return there. But I can rebuild. It's what I was born to do and trained to do.

If this California Rogan had a hand in your death, I will avenge you *Papa*.

2

STAMMO

We don't get a lot of clients looking like this one, that's for sure. She's one of the rich ones Rogan's limey buddy often sends us. Not that I'm complaining; we made a fortune out of that Bradbury woman for finding her kid. And this one looks like she can spare a buck or two. I wonder what she needs us to do. I can't help noticing her looks. She's like a model but right now she looks troubled and sad. I smile at Adry and wheel over to where the client's sitting.

"Good afternoon. Ms. Summers?" I ask.

"Mr. Rogan?" she smiles. It's a real warm smile and it brightens up the whole reception area.

"No," I manage to say through the catch in my throat. "I'm Nick Stammo, his partner." The last word brings the flood of emotions I can't seem to shake. I push them down. "Cal's been delayed so I'll be taking the details of your case." Delayed, that's a polite word for it.

She puts out her hand. "Marly Summers," she says. Her hand's cool and slim but her grip's firm. I find myself wanting to just hold on to it. It's something steady.

"Nice to meet you," I say. "Before we start, would you like a coffee or water?"

"Do you have tea?" She smiles again and doesn't seem to be annoyed that Rogan's not here.

Before I can ask, Adry gets up from her spot behind the reception desk and says, "We have English Breakfast, Earl Grey and some herbal teas. What would you like?"

"Earl Grey would be lovely; black please."

Adry goes off to our office kitchen.

"Well, follow me please," I say, wheeling toward the tiny conference room we use on the odd time a client comes to the office. Rather than follow, she takes an extra step and walks along beside me.

"Arnold Young spoke very highly of your firm," she says uncertainly, "I feel rather embarrassed talking to a detective agency."

From some people I might not like that sort of talk; it's like there's something shady about us. But from her it was said OK.

I look up at her and smile. "Don't worry. We're

very discreet. You don't need to worry that anyone will even know you've been here."

I wheel up to the conference room door. "After you," I say. She pushes the door, walks in and holds it open for me. Damn wheelchair. I'd give anything to hold the door open for her, or for anyone for that matter.

She sits down and smooths her skirt. The movement's elegant, like her. I need to focus on business now. "How can I help you?" I ask.

She looks at me for a moment and smiles nervously. "You'll probably think I'm being very silly," she blushes.

"I promise you I won't," I say just a bit too quickly, wondering why this woman is making me nervous. "Just tell me what's worrying you," I manage to say.

She smiles again but this time she just looks sad. She pauses for a second or two, takes a breath and then the words tumble out. "It's my husband. Something's wrong but he won't talk to me about it. I think he may be having an affair or maybe I'm just being paranoid. Maybe it's something at work. I've tried so hard to get him to open up and tell me but he insists nothing's wrong. But I know there is and I need to find out what it is. I need you to find out for me."

I can see a hint of tears starting in her eyes. I

lean forward and push a box of tissues toward her. We get a few tears in this room.

"You did the right thing to come to us," I say. "I doubt he's having an affair." I can't imagine your average man would have an affair if he had her as a wife. I want to tell her this but I know for sure it would come out all bollixed up. Talking to women has never been my strong point. "Tell me what he's been doing that has you worried." There's something in her face I can't quite read. Maybe this is more than the usual cheating husband case.

"He's always worked hard but recently he's been staying late at the office and sometimes he doesn't even come home. If I ask him about it, he just says they're slammed at work and he's got to put in the hours if he's going to make partner. He's a Chartered Accountant."

Her words stir up a bit of guilt in me. I said the same stuff to my ex when I was fooling around on her, except it was to make sergeant, not partner. "When he comes home late, does he smell of alcohol?"

"Sometimes. He usually says he just went for a beer with one of his colleagues. But he's never drunk. Dale's not much of a drinker."

"Does he ever smell of perfume?"
She shakes her head. "Never."

Nor did I. It makes me wonder if it's the same thing with Dale.

"So what makes you think something's wrong?" Maybe she *is* just being paranoid. She looks at the box of tissues and takes another one but just holds it in her hand, worrying it with her fingers. Now we're getting to it and I'm betting I know what she's going to say. I give her time.

She's just about to speak when Adry walks in with coffee, tea and my favourite cookies. Everything's on a tray with elegant china cups, saucers and plates. Adry made me spring for them. *'You can't serve clients out of paper cups or those disgusting old mugs you and Cal use,'* she insisted.

When Adry leaves, I prompt her, "You were saying..."

She sips her tea once... then again... then nibbles at a cookie until finally she speaks. "He's stopped, you know... having relations with me." I was right. Something must be seriously wrong. She moves the tissue to her face and wipes away a tear trickling down beside her nose.

"Don't jump to the wrong conclusion," I say in an attempt to comfort her. "It may just be the pressure of work. Some of those accounting firms are pretty high pressure places. Sometimes the stress of—"

"It's been over a year since he..."

"Oh... I'm sorry." It's all I can think to say.

She wipes her eyes and blows her nose, then smiles at me but all I can see is her sadness. "Anyway, he hasn't been home since Thursday morning. I've texted him several times and all I got was 'I'm working'; he hasn't even replied to the last two. It's the first time he's been gone so long." She takes another tissue. "Yesterday was our fifth wedding anniversary."

What a bastard! My heart really goes out to this woman. It makes me wonder if I hurt my ex this much when I was fooling around on her. I hope not. She was no angel herself, probably still isn't, but nobody deserves this kind of pain. I'm gonna make sure we get everything there is to know on this woman's husband so she can sue the ass off him.

I grab a notepad and pen off the table. "What's his full name?" I ask.

She hesitates for a moment, knowing this is the point of no return. She takes a deep breath. "Matthew Dale Summers, but he goes by Dale." I pull the notepad onto my lap and start to take notes. "He's a manager at Beloff and Plasker," she continues. He must be good. They're one of the big five accounting firms, a detail I never knew as a cop but have learned about since Rogan and me started the agency. She gives me all the usual details: addresses, there are three, a West Van house on the waterfront, must be five million at least, weekend places in Whistler and on Salt Spring Island, two prime destinations for Vancouver's rich and famous; date of birth; email addresses and phone numbers; Social Insurance Number; social media handles; cars and license plates, a Merc and a Lamborghini, both with personalized plates, must be nice; favourite restaurants and bars which I know are all expensive hangouts.

I'm going to ask the obvious question but I need to word it just right. "You seem to be uh... quite wealthy, so I need to ask you this because it could be important and I hope you won't take offence How do you afford all this when your husband earns what, a hundred and twenty, a hundred and fifty grand a year?"

She gives an awkward little smile but there's no humour in it. "Dale's from the Summers family who own the hotels."

Enough said. Everyone in the world knows the Summers hotel chain. "So why the hell does he work for a CA firm?" It's out of my mouth before I even think about it. "Sorry, I hope that wasn't..."

"No problem Mr. Stammo, it's a fair question." She smiles and I feel something I haven't felt for a long while. It makes me doubt everything; doubt my reason for finally leaving my ex; doubt my reason for quitting the OPP in Toronto and coming out to

Vancouver; doubt the fact that... She rescues me from my thoughts. "Dale's money comes from a trust which his late father set up. However, Dale does not get on with the rest of his family, especially his older brother Luke, who's CEO of Summers Holdings. He won't have anything to do with them and he feels he has to make his own mark in the world and decided being a partner in a CA firm would be a good first step."

"That makes sense." I don't know if it does but it's the only thing I can think to say.

"Is there anything else you need to know?"

"I don't think..." I start to say then realize I almost forgot the obvious question; I must be losing it. "Why is he estranged from his family?"

She pauses and the smooth skin of her forehead wrinkles. "You know, it may sound strange but I don't really know. He says things like 'we never got on' or 'I was always the odd one out' but he's never really discussed it with me. I've never met any of them. He's really very private. It's why I need you to find out what's going on with him."

It does sound strange. Surely if you met and fell in love with someone like her you'd tell her everything. I'm beginning to wonder if there's something very big and very wrong in Dale Summers' relationship with his family. Maybe it's at the bottom of his problem.

I take a business card from the breast pocket of my jacket and slide it across the table to her. "Please call me as soon as he returns home. I promise we'll find out what's going on with him." Another rule broken: never promise anything to a client except best efforts. What the hell, it's the least of the rules we've broken in the last couple of weeks. "Oh, and please can you email me a recent photo?"

She puts my card in her purse and removes two items which she slides across the table to me. "Your retainer as outlined in your email and a recent photo of Dale."

"Thank you." I resist the temptation to look at the cheque. I just put both items on the notepad on my lap and put the pen on top.

As she stands, I wrangle the conference room door open. It's one of the tricks I've learned to do in a wheelchair but I can only do it from inside the room.

She walks through the door and as I follow, I almost run into the back of her. She's stopped in the hallway face to face with Rogan. It's the first time I've seen him since Matt's funeral. A perfect storm of emotions starts to boil up inside me.

3

CAL

My continent of beauty. Shakespeare must have been thinking of this woman when he penned those words. But for all that, I wish she weren't here; it's Stammo I need to talk to right now. I force my eyes from hers to Stammo's. I can't get a read on him.

He looks up at her. "Ms. Summers, this is my partner Cal Rogan."

She extends her hand. I take it and enjoy the firmness of her shake, which is over more quickly than I would have liked.

"Nice to meet you," I say. It sounds inane. I wanted to leave a better first impression.

She just smiles. Wow!

She turns and looks down at Stammo. "Thank you so much for being such a good listener."

Stammo grins like a kid. "My pleasure, we'll be in touch very soon. And don't worry I'm sure it's gonna be OK." If I didn't know better, I'd say he was blushing.

She touches him gently on the shoulder, says, "Thank you Nick," gives me another smile, smiles at Adriana—our new receptionist, office manager and all-round factotum—and lets herself out the main door.

I kick myself for not thinking faster and opening the door for her.

The silence left by her departure is broken by Adriana. "Nice to have you back Cal."

"Yes, thanks, it's nice to be back." Nice is a huge understatement. A week in a jail cell at the Surrey Pretrial Centre seems to have robbed me of my vocabulary.

"Let's talk." Stammo wheels his chair into the main office area and parks himself behind his desk. I sit at mine.

Keeping my voice quiet so Adriana won't hear, I say, "They dropped the first two murder charges, for the moment anyway. No evidence, thanks to your planning." I look at him for a reaction. None. "We admitted I was on the island but just to find evidence that Ariel was actually there." He just nods but gives nothing away. "The third charge still stands but Jim Garry, my lawyer, says that with your evidence, any judge will agree it was self-defence and find me not guilty."

He nods again but this time he says, "OK."

"Thanks for doing the affidavit, by the way. It was the thing that convinced the judge to give me bail."

He looks down at his desktop and nods for the third time.

All the things I thought about while sitting in my cell start to bubble to the surface. "Listen Nick, about Matt, I just want to say—"

"NO." His tone of voice cuts me off. "I can't talk about that right now." I can see the emotions wrestling on his face but I can't begin to read each one of them. All I can see is an overwhelming sadness.

"I'm sorry Nick." It's little more than a whisper.

He shakes his head. "Let's talk about the new case." He takes a notepad off his lap, puts it on his desk and looks at the cheque lying on top. "Remind me to tell Adry to deposit this." We hired Adriana when her former boss went to jail awaiting trial on charges of child pornography and voyeurism offences During the week I was in jail, Stammo seems to have forged a good relationship with her. Just as I think it, she brings in two coffees and two plates of those half-chocolate digestive cookies Stammo loves.

She takes the cheque and says, "If it's OK with you guys, I'll go down to the bank and deposit this before they close." She leaves us alone.

"Right," says Stammo through a mouthful of cookie, "I'd better update you on what's happened with our cases while you've been goofing off on vacation."

For the moment at least, it's business as usual.

———

I STAND before the door undecided. I know the smell of jail is on me and on my clothing but this can't wait. On the other side are the two people I love most in the world: my daughter Ellie and my ex-wife Sam. The last time I was here it was blissful. Now I have no idea of the welcome I'll get. Finally I summon up the courage to ring the doorbell. I can hear it ringing in the house but that's all I can hear.

I ring again.

Silence.

I should have called first but was afraid I might get rebuffed. *Thus conscience does make cowards of us all.*

I press my nose to the stained glass semi-circle in the door. The distorted view of the hallway looks bare. It's as if they don't live here any more. My heart speeds at the thought. Is it my worst fear? Has Sam taken Ellie and just left? When I was taken into custody accused of killing three people, the look on Sam's face was stricken and during my week at the pretrial centre she made no attempt to contact me, let alone visit. Could the knowledge that the man she fell back in love with is a stone cold killer have shattered any possibility of me being in her life?

I walk across the verandah to the door of Sam's neighbour I ring and it's answered almost immediately.

"Hello Detective Rogan. How are you?" Cora Hunt has either forgotten or never knew that I'm no longer a VPD detective.

"I'm fine thank you Mrs. Hunt. I'm looking for Sam and Ellie, do you know if they will be gone long?"

She look puzzled. "Didn't you know?" she asks.

I feel my heart sink into my gut. "Know what?"

Her puzzlement morphs to confusion and then fluster. "Oh, dear! If she didn't tell you it's hardly my place to—"

"Please Mrs. Hunt, I need to know where they are. Has something happened to one of them?" She can hear the note of panic in my voice.

"Oh, dear!" her compassion is fighting with her loyalty. "Oh, dear!" Then compassion wins out. "Sam has some trouble. I don't exactly know what it is but she left a few days ago saying she wouldn't be back for a while. She asked me to take in any deliveries she might receive."

"Do you know what sort of trouble? Was it her MS?"

"No nothing like that and nothing to do with Ellie so you don't need to worry on her account. It was something else. She didn't exactly say but I have a sneaking suspicion it might have been something to do with money."

This is not making sense to me. "When was this? When did they leave?"

"Let me think... it was early last week, Monday or Tuesday." She knits her brow. "Tuesday," she decides. "Almost a week ago." Three days after I was taken into custody. Now it's making sense. The knowledge that I'm a killer is what has decided her to run away with Ellie. She took three days to get organized and now she's gone.

"Do you know where she went, Mrs. Hunt?"

She blinks twice. "No." She's a poor liar but a good person and I hate to pressure her but I must.

"Please I have to know she's safe. I must know where she is."

"I'm sorry, if she hasn't told you, I don't feel I can."

My gut is in turmoil. "Please Mrs. Hunt."

"I'm sorry." She closes the door and I hear the deadbolt click into place.

I can feel rising panic but one thought keeps pushing to the fore: you're a detective, if anyone can find them, you can.

4

CAL
TUESDAY

As I step off the elevator, I'm impressed by the silence. There's a seating area with leather chairs, sofas and elegant coffee tables and a double reception desk backed by a black marble wall bearing the logo and name proclaiming to the world that this palace is the domain of Beloff and Plasker, Chartered Accountants. There's a glass spiral staircase leading down to the floor below. A while back I would have felt intimidated by an office like this but in my last few cases, both in and out of the VPD, I sparred with some very sketchy criminals who inhabited such places.

I'm wondering whether I will be able to find out anything useful from the gatekeepers.

"How may I help you?" The younger of the two receptionists gives me a big smile.

"Good morning, I'm John Falstaff." I smile, partly at her and partly at my choice of the first pseudonym that popped into my mind. "I have an appointment with Dale Summers."

She examines her computer screen, taps a few keys and frowns. "You're not in his calendar. Are you sure it was for today."

"Very sure. Maybe you could check with him."

"His calendar shows he's in a meeting." Her frown deepens. She turns to her more senior cohort. "Maddie, did you just see Mike Jarvis leave the office?"

"Yes, he went to a client meeting."

"It says here he's in a meeting with Dale."

Maddie clicks her mouse a few times. "Huh," she announces, "He's not logged into the system. Let me check with Janine."

"That's Mr. Summers' personal assistant," the younger one informs me, *sotto voce*.

Maddie's slightly wrinked brow becomes more puzzled as she speaks with Janine. "Well, there's a Mr. John Falstaff here who says he has an appointment with him."

I see my chance. "I wonder if I might talk with Janine?" I ask.

"Hold on Janine, the gentleman would like to speak to you." She directs me to one of the coffee tables with a telephone on it. "I'll put you through to her."

I stay put. "I'm afraid it's rather a confidential matter, I wonder if I might speak with her in person."

Maddie clearly takes her job as gatekeeper seriously. She hesitates for a moment so I give her my best smile and she caves. "Could you come up to sixteenth floor reception and speak with him? He says it's a confidential matter." Her tone of voice puts the last two words in quotes but after a pause she says to me. "Take a seat, she'll be right up."

Just out of orneriness I stay standing.

I go through in my mind my initial attempts to try and track down Sam and Ellie. Sam's step-father just flat wouldn't tell me anything. He clearly knows something but he also knows I was accused of murder—a fact he revealed with some relish—and his advice before he hung up on me was, "Just stay out of their lives." I can't help wondering if they're holed up with Sam's parents. But the thought of staking out their place feels a bit too much like stalking. Maybe if I get desperate enough...

I've received no response to my texts and emails and a search of Sam's and Ellie's social media accounts revealed nothing. There was nothing on Sam's website to give any clue. I don't relish the idea of getting Stammo involved but I will need his help trying to track Sam via her digital footprint.

On top of my worry for Sam and Ellie, when I got home last night I found out my apartment had been searched. The place was a mess and there was a search warrant on the dining table. I wonder if—

My thoughts are suspended as I see a woman of about my age come up the spiral staircase clutching a small spiral notebook and a pen. After we introduce ourselves, I ask if we might talk privately and she leads me into a small meeting room.

"How may I help you Mr. Falstaff?" she asks without offering me a seat.

I need to take charge of the conversation. I just look at her for a moment as if trying to make a decision about her. Just as she starts to look a little flustered, I ask her, "Has Mr. Summers gone missing?"

"How do you—?" She cuts herself off quickly, then amends the question. "Why do you ask?"

"Why don't you sit down." I suggest in a tone that says I might have some bad news for her. I feel a twinge of guilt. She seems like a nice person but I need to get to some truth about Dale Summers.

She complies and I sit opposite her.

"I'm a friend of Dale's and I'm worried about him." As always I wonder at how easy it is for me to lie to witnesses. "When was the last time you saw him?"

"Friday afternoon."

I just nod and stay silent. People can't stand silences, they just have to fill them.

As does she. "He spent the afternoon in a meeting with one of our US clients. They left at about four and he told me the meeting went very well and that he was going to have a celebratory after-work drink at the Railway Club. Quite often the managers meet there on Fridays."

Her words say it was all normal but there's something in her face that belies it. I cock my head on one side and give her a slightly puzzled look.

Again she fills the silence. "Well, the thing is, after client meetings, he would always come back to his office and review any notes he'd taken, maybe scan them and maybe email a summary of the meeting to the partner responsible for the client. But on Friday, he asked me to log him off his computer and he just left. He's never done that before. Never."

I nod wisely and say, "That makes sense." Now *she* has the puzzled look. "I've noticed recently Dale has been behaving a bit, how shall I say... erratically." She nods unconsciously. "Has it been the same at work?"

She leans forward and glances through the glass wall of the meeting room as if someone outside might be able to see what she was saying. "Well, yes.

He has been rather moody which is not like him at all."

"I've noticed that," I tell her. She nods and smiles at the validation.

"Not only that," she adds, "but recently he has left early some afternoons for outside meetings with clients but hasn't logged the hours on his billing forms. When I questioned him about it he said it was a marketing meeting, or that he was dealing with a client problem which wasn't billable. But even so, he should *show* that on the forms." She looks crestfallen. "I marked them in as visits to the dentist."

"You're a good friend to him," I tell her.

"I try to be."

"Was there anything else?" I ask.

"Not that I can think of."

Well she's not offering so I'm going to ask, "Change of mood is often an indicator of something specific. Do you think it's possible there's another woman in his life?"

She looks shocked. "Dale? No. He would never. No, not Dale." Her emphatic response waves a little red flag.

"How can you be so sure?"

She looks at me. I can't quite read her expression. Suspicion maybe?

Finally she answers, "I just am."

Without thinking it through I ask, "Did you and he ever—"

"Certainly not!" she snaps and stands up. "I don't know who you are. Any friend of Dale's would know there could never be another woman in his life except Marly. As far as I'm concerned this interview is over."

"OK. Look, I really apologize if I offended you. I didn't mean to." I stand up. "Listen, if I track him down I'll tell him to call you."

"Thank you." She's tight lipped and quivering with anger.

We say our goodbyes and I leave with the suspicion that Marly Summers' worst fears are in fact right: her husband's having an affair, maybe with the woman standing glaring after me.

But maybe I'll know more this evening.

5

STAMMO

Something's up with Rogan. I've known him too damn long to not see when he's worried. I've also known him too damn long to bother asking him, he'll get to it when he gets to it. I just hope he doesn't try and talk about Matt again. It's not my job to soothe his damn conscience. Besides, I've got a worry of my own and I don't know whether to share it with him or not.

"So what did you find out about Dale Summers?" he asks.

It's a more interesting question than he suspects. "He's an anomaly," I say.

"How so?"

"He's twenty-nine, rich, in a solid profession, married to a doctor—yes, she's a doctor, she just qualified—and yet he has a tiny digital footprint.

Unless he's using a pseudonym, he's not on Facebook, Instagram or Twitter. He's got a LinkedIn account but he hardly ever posts anything and when he does it's only about work, all pretty standard stuff."

"What about other stuff?" he asks.

"Nothing there. He's never been in trouble with the law, not even a parking ticket. He's got a great credit rating. His family has more money than God and none of them seem to be in any sort of difficulties, legal or otherwise. I tried to find out why he's estranged from them; I had a good dig in all the tabloid and fake news websites but there's nothing except one whack-job site claims his brother's one of the lizard people who run the government." I give a smile, not at the lizard people thing but at the fact that I'm holding the best bit back for a while.

"It's a bit unusual, the social media thing."

"A bit?! It's bizarre. Everyone in his demographic is all over Facebook, Twitter and Instagram. I'm thinking he's hiding something, in fact I'd bet a bottle of Jack Daniels on it." I wonder if he'll take the bait.

"Yeah, but what? Maybe I should ask Marly." Bingo! He looks pleased at the thought of talking to her.

"I already did." His face drops just a bit. "I asked her if he used a different username for social media.

She said he always claimed social media was an invention designed by the devil to waste time and that he wouldn't have anything to do with it. But then she said something interesting." I pause, just to irritate him. I don't know why we do this to each other but we do. Just as I see the frustration appear on his face, I continue, "She said she walked up behind him one time and he didn't hear her. She said he was on his phone, on Facebook, thumbs tapping away. When she said something, he stopped and blanked the screen. Said he was doing some checking on a client. Only reason she mentioned it was that he looked a bit guilty and when she asked which client, he hesitated a bit too long before naming one."

"So are you thinking he might be using a fake name?"

I nod.

"Can you dig through Facebook and find what name he's using?"

I snort and shake my head. For such a smart guy, Rogan knows jack shit about the internet.

"I wonder what he's hiding?" he asks.

I hold back on my growing suspicion. I'm not ready to bring up the subject just yet. I leave it at, "Dunno. I'm betting it's another woman. Though why the hell..."

He shakes his head. "If it is, I don't want to be the one to tell her."

Like *I* do?

He's got that faraway look in his eye he often gets when an idea's forming. I know to keep quiet, I don't want to break his chain of thought. He looks at me as if trying to decide something.

"Can you do something for me Nick?" he asks.

"Sure."

A long pause. I get the creeping suspicion this isn't about the Dale Summers case. He looks worried. I'm betting it's about the killing but I can't go there right now. I gotta tell him.

"Doesn't matter," he says before I can open my mouth. "It'll keep." He sits up in his chair. "I've got one lead on Dale Summers which I can follow up this evening. For right now I've got some ideas about the other cases we've got on the go."

I feel a wave of relief that we don't have to discuss the elephant in the room. "Sure," I say and I can see the relief in his face too.

But we're gonna have to talk about it some time.

6

TOMÁS

T he lawyer says that Rogan used to be a cop, *Patrón*. But he was released yesterday." The news spears through me. How can a triple murderer be released? No one has that level of clout.

"How so?" I keep the words as even as I can.

"Our lawyer says the charges for killing your father and the politician have been dropped but the charge of killing the Bookman stands."

"What?!" I cannot keep the anger out of my voice. It's a mistake. My father never showed anger unless it served a purpose. I need to remember that.

He says nothing. Just stands in front of me. He's measuring me against *Papa*. That's OK. Just because I went to Harvard Business School doesn't make me any less ruthless than my father. Maybe it makes me more so. It's one of the reasons he sent me there.

"It's good. Out in the open he will be more vulnerable. Remember, I don't want him killed. That would be too easy on him. I want him to suffer like we suffer. His family, his friends: at least three lives of people he loves in return for the life of one Santiago."

"Si *Patrón*." He has a cruel smile. Good. It's the last thing Rogan's loved ones will see in this lifetime.

"I want the details of everyone close to him. When you have tracked them down report back to me. I will give you the details of how I want this done."

I nod and he leaves.

Now another task to organize: how to cause the maximum possible pain for Mr. California Rogan. And how to observe him while he suffers. Yes. That feels right.

7

CAL

The offices of Beloff and Plasker were palatial but this is in a whole other league. The furniture in the reception area looks like it's worth more than the annual revenue of Stammo Rogan Investigations. I'm surprised I was able to get an appointment to see Luke Summers without having to get Arnold Young to broker it. Luke is the CEO of Summers Holdings Inc. which owns the hotel chain bearing his family name. My surprise gives way to something else. Something I will need to probe for.

He strides into the reception area and I know without asking that this is Luke Summers. He's as tall as me with fair hair, cut like a Marine, and a face that resembles the picture of his brother. Yet he's subtly different; slimmer and more confident looking. He has a bearing that speaks of money and power yet he seems relaxed and approachable. I can sense this is a person whom his subordinates would follow through the gates of hell if he asked them to do so.

"Mr. Rogan. I'm Luke Summers, welcome."

I stand and take the proffered hand. He has a firm but not overwhelming grip and I'm struck by the genuine tone of his welcome. "Please, call me Cal. I really appreciate that you could see me so quickly."

"My pleasure Cal. Come with me please." We walk down a corridor, lined with pictures of Summers Hotels from around the world, and go into a corner office facing the North Shore mountains. It must be at least a thousand square feet. He leads me to a seating area comprising a circular coffee table surrounded by six deep leather armchairs. "I was about to have an after-lunch *Americano*. Would you join me?"

Before I can think, I have answered in the affirmative. It's a gentle reminder to me that I must not get seduced by this man's charisma and urbanity. As I sink into one of the chairs, he marches over to an expensive espresso maker. "So you wanted to talk to me about my brother Dale," He says as he starts pressing buttons and placing china cups in position under two of the six spouts. "How can I help you?"

"I'm afraid your brother seems to have gone missing."

"Uh-huh." He still has his back to me as he turns two dials and presses buttons directly above the waiting cups.

"His wife came to our offices yesterday afternoon. She hasn't seen him since Thursday morning."

He turns from the hissing coffee machine and makes his way back to the seating area. "Ahhh, Marly. The ever concerned wife." He sits down. "Sorry, I didn't mean for that to seem harsh but she *is* a bit of a worrier." His apology seems forced. I don't think he likes his sister-in-law one little bit. Then it hits me. Marly told Nick, she had never met any of Dale's family. Unless Nick misheard her, either she or Luke is not telling the truth. I'll probe that later.

For now I just say, "Well in this case she might just have a point. He's not been seen at work since Friday afternoon."

"Mmm. That's unusual. He's always seemed overly concerned about that job of his." I sense that perhaps his urbanity's slipping a bit.

"You don't approve of his work?" I ask.

"Not *per se,*" he responds and I try not to show my irritation at people who use *per se.* "Dale's a *bona fide* genius when it comes to corporate finance," he continues, again with the Latin, "that genius is wasted working for a CA firm. If he were in the family business, he would be CFO earning four times what he makes at Beloff and Plasker."

"So why *doesn't* he work here?"

His face goes hard. "Stubbornness," he says. I sense I'm getting somewhere.

"How so?" I ask mildly.

"Because he—" He stops himself for an instant, then, "Because he's just not prepared to make some changes."

"Changes...?"

"It's a family matter. I would rather not discuss it and I doubt it's relevant to his going missing."

I'm not going to give up that easily. "Does it have anything to do with Marly?"

"Ind—" He stares at me and his look of irritation abates. A small smile plays on his lips. "You're good," he says. "You almost got me to say more than I want to on the subject of my brother. Anyway our family history is not relevant to the fact that he's missing right now."

The way he says it convinces me that exactly the opposite is true but I'm equally convinced I'm not going to get anything out of him on the family history. However, I think the curtailed word might have been 'indirectly'. "You don't like his choice of spouse do you?" I ask.

"I've never met the woman," he replies and I note he neither confirmed nor denied it.

"Really? You said before she was a bit of a worrier."

"I've never met her but I know a lot about her. When I learned of her relationship with Dale, I had her checked out thoroughly."

"And what did you learn?"

He smiles grimly. "That's for me to know and you to try and find out." He stands and extends his hand to me. "I haven't seen my brother in years so I doubt there's anything I can help you with however, when you find him, please let me know." I too stand and shake the proffered hand. There's no way I'm going to get anything more from Luke Summers. But I'm going to find out what's the deal between Dale and his family and I'm betting it *is* relevant to his disappearance despite what his Latin-quoting brother may say.

As I leave I realize I never got the proffered *Americano*.

———

"HELLO. I'm Cal Rogan, Ellie's dad. I'm sorry for any inconvenience but I need to take her out of class early today." As soon as the words are out of my mouth, I know something's wrong. Her face changes, she looks across at her fellow worker and they exchange glances. Not good glances by any stretch of the imagination.

"I'm sorry Mr. Rogan, your ex-wife has taken Ellie out of school for the balance of the term. Didn't you know?" The last three words are laced with vitriol. Now she's looking at me like I'm a child molester.

What the hell is Sam up to? She knows what I did on that island but she can't think I would do any harm to her or Ellie... Can she?

I look at the guardian of the school office and know what she's thinking about me and to make matters worse, I feel a flush rising in my cheeks. Why is it that we blush when innocent as readily as when guilty? She doesn't know *That blushing red no guilty instance gave.* To her I'm just some deadbeat father and husband.

I turn, walk out of the office and stride down the hall. I can feel tears rising to my eyes: tears of sorrow, love and anger mingled. Suddenly a cold hand of desire for a hit of heroin sweeps through me. I long for the unworried bliss only it can bring. As I push through St. Cecelia's school doors into the spring drizzle, I can see my car parked across the street. In fifteen minutes I could be in the downtown east side; in thirty minutes I could be safe at home in the arms of the Beast free of all cares... for a while anyway. I really need it. Right now.

I get into the car. To get downtown I need to go in the opposite direction. I fire up the engine, taking no joy in the throaty roar of the Healey's exhaust. As I do the u-turn, I look at the school. The front doors swing open. Have they sent someone to ensure I'm off the premises? No it's a kid. Not just any kid either. I hit the brakes and get out.

"Ashleigh," I call.

She looks up guiltily from her phone but when she sees me she smiles and walks over.

"Hello Mr. Rogan," she says and extends her hand. Manners are a big deal at the school. I shake her hand but let go quickly, aware of the accusations that might be levelled at a father whose kid has been removed from the school by her mother.

How do I do this? It can't be an interrogation as it was the last time we spoke.

"You must miss Ellie," I say.

"Yes," she smiles. "But she'll be back in September, right?"

"Oh, yes. You must have been in touch with her on Facebook, right?"

"Instagram," she corrects me. "It's funny, I was just texting her."

Perfect! "Where is she right now?" I ask.

"I'll ask her." Her fingers fly over the screen. I

can't believe how lucky I am. She stops typing. I wait patiently. She looks at me and I feel as if I need to say something. But what? Just as it starts to get awkward, her phone buzzes. She frowns and purses her lips then her fingers fly for less than a second. When the reply comes she looks somewhere between puzzled and annoyed.

"She said she's not allowed to say."

Before I can question her further. I hear a man's voice. "Hey." It's a shout. I look up. A less than fit security guard is making his way toward us, eyeing me unpleasantly. I weigh my options and choose the most sensible.

"Thanks Ashleigh," I say, then turn and take the six paces back to my car. I'm one hundred meters down the road by the time the panting guard reaches the sidewalk.

My frustration at the lack of information from Ashleigh is tempered by the knowledge that I may have found a way to track down Ellie and Sam. That faint hope somehow gives me the strength to resist the siren cry of heroin, at least for today.

I hope.

8

SAM

Mommy. I'm texting with Ash and she says Daddy's there." The excitement in Ellie's voice sends a maelstrom of emotions through me but the biggest one overwhelms all the others: fear. In my rush to get from the kitchen to the living room, I forget my cane and stumble, almost sprawling on the hardwood floor. The stress of the last few days has aggravated my MS, damn it.

"DO NOT text her back," I yell.

Ellie looks puzzled at first but then her stubborn streak shows. "Why not?"

"Because I say so." It's a lousy answer, one I promised I would never say to a child... until I actually had a child. I limp unsteadily over to her and drop down on the couch. She has started to type and I just manage to grab the iPad from her before she finishes.

"Hey." She's angry now. "That's private."

I look at the text. The *Your dad says where r u?* from Ashleigh is followed by Ellie's unfinished response of *Tell him we are at...* Fingers trembling, I backspace over the text and type *Tell him I'm not allowed to say* and hit Send.

Why?

I can't say. Sorry Ash. I reply.

There's no response to that.

Ellie's really angry now. "When you said I couldn't have a phone but could have an iPad, you said it would be private. Why can't I tell Daddy where we are? I want to see him."

How the hell do I answer that question without scaring the life out of her? Do I say because it's safer for us and for him that we stay apart for a while? That's partly true. Or do I just tell her an outright lie? And if so, what lie? I guess I'll fall back on that other parental standby.

"It's difficult to explain sweetie."

"Why?"

The inevitable question, which I evade. "It's just very important that Daddy doesn't know where we are for the moment, OK?" She looks not in the least mollified. "Listen El, I'll try and arrange for us to meet up with Daddy soon but until then, you must promise me two things: one, you won't let *anyone* know where we are and two, you will not talk to or text Daddy until I say it's OK. Do you promise?"

"OK." Her voice is quiet now. "But you have to promise we'll see him soon, OK?"

"Yes, I promise." That may be a cheque too big to cash. I cannot put our lives in danger by meeting up with him. Or *his* life for that matter.

Oh Cal, why, why why? Didn't it occur to you that killing a drug lord might just have consequences?

9

CAL

The Railway Club is a Vancouver institution. Except for about nine months in which it changed hands and got a facelift, it has been in business since 1931 when you had to work for the Canadian Pacific Railway to get in. It's known for it's great music and gave a start to k.d. lang, The Tragically Hip and the Barenaked Ladies among others.

I like that the current owners didn't renovate the character out of the place and also that they installed twenty taps of local craft beer. I'm propping up the bar and enjoying a Dageraad blond ale.

There's no band playing tonight so it's a bit quieter than normal and the bar staff are not slammed.

"How's your beer?" the barman asks. He's young, intelligent looking and more than a little tattooed.

He's worked here for a while and served me quite a few times before.

"It's a Dageraad, so it's great, right?"

"I hear you," he says with a broad smile and broader Irish accent.

I finish my glass and say, "Good enough for a second one."

While he pours it, I pull out the photo of Dale Summers. "Do you know him?" I ask as he places the fresh glass in front of me.

He looks at the photo and back at me, undecided. Sometimes bar staff can be protective of the privacy of their regular clientele.

"It's just that he's gone missing. No one's seen him since Friday evening." His expression doesn't change so I add, "His wife and kids are beside themselves with worry." Again with a lie, this time about the kids. But it seems to work. His face softens. Worried kids can melt harder hearts than his.

"He was here Friday. It's a regular thing, he comes with a bunch of guys. I think they work together. They start to drift in around four-thirty, five, but they always leave by seven before the main band starts." He shakes his head at the sacrilege.

"Do you remember what time he left?" I ask.

"Well, that's the thing. Normally they all leave together. But on Friday, they were all standing around the end of the bar, there were six or seven of them. It was around six-thirty when this other guy shows up. He comes up to the bar and orders a Fat Tug when your man notices him and comes over to chat to him; they obviously knew each other from before. A few minutes later, I notice he's introducing him to his pals but what was funny was, right after, the others settled up their bill and all left but for the two of them. They sat down at the bar and got into a deep conversation. Stayed there, had another beer and then left around seven."

"Any idea what they were talking about?" I ask.

"Funny you should ask. I got the impression it was something important or maybe urgent would be a better word. Anyway, when they left it was like they were eager to get somewhere."

"Any idea where?"

He just shakes his head.

"Anything unusual about the other guy?"

"Not really. Average looking, thirty something, about six foot give or take, expensive looking suit though. I didn't recognize him, so I don't think he's been in here before."

Someone at the bar, makes the universal signal for the bill and he goes to the cash register to get it and the payment terminal. While he does it I enjoy my beer and think over the conversation. Nothing useful. Dale Summers comes to the bar as always, runs into a friend and leaves with him. Nada. I was hoping to get something but the hope is pretty well dashed... except for one thing. As the barman comes back to my end of the bar to replace the payment terminal, I stop him.

"You must get a ton of people in here, how come you remember he ordered a Fat Tug?"

"Ah well, he asked me what I'd recommend and I noticed he had a strong Irish accent; when I remarked on it, turns out he was from Galway not too far from my granddad's place. He said he liked a strong, bitter taste and when I suggested a Fat Tug, he laughed, said his father used to work on a tugboat."

I smile and nod, hoping he might add more. But he doesn't.

I show him the picture of Janine, Dale's personal assistant, which I downloaded from Beloff and Plasker's website. "One last thing. Did you ever see him in here with this woman?"

He shakes his head. "Never."

Well the stranger from Galway is the last person I know to have seen Dale Summers alive and I have just one chance of tracking him down but that will have to wait until the morning. And it will only work if I can be persuasive enough.

10

CAL

WEDNESDAY

There's a lot of controversy about this place. It used to be a quintessentially Canadian department store but now it's just a vast cavern under renovation. The American giant Southbrook is building a new high-end store in its place. I'm here to meet with Sean O'Day, Southbrook's project manager.

After a good deal of persuasion Dale Summers' personal assistant, Janine, revealed that Dale did have a contact with a strong Irish accent, a client in fact. Only when I expressed a high level of concern for Dale's safety, coupled with a promise of complete discretion, did she volunteer that Sean O'Day worked for Southbrook, one of Beloff and Plasker's international clients.

The foreman, who let me onto the site and decked me out in a yellow hardhat, is leading me across the bare concrete floor toward a man in a suit poring over blueprints with a young man whom I suspect is an engineer.

"Mr. Rogan to see you Sean," the foreman says.

The man in the suit turns toward me. Sean O'Day looks to be about thirty-five, he has a mop of jet-black hair protruding from beneath his hardhat and he has blue eyes. His looks match his deep voice and Irish accent. "Mr. Rogan," he says extending his hand, "how can I help you?"

There's something about him that tells me to be straightforward with him. I suspect he would spot any subterfuge quickly.

"I'm a private detective. I understand you know Dale Summers."

"I do."

"I've been retained by his wife to try and find him. He appears to have gone missing and you're the last person I know who was with him."

He doesn't react to this in any way, no expression of surprise, no expression at all. Strange. He just says, "How so?"

"I believe you were with him at the Railway Club on Friday evening."

"I was."

I wait but he doesn't offer any further information.

"What were you talking about?"

"Business."

His terseness is starting to get to me. "What specifically?"

He thinks for a bit and looks like he's deciding whether to answer. "There were some cost overruns with the contractors, I needed to make sure he factored them into the financials."

"You could have done that by email, surely."

He looks irritated. "Yes, I could have but I needed to ask him some questions too and I thought it was better to do it face-to-face."

"What questions?"

"I beg your pardon?" The irritation's in his voice now.

"What questions did you need to ask him face-to-face?"

"I'm afraid I can't discuss that with you for reasons of company confidentiality." He says it evenly, the irritation gone as quickly as it appeared.

"You and he left together at about seven o'clock."

"That would be correct."

"Where did you go?"

He looks me in the eye. No expression. I think he's trying to gage how much I know about his movements on Friday night.

"I went back to my hotel." I have a sudden intuition this is not one hundred percent accurate.

"Where did Dale go?"

"Home, I assumed. But if you say he didn't, well I don't know."

Again the intuition. I play along with it and just look at him with the hint of a question in my expression.

His gaze flickers away from my face and over my right shoulder for a second. "Well, if there's nothing more I must get back to work."

"Just one thing: which hotel are you staying at?"

A slight pause. "The Hotel Vancouver." It's said almost as a question.

I take out a business card. "If you see Dale, will you ask him to call me please?"

He takes the card and puts it in his pocket. Again he looks over my right shoulder and this time he smiles. I turn to see a woman in a pantsuit and a white hardhat, the latter of which she somehow manages to make into a fashion statement.

"This is Ms. Audley, our Vice President of Development," O'Day says. "She's overseeing our expansion. Em, this is, uh," he consults my card, "Mr. Rogan. He's investigating the disappearance of Dale Summers."

She extends her hand and takes mine in a very

firm handshake. "I'm pleased to meet you Mr. Rogan. Please call me Em. Disappearance you say?" Her voice is pure southern US, deep and vibrant. I find myself viscerally attracted to this woman. She's not classically beautiful like Marly Summers but there's something infinitely sexier about her. She's about five-nine or -ten, with blue eyes, short, almost cropped, blond hair showing under the white hardhat and a playful smile.

"Nice to meet you Em, I'm Cal." I can feel the silly grin on my face as I hand her my card. "Mr. Summers hasn't been seen since Friday evening. I'm investigating on behalf of his wife."

She puts my card into her purse. "I met with Mr. Summers on Friday afternoon but haven't seen him since. He's a very nice man, I hope nothing has happened to him." She looks from me to O'Day and back. I notice O'Day is looking at me with a very measured gaze. Can he see the silly grin for what it was?

"Was there anything else?" There's a playfulness in Emily Audley's voice but it doesn't stop me from feeling like I've been dismissed.

"No," I say. I nod to Sean O'Day. "Thank you for your help. I'll let you know if anything comes up."

With a smile to Emily, which is returned warmly, I head toward the exit door. As I go through it, I look back. She's leaning over the plans with the engineer but Sean O'Day is looking directly at me with that expressionless face of his.

I wonder what's going on behind his blue Irish eyes.

11

STAMMO

H i Cal." I hear Adriana's voice followed by a "Hi" from Cal. My partner's back. He walks into the main part of the office. Some days I can read him like a book. Today's one of those days. I'm betting his meeting with the Irish guy didn't get us any further ahead. He flops down at his desk. Yep, I'm right.

Adry's voice floats over from the reception area. "Coffee and cookies?"

"Yes, please." We say in unison. Cal chuckles but it's not a completely happy sound.

"Got nothing from the Southbrook guy, I'm guessing."

"Not really, I just had a feeling he was holding something back. Probably nothing; maybe I'm just being paranoid."

"So where do we go from here?"

"Damned if I know." He looks really down. More than just the ups and downs of a case. I think he secretly likes it when a case is going off the rails, it makes him try harder. This is something else.

"So what's up?"

He puts his elbows on the desk and his head in his hands. He massages his scalp with his fingertips and I notice he's got a couple of grey hairs. I never saw them before. Finally he looks up. "I need you to help me find Ellie and Sam."

"What?"

He tells me the details and I can see he's really worried. He ends with, "Can you maybe track their social media posts and find out where they're posting from? Their IP address or whatever it's called."

"No, to do that I'd need to hack into Facebook or Twitter or whatever and there's no way I've got the skills to do that. Not to mention it's illegal."

"Do you know anyone who could?"

"No," I lie. I'm not going down that rabbit hole.

"Coffee." Adry comes in with three cups of coffee and cookies. For the first time she sits down with us. She's changed since she came to work for us a couple of weeks ago. She's lost the corporate look and is a lot less formal and reserved than she was. She wears her brunette hair down and her clothes are much more casual than on her first days here. I kinda like it. Right now she's got a big grin on her face. Rogan's noticed it too.

He laughs. "You look *full-replete with choice of all delights*." he says, whatever that means.

"I am... I think." She giggles. "I was looking through the stuff on this Dale Summers guy. Now I know you two were falling over yourselves to try and impress her, her being so pretty and all," the sarcasm's pretty much right on so I can't suppress a chuckle myself, "but she wasn't exactly truthful with you guys."

"Tell me more," I say.

"She didn't tell you about a prime piece of real estate her husband happens to own. I wonder why she kept it from you."

"What real estate?" Rogan asks just as I say, "Maybe she doesn't know about it."

"You're pretty quick to defend her there Nick," she laughs. I can feel a flush of anger coming to my cheeks and part of me is a little bit irritated by it, and therefore at her, but a bigger part of me is intrigued.

She continues. "I checked the city property records and found out that Mr. Dale Summers owns a townhouse in Kits with an assessed value of a cool two point two million dollars."

"Maybe he's had it for a long time and his wife doesn't even know about it," I say.

"He bought it two years ago. They've been married since twenty-thirteen. Sooooo, no. He bought it four years into the marriage."

"Oh." A big part of me wants to believe Marly Summers was being straight with us but I've gotta be sure. "You live in Kits Rogan, why don't you check it out on your way home. See if he's holed up there. I'll contact Marly and ask her about it."

"Well done Adry," says Rogan. I think it's the first time he's called her by her shortened name.

"I live to serve you guys," she jokes but I can see she's pleased. "I'll see what else I can dredge up on him." She takes her coffee and two of the chocolate digestive cookies and heads back to her reception desk.

Rogan goes all thoughtful on me, doing that staring off into space thing. I leave him to it and wiggle my mouse to wake up my computer. I'm going to do some digging into Marly Summers and see what I can find. Maybe I'm wrong about her. I hope not.

Rogan springs to his feet. "I'm going to check out that townhouse. Maybe she doesn't know about it. It could be a place he keeps for a mistress or maybe he goes there to get away from it all. But if it checks out we'll have an answer for her and will have earned our fee. I'll text you when I find out what's happening." He takes something from his desk drawer, grabs the last two cookies and heads for the door.

Now I need to see if I can track down Sam and Ellie for him but I don't have a good feeling about it. Sam knows what Cal did on that island and I figure she doesn't want to be found by him.

12

CAL

Sixth Avenue in Kitsilano is one of the nicest streets on the Westside of Vancouver. West of Balsam, large trees line the sidewalks and form a canopy over the road where, even on the hottest days of summer, they provide cool shade for walkers and joggers. And shady parking for Austin Healeys.

Dale Summers' townhouse is in a small but expensive-looking development not too far from Alma. The townhouses are tall and narrow with flights of six steps up to the front doors.

Pressing the doorbell produces a muted and elegant chime but no answer. I try it again. No answer again. Just on the off-chance, I try the door. Locked. I feel a tingle of relief. A couple of times recently, when I've found front doors open it has not led to a happy encounter.

I descend the steps, walk to the end of the block, do a couple of left turns and head down the alley. As I thought, there are garages behind the townhouses. One of them is open revealing a Lamborghini Aventador SV with a personalized plate: DALE CA. So far, so good. I walk in and try the handle of the door leading into the house. Locked. Well, I've come this far. I press the button to close the garage door and it clatters down. Now I'm shielded from prying eyes. It's one of those doors with the lock inside the door knob. Easy-peasy. I take my trusty lock-picks—confiscated from a petty thief years ago when I was a uniformed constable and kept in my desk drawer—and I'm in the house thirty seconds later.

Unfortunately, I can hear a persistent triple beeping. A security alarm will be blaring in thirty seconds. When that alarm goes off, the monitoring company will call the police and in Kits the police don't take long to arrive at the scene of a property crime. All my senses tell me to get out of there fast. All except one. Smell. An all too familiar smell. A grim reminder of another townhouse at another time. It takes me seven seconds to head up the stairs to the main floor. Ten more seconds to check the main floor. Seven seconds to the second floor. There are three doors. One's open. The smell's stronger. Taking a deep breath I walk through the door.

Dale Summers is secured to a bed with rope and duct tape. He's very, very dead.

I take several deep breaths to calm me.

The alarm's beeping speeds up.

I look closely at the body. He's naked. The ornately carved, bejewelled handle of a knife is jutting up out of his chest. His stomach is a mess. It looks like it's been branded and as I move closer I can see it has indeed. The numbers two, zero, one, three, written in a square pattern, in digits four inches tall have been scorched onto his flesh. I'm betting they were burned there before the *coup de grâce*. While he was still alive. I shudder at the thought. I've been to a bunch of crime scenes before, even a dead child, and I've never thrown up. My roiling stomach tells me this may be a first.

The sound of the flies is drowned by the ear-shattering peel as the security alarm blasts into life.

I figure I've got five minutes to check the crime scene.

First the body. The knife has been placed precisely over the heart entering the ribcage between the third and fourth ribs. There's a lot of blood but the stomach has been wiped clean, presumably to show off the killer's handiwork. The killer's obviously a sadist. The numbers look like they have been carefully and probably slowly branded with some red-hot blunt instrument. The pain must have been excruciating. The queasiness ramps up a notch. As an added insult, the digits are surrounded by a square also branded on his flesh. The hands and feet are tied to the four bedposts with ropes. The ropes are further secured to the body with lots of duct tape. They are tight, forcing the arms and legs far apart. The genitals are shrivelled, almost certainly as a result of the victim's fear and pain. His mouth is secured with more duct tape which is wrapped across the mouth and around the back of the neck several times. It's a very thorough job.

The murder weapon's ornate; it looks medieval. The blade seems to be ten or twelve inches long because there's a good six inches of blade between where it enters the chest and the hilt.

Everything else in the room looks incongruously normal. The killer must have tidied up before he left. There's nothing on the floor and the only thing under the bed is a pair of red leather slippers. There's nothing else here which catches my attention.

With a selfish little twinge, I realize this has ruined my afternoon. I was planning to spend the time trying to track down Sam and Ellie. I have a couple of ideas on how to do it. But as much as I want to, there's no way I can do it now.

I guess I'll go downstairs and open the front door for the cops. Hopefully I won't get arrested for murder again. However the shakes that have started in my body are not at the thought of arrest; it's the full horror of what I experienced upstairs. I think I'm going to need to throw up. It's seeping into my bones and the old feeling's on the rise: I *am* going to get whoever did this.

———

AFTER EIGHT HOURS with the VPD's Major Crime Section, during which time I was debriefed end-lessly about my investigation into Dale Summers' disappearance, all I really want to do is go home and sleep. Except I just need to scratch a mental itch which is irritating me.

Marly Summers looks wrecked, I'm surprised she agreed to see me at this late hour at her home.

"Thank you so much for seeing me. I won't take up too much of your time."

"No problem Mr. Rogan. I don't think I'll sleep much tonight."

"Yes, I understand. I'm so very sorry about your husband."

She doesn't respond but walks me into a large living room overlooking English Bay with the lights of the Westside reflecting in the water. She sits on a long sofa facing the view and indicates for me to sit at the other end. But I don't and I'm not sure why.

"The police told me it was you who found him." It's said in an almost matter-of-fact manner. Her emotions don't seem to match her appearance.

I won't go straight to the mental itch and besides there are some other things I want to know. "Dale owned the townhouse where I found him." Her eyes flutter. Maybe tiredness, maybe something else. "Did you know about it?"

"No." She says it quickly, like she was expecting the question.

"Your husband never mentioned it?"

This time she doesn't answer immediately. She's trying to see where I'm going with this. "No," she says, more emphatically. With an elegant movement, she puts her feet up on the coffee table between us.

"Did he keep his financial affairs secret from you?"

"I didn't think so but now I'm beginning to question that." Honest sounding answer.

"Did he have any enemies?"

She pauses before answering. "Yesterday, I would have said no, but I'm starting to realize I know even less about him than I thought. It seems he had many secrets."

"Did you have any secrets from him?"

She reacts to the question. "What exactly do you mean, Mr. Rogan?" There's an odd tone in her voice.

"You told my partner you and your husband hadn't been intimate for a year or more. Is there anybody else in your life?"

"No. Nobody. I'll admit I thought about it once or twice, but no, I could never do that to Dale." Either she's sincere or she's thought this through in advance.

Time to scratch the itch but first, "Well thank you again for meeting with me so late, I really do appreciate it." She takes a deep breath and relaxes; she looks glad the questioning's over. Now to slip in that last question.

"Would you like a drink before you go?" Her question throws me. She sees the surprise in my face. "It's been a long day for you too. What would you like?"

This might work better. "Do you have a local beer?"

"No, Dale hated beer. How about a Scotch?"

"Sure, thanks."

She walks over to a cabinet and opens a door to reveal an array of expensive spirits. She grabs a bottle of eighteen year-old Johnny Walker and two glasses. "Please, sit." This time I comply and she sits down too, but not at the other end of the couch. Her knee's inches from mine.

She puts the glasses on the coffee table in front of us. The bottle has never been opened until now. She cracks it open and pours two very big drinks. "My husband hated blended Scotches too." Said defiantly. She hands me one and clinks hers against it. "Cheers."

I respond and take a sip; like her late husband I usually prefer single malts but this is wonderful. She takes a gulp and then another. I'm confused. Where's she going with this?

She rotates toward me and brings her knees up onto the sofa and as they brush against the outside of my thigh, she gives me that wonderful smile I first saw in our office on Monday afternoon. Despite not wanting to, I feel my body reacting. She takes another drink of her Scotch and, unnecessarily, the tip of her tongue slowly licks the right side of her upper lip and traverses to the left.

I get the feeling I'm being manipulated but I have no idea why.

"You know it's been a long time for me," she says and puts her hand on my knee.

My common sense tells me that what I'm thinking is insane. She runs her nails up the inside of my thigh; now my body's really reacting. I'm lost... until King Lear comes to my aid: *O, that way madness lies; let me shun that!*

"I'm sorry," I mumble as I struggle to my feet. "I have to go."

I walk awkwardly out of the living room and without looking back, head for the front door.

Then I realize with annoyance, I never got to scratch the itch which brought me here in the first place. Maybe *that* was the manipulation.

13

CAL
THURSDAY

I haven't been on this doorstep in over a year and the welcome is even more frosty than the last time I was here. "What do you want Cal?" Sam's mother has always disliked me, which I can't actually blame her for; I did after all ruin my marriage to her daughter by shooting enough heroin to numb my brain for over five years.

"Hello Miriam. I'd like to speak to Sam please." I try to sound as friendly as I can.

"I thought when you called the other day my husband told you she wasn't here."

"He did but I kind of hoped..."

"Hoped he was lying? I thought that was in your character, not his."

"Please Miriam, I'm worried sick about her and Ellie."

"Well you should have thought of that before you went and killed a drug dealer."

"Those charges have been dropped," I tell her just a bit too quickly.

"Oh well that's OK." The sarcasm drips from her tongue. "The gang will know you're not the one who killed their leader if the charges have been dropped. Samantha's petrified they'll try and extract vengeance on you and maybe on her and Ellie too, so she's gone into hiding and I'm the last one who's going to say where she went."

It hits me like a truck. Why did it never occur to me? Just because Santiago's dead doesn't mean the gang's wound up. They arrested several of them when they raided his place on Samuel Island but they couldn't have got all of them. Those who are left won't want his death to go unavenged.

"You didn't think of that did you?" It's her parting shot as she slams the door in my face.

But she's right.

I stand on the doorstep. Sam's right. Of course they're going to come after me and maybe her too and even Ellie. My God, what have I done?

In a daze, I turn and walk down the path to the front gate.

I get into the Healey and fire up the engine. As I pull away from the curb, I hear the squeal of brakes. In my altered state, I pulled out in front of a black

Escalade without looking. I wave my apologies to the driver and take off down the road. I know what I have to do now.

I have to let them go.

————

"I GOT some good news for you Rogan." Stammo has a big grin on his face. "I might know where Ellie and Sam are." Then he sees the look on my face. "What?" I tell him about my meeting with Sam's mother.

He looks at me and his face drops. "Why didn't we realize? Sam's smarter than the two of us put together. We've been so worried about the VPD finding out, we never thought that once you got arrested the news might get back to the remnants of his gang. It's just possible they could get it into their minds to come after you, me, Ellie and Sam." He thinks for a while. "Once you left your DNA on the island, we were screwed."

I don't know what to say to him. My DNA was there because... But there's no point in rehashing all that. There's a far more pressing problem.

"You said you may have tracked down Ellie. Where is she?"

"When you found out last month she was on Instagram I started following her. I just checked and she has been posting some selfies. I recognized one of them. Here, take a look."

He swivels his screen toward me and clicks a tab in Chrome. Ellie's smiling out at me from the deck of a boat. It's the car deck of a ferry and behind her I can see Sam's car. The ferry's approaching a dock. "You know where this is?" I ask him.

"I'm pretty sure it's on the ferry over to Gibsons."

He's right. The Horseshoe Bay to Langdale ferry takes people over to the aptly named Sunshine Coast. Of course! Sam's parents have a summer cottage on Hardy Island. That's where they're headed. A wave of relief washes over me. I know where they are. They're safe on a remote island a hundred kilometres from Vancouver. I tell Stammo but he doesn't look so happy.

"They could still come after you and me. From now on I'm gonna be carrying my Glock wherever I go. The law be damned. You ought to get yourself one too."

His words take the edge off my relief. I grab my phone and text Sam. *Tell Ellie to stop posting pictures. They might be able to find your location. PS I love you both.* It wooshes and the 'Delivered' message comes up. She hasn't replied to any of my other texts or emails so I don't expect her to reply to this one. I'm not too worried about the gang tracking them. Even if they find Ellie's Instagram *and* recognize the Langdale dock, there's no way they could make the connection to Hardy Island. It's me they'll want to catch. Maybe I should follow Stammo's advice and get myself a gun. It just seems so, I dunno, so un-Canadian.

He breaks into my train of thought. "So, you closed the Dale Summers case. Not the ending Marly Summers was hoping for."

"No, but you know what, something's been bothering me. The killer branded him with the numbers two, zero, one, three. Didn't you say they'd been married for six years?"

"Yeah." He looks at me then it dawns. "Twenty-thirteen, the year they were married." A shocked look slides onto his face. "You don't think she killed him?"

"No. But I've got to believe there's a connection."

"I wonder if she has a lover?"

"I asked her that and she said not. I think she was telling the truth."

"When did you ask her?" he asks. There is a tone in his voice.

"Last night. I went over to her house after I'd finished at Major Crimes Section. It was one of the things I asked her."

"Oh." I can tell he's not happy that I went to see her. "So what did she say about the twenty-thirteen thing?"

"I never got to ask her." I can hear the hint of embarrassment in my own voice.

So can he. "Why the hell not?"

And the truth will set you free. Not Shakespeare, but from the other oft-quoted verses. We'll see if it does. "If you really want to know, before I could ask her she came on to me."

"You are joking!" He laughs. It's not a nice laugh.

"No."

"Why would she do that?"

I decide not to take that too personally. "I dunno. Maybe in a weird way it was to get back at her husband. Or maybe it's the thing that happens when we're exposed to death: the deep evolutionary need to procreate, to create a life that replaces the lost one."

He looks at me with his interrogator's look. "And did you?" he asks slowly.

"No."

"Huh." He seems placated. "Then you're a stronger man than most." After a pause he adds, "Anyway the case is closed. She called this morning and asked if there was any final billing. I told her no, the retainer covered everything. It was a big fee for only two days work. I'm happy."

I should be too. But I'm not. The cop in me wants to continue the investigation, question her about the twenty-thirteen branding, dig into her life, find out if she's got a lover, find out how much she inherits from her husband. For the hundredth time I question my decision to leave the VPD.

"You've got that look again."

"What look?"

"Like a dog that won't let go of a bone. Let it go Rogan. Call Major Crimes and tell 'em about the twenty-thirteen connection and let them do their thing. Do it now."

He's right. As much as I may want to investigate the murder of Dale Summers, it's a job for the VPD now. I need to just tell them what I know and get on to other things. Anyway, my next move would have been to get Stammo to do some research for me and there's no way he's going to do that if it's not billable. Reluctantly—and it's more like a gut-wrench than mere reluctance—I pull out my phone to dial the familiar number but before I can, it rings.

"Cal Rogan."

A newly familiar voice says, *"Mr. Rogan, I need your help with something."*

14

TOMÁS

He looks pleased. "Our men have some news *Patrón*." I nod for him to continue. "We found Rogan. We Googled him and found his company. He's a private investigator now. The photos of him and his partner were on the website and so was the address of their office. We followed them and we know where they both live. Now here's the odd thing. His partner's name is Nick Stammo."

"Stammo? That was the Bookman's last name wasn't it?"

"Yes *Patron*. He's the Bookman's father."

"Very interesting. He and Rogan are responsible for his own son's death. Go on Javier."

"We also discovered he has a wife and daughter though they don't live with him. We have a man staking out their address but they have not been there. And the daughter is not at her school."

"A wife and daughter? Good work Javier. I knew I could rely on you." A little praise is good, something my father often omitted.

"Thank you *Patrón*," he smiles and there is pride in his voice. "There is more. This morning, just an hour ago, Rogan went to a house in Burnaby. I saw him there myself. We checked the property records; it belongs to a woman who has the same last name as Rogan's wife. It could be her mother. If the wife and child don't show up soon, maybe the parents will know where they have gone."

"Excellent. When it comes time to kill them, you can have the wife as a little bonus. It will increase the level of Rogan's pain."

"Thank you *Patrón*. I have seen a picture of her. It is a bonus I will enjoy."

Knowing Javier's proclivities, I'm sure he will and am equally certain she most definitely won't.

15

CAL

The coffee shop is opposite the site where they're renovating the building which will become the new Southbrook store. While I wait, I look through the rain across Granville Street at a small group of people with placards objecting to the fact that another iconic Canadian department store is being replaced by an American behemoth. As much as we really do love our neighbours to the south, there is a small group of Canadians who like to object to every encroachment of US business into Canada. I personally don't really care about the lost department store; I do most of my shopping online these days. Somehow being online anonymizes the nationality of the stores. As I think about it, I have no idea where some of the sites I use are located and who might own them.

My train of thought is derailed by the voice I heard on the phone. The sweet, southern sound says, "Thank you so much for seeing me at such short notice, Mr. Rogan."

Emily Audley, Southbrook's VP of Development, puts a huge cup—it's almost a bowl—of cappuccino on the table and sits down opposite me. I stand and shake her extended hand. "It's my pleasure Ms. Audley."

She gives a big, room-lighting smile. "Now Cal, as I told you when we met yesterday, I want you to call me Em." I don't know whether it's the accent or the playfulness in her voice or what, but I find myself again attracted to her.

"It's my pleasure, *Em*." I correct myself.

"Now that's better, *Cal*." She matches my tone and gives me a big grin, which I call and raise her a chuckle.

She takes a sip of the cappuccino and licks the foam from her upper lip. It's not overtly sexy like Marly Summers licking the scotch from *her* lips but it's sexy nonetheless. She is a very attractive woman. I usually go for women with long hair but seeing Em without her white hardhat shows her short hair off beautifully.

"You said on the phone I could help you with something. I've been trying to imagine what that might be," I say.

Her face becomes serious. "I got a call this morning from the managing partner at Beloff and Plasker. He told me Dale Summers had been murdered. He didn't really know the circumstances or any details."

I nod but don't tell her it was me who discovered the body.

"Well I was shocked," she continues. "Dale and I have been working together for some months now and we have got to know each other quite well. He was a real gentleman and I truly got to trust his opinions."

She pauses and in the gap in conversation, I wonder what the words 'quite well' might mean. Was she the one having an affair with him?

"Anyway, Cal, I would like your firm to pursue an investigation into his death on Southbrook's behalf."

I can't cover my surprise. "Could I ask why?" I ask. "I'm sure the VPD are putting every effort into finding his murderer. Most murders in Vancouver are gang members killing each other off. I'm sure they're giving Mr. Summers' case high priority over others."

She sits a little straighter and her demeanour changes. Suddenly she's one hundred percent businesswoman. "Before I answer that, can I rely on you to keep this confidential?"

"Of course. It will just be between you and me and my partner, Nick Stammo."

"Good. When we decided to open a store in Canada, we had to create a Canadian subsidiary company to own and manage the operations. The subsidiary is one hundred percent owned by South-brook US but we needed two Canadian directors and wanted a lawyer and a CA. We asked Dale—partly, I will admit, because of the Summers name —and he accepted. My concern is that if his murder could, in some way, give rise to negative publicity for Southbrook, I would like to know in advance, so we can get out ahead of it. I talked to my head office people. They agreed with me and gave me authorization to hire you."

The old need to follow through on the case clicks back in. It was thwarted this morning but it's back, front and centre I don't know what she expects I'll be able to discover that the police can't. Even I don't have the hubris to believe I can solve this ahead of my former colleagues... well maybe a little.

She reads my thoughts as indecision. "Maybe this will help you decide." She opens her purse, re-moves a slip of paper and hands it to me; it's a money order for ten thousand dollars, US dollars at that, a thirty percent bonus. "That's a week's retainer. I expect you to handle this as a priority and report back to me on a daily basis."

Stammo can't object now. I can get him to do the research I want. It's on!

"Thank you Em, we would be delighted to take the case on Southbrook's behalf."

"Well that's good. It will be good to have you on our team." She smiles, takes a sip of her cappuccino and relaxes back into her chair. "Now is there anything else you need from me?"

There is and it will effect the way I do the job. But I'm loath to bring it up and, if I'm honest with myself, I feel a little bit guilty about wanting to know personally. Well, here we go.

"Please don't take this the wrong way Em, but were you and Dale... uh, well, more than just business associates?"

"Why, Mr. Rogan! You do ask some, shall we say, penetrating questions." To my surprise she is not at all offended by my inquiry. In fact there is laughter in her southern drawl. "No, Dale and I were not involved in that way. Truth-to-tell I didn't find him attractive. He was good-looking but just not my type." It makes me wonder what is her type. She continues, dropping the volume of her voice a little, "Besides, Dale was married and I make it a rule never to date married men, especially those with jealous wives."

I'm starting to think that Stammo and I might

have been a bit blinded by Marly Summers. First Dale's brother and now Emily Audley have cast some doubt about her; doubt I need to look into. But for now, I'm going to enjoy the bonus of this case: spending some time every day with Em.

16

STAMMO

Cops have a natural suspicion of defence lawyers but Jim Garry is one I trust. Although he whooped my ass in court a couple of times, he did it fair and square which is a lot more than I can say for some of his colleagues. Still, I'm suspicious of why he's here to see me right now.

We're in the conference room because I don't want Adry to overhear us. I trust her but I'm not ready to have her learn about what Cal and I have done.

"I'll come straight to the point Nick. So far the police have no evidence to connect Cal to the assassinations of Carlos Santiago and Ed Perot but if they find anything, like the murder weapon, he will be in a lot of trouble." He looks at me with a question on his face, a question I don't want to answer. I know the murder weapon is under a hundred and fifty meters of water in the Strait of Georgia but if I tell him it makes me complicit in the assassinations. Maybe I need to find myself a lawyer of my own. I just shrug.

"However," he continues, "there is all sorts of evidence that he did kill your son Matt." He looks at me for a reaction but I was a cop too long to give away what's churning my gut. "The forensic evidence supports his claim of self-defence but the thing that will make the difference is your evidence. I'd like to go over it with you again now, if that's OK."

"Sure," I say... but I'm not sure.

"I understand Cal was on the island just to observe if the kidnapped girl Ariel Bradbury was there, is that right?" We both know it's not but we have to play the game.

"Yeah."

"And you and he were in radio contact?"

I nod.

"Did you speak to Matt on the radio?"

I just need to say yes. It's true. Matt took the radio headset from Rogan and spoke to me. He was planning to kill Rogan right then. Rogan didn't have a choice. A pain lances through me and I feel a tightening in my chest. I have to make a decision. I look at Garry and there is worry on his face. I failed my son in life but can I fail him in death? I'm as much to blame as Rogan for what happened; maybe we both need to pay for it.

Garry breaks into my thoughts. "In the affidavit you swore, which got the judge to approve Cal's bail, you said Matt had taken control of Cal's radio and that you feared for Cal's life. Is that correct?"

"That's what I said in the affidavit."

"Are you prepared to swear to it in court?"

I'm on the edge and don't know which way to go. I'll take the Canadian way out: compromise.

"I'll have to think about that." I say with finality.

Garry strokes his grey beard and the usual twinkle has gone from his eye.

———

GARRY HAS BEEN GONE for over an hour but I haven't been able to do any work. For what feels like the tenth time, I open the bottom right desk drawer and stare at the bottle of Jim Beam Devil's Cut. It would take the edge off just fine. This time, I don't slam the drawer shut. I push my wheelchair back so I can reach down, pull out the bottle and a glass and pour myself a good shot. I shouldn't be doing this at eleven in the morning but what the fuck.

I look at the amber liquid and lick my lips in anticipation. Or is it in doubt?

I hear the front door open. "Hi Adry, can you deposit this when you get a minute?" Rogan sounds a hell of a lot more chipper than he did earlier this morning. He breezes into the main office and stops, eyeing the glass in front of me. It ratchets up my anger; I grab the glass and down it in one gulp, a hell of a way to treat six-year-old, ninety proof bourbon but I don't give a damn.

"Are you OK, Nick?" he asks.

Stupid question.

I think about pouring a second shot but don't.

"Yeah. I'm just aces," I shoot back at him, angry at both of us. "What was that you were telling Adry to deposit?"

Glad of the question, he smiles. "A retainer of ten grand US," he says.

I don't know if it's his answer, or the Jim Beam hitting my bloodstream on an empty stomach, but the emotions deflate with a sigh. "What for?"

"Emily Audley, the VP of Southbrook, gave it to me as a retainer," he grins.

"What for?" I ask again.

"She wants us to look into the murder of Dale Summers."

"What! Why? What's the connection?"

He sits down at his desk and tells me about his meeting with her. "So how do we go about it?" I ask.

"I've been thinking about that. I want to go and talk to Marly Summers again. Both Dale's brother and Em Audley have expressed reservations about her. The brother said he had checked her out but he wouldn't say what he found and Emily said she thought Marly was the jealous type. I want to grill her about the fact that the year of her marriage was branded onto her husband's stomach. I think you should do a detailed background check into her; find out if she's the nice girl we both think she is. And have a word with whoever's got the case at VPD; maybe they've checked her out."

Sounds reasonable. "What if she won't see you? You said she came on to you last night but that you walked out. Didn't your Shakespeare say something about the fury of a scorned woman?"

He chuckles. "No, it was a different William. But you've got a point; she might well refuse to talk to me."

Adry's voice chimes out from the reception area. "Nick, call for you on line one."

I pick up the phone.

And the caller settles it for us.

17

SAM

Now we have arrived here I feel kind of foolish. Are we really in danger from a drug gang or am I just being paranoid? Ellie is mad at me: one for taking her out of school, two for bringing her here, so far from all her friends and three for refusing to let her post about it on Instagram or text with Cal.

On the plus side, it *is* beautiful here. When I was a kid, Mom and Dad would bring me here most weekends in summer. There are only a handful of houses on the entire island, all connected by trails. There are no roads and no vehicles other than the odd tractor or two. We came here by car and ferry and finally on Dad's Boston Whaler to our own dock. It's a perfect spring day and after a late breakfast, El and I have been sunning ourselves in the garden. It has only slightly improved her mood. The lawn reaches down to the dock where the Whaler is moored. I look across the little bay and can just make out traffic on the mainland road less than three kilometres away. There are some fluffy white clouds in the sky and it's warm and peaceful.

Best of all being here has given me time to think. I know I love Cal and there will never be anyone quite like him. But he's high maintenance emotionally. I guess I can handle the fact that he's an addict; he seems to have it under control, although there's always the danger he'll reuse. And his obsession with his work was always something which got between us. But this new thing is too much. I don't think I can live with someone who has killed people and killed them in cold blood. For God's sake he's accused of killing a drug lord and a Federal MP. I don't know the details but all I know is that I don't think I can be with him anymore and I don't think Ellie should be either. He has put us in danger too often and here we are hiding out on Hardy Island in case a vengeful drug gang decides to come after us. But where do we go from here? Toronto? The States? It would have to be the West Coast, I don't think I could handle the winters east of the Rockies. But with my MS, I couldn't get health insurance, so the US is probably out anyway. It just all feels so hopeless.

"I'm hungry Mommy." Ellie brings me out of my thoughts. She looks so beautiful sitting in the deckchair with her book in her lap. My mood lightens.

"Me too. How about we go down to the beach. The tide's low enough for us to get some oysters. I'll fry them up for lunch."

"What are oysters?"

"You'll see. Come on."

She jumps up and drops her book on the floor.

As she stoops to pick it up, our familiar Beatles song comes to mind. I'll see how far I get this time before she stops me. "Eleanor Rogan, Picks up her book, Off the ground where she let it fall down, Oh what a clown—"

"Mommy!" she says and then, in a pretty good imitation of me, she adds, "How many times do I have to tell you not to do that."

Giggling, we head toward the house to get a bucket and a screwdriver to pry the juicy delights off the rocks. Maybe we can spend the spring and summer here and see what happens. We'll probably get bored from time to time but at least we're safe from the outside world.

18

CAL

Bob Pridmore looks more like a linebacker than a lawyer. He's a good six foot six, he must weigh two-fifty and it's mostly muscle. He makes our conference room feel a lot smaller than it already is; it feels like the four of us are on the Skytrain in rush-hour. His face doesn't fit either; he looks like a mean version of Robert Redford, who hardly ever played a lawyer.

He takes charge from the get-go. "We are here because Ms. Summers needs your assistance." He says it like he doesn't think much of Marly's choice of Stammo Rogan Investigations Inc.

I look at Stammo, the obvious question in my mind. He looks back, he's thinking the same thing as me. He shrugs. "Go on," he says.

"First thing this morning, she had a visit from

the VPD, a Sergeant Waters and his partner. They asked her some very pointed questions which indicated she's a suspect in the murder of her husband."

"What questions?" Stammo asks gently, looking at Marly.

"First, they asked her—"

"I'd like Ms. Summers to answer," Stammo interrupts. Atta boy, Nick; this lawyer is getting on my nerves too.

Marly looks at her counsel as if asking permission. I can't help feeling it's what a guilty person would do. Pridmore gives her the smallest of nods. They have rehearsed this.

"They asked me a lot of questions about my relationship with Dale. They were very explicit." She blushes.

"What did you tell them?" I ask.

She glances up at her lawyer again. "I told them what I told you. That I haven't had any uh, intimate relationship with him. Not for a while, anyway." She stops and purses her lips and her left index finger reaches up and rubs the front of her chin. She makes a decision. "I told them I've been having an affair for the last six months."

"Is that true?" I ask. "You told me the opposite." Right before you ran your fingers up the inside of my thigh. I think it but don't say it.

She blushes. "Yes, I know, and I'm sorry I lied to you."

Stammo jumps in, "We can only work for you if you tell us the truth." His voice has lost its gentleness.

"Yes, I understand."

"Who have you been having an affair with?" I ask realizing I have a touch of aggression in my voice. Is it jealousy?

Again with a glance at her lawyer, she says, "I would rather not say."

"Listen, Marly, you have to tell us who it is," says Stammo. "He could be a suspect in the murder of your husband."

She thinks for a moment, her eyes down, looking at her hands. She moves her head toward Bob Pridmore but then seems to think better of it. I wonder what's going on behind that beautiful face. Finally she looks back up at Stammo. "Nevertheless, I won't say. But I will say this: I can assure you my lover did not kill Dale."

"You can't know that, he—" Stammo starts to say.

"My client has nothing more to say on the subject," Bob Pridmore reasserts his position of being in charge of the narrative. "Your job here is two-fold. One: find out who actually killed Dale Summers, thus exonerating my client, and two: investigate any evidence the police might have against her and report back to me."

Stammo starts to speak but I interrupt. "Before we accept the assignment, my partner and I need to discuss this. Please excuse us for a moment."

Marly's lawyer looks at me and scowls. Stammo looks at me and smiles. He maneuvers his wheelchair deftly and pulls open the door for me, we head into the open area as far as possible from the conference room. "Adry, see if they want anything. Water or coffee," I say.

"Don't offer them my cookies," Stammo growls.

Keeping my voice down, I ask the question we both had when we learned Marly wanted to hire us. "We just accepted a big fat cheque from Southbrook to do the same investigation. If we take the same assignment from Marly is it a conflict of interest?"

"Yeah, I wondered about that. I don't think so. The only conflict would be if Marly turns out to be the killer but that wouldn't be a conflict with Southbrook." He chuckles. "It'd be a conflict for her. If she *is* her husband's killer it'd be her own damn fault for hiring us."

"You didn't see the body. I can't imagine Marly doing that."

"Don't be too sure. I've seen too many ugly murders by jealous spouses."

I shrug. "What about the second half of the job

her pet shark described? What did he say? Something like *'find out any evidence the police have got against her and report back to me.'* We can't agree to that. He probably went along with hiring us because he knows we're both ex-VPD members and assumes we have an 'in' with the Department. If we did learn anything from Steve about what they've got against Marly, there's no way we'd be able to share it with her or with him."

Stammo nods slowly and then smiles. "For now, let's make them think we're taking the case and find out what happened when Steve and his partner interviewed her."

"Sounds like a plan."

We cross the office and go back into the conference room. There is a tension in the air. Is it because we left the room or is there something else going on? Oh. I wonder if—

Stammo breaks my chain of thought. "Tell us about the interview with the VPD," he says. "You said Steve Waters was the senior officer, we both know Steve well. We were both partners with him at different times." Bob Pridmore nods and gives the shadow of a smile. Good move Nick, get the lawyer on side. "Do you remember the name of the other officer?" Good. Easy question. Get her talking freely.

"Yes, I think so. I think his name was Detective Street."

We both try and cover our surprise. Detective Eric Street is a very ambitious young cop who screwed me over badly when I was back in the Department. I'm surprised he's still with the VPD, let alone Steve's partner. I guess the scum, like the cream, rises to the top.

"Can you remember the questions they asked you?" Stammo continues.

"Well yes, first they asked me where I was at the time of Dale's murder."

"His body was found at midday yesterday," I say, wondering if she knows it was me who found him. "Did they tell you the time of death?"

"Between six and midnight of the previous evening," she says.

"What did you tell them?"

"That I was home in bed... alone." She puts an emphasis on the last word.

"What else did they ask?"

"They asked why I was angry at my husband. I don't know why they thought I was angry at him. I told them that and added I was just worried because he had gone missing. They didn't seem to accept it. The younger one asked if I had threatened Dale."

"Had you?" Stammo asks.

"No, of course not."

"Did he say why he thought you had?"

"No, but he kept asking me in different ways."

"Why would he think that?"

"I have no idea." She looks like she's close to tears. I believe her. Maybe Stammo can find out from Steve why they thought that. "Then they asked me when was I last at the townhouse where Dale was found. I told them I'd never been there, that I didn't even know it existed. That was when they accused me of lying, they said they had DNA evidence I had been there. The younger one was really nasty about it. So when they asked me if I had a lover, I was scared to deny it. I didn't want to be caught in an actual lie in case they thought I was lying about never having been to the house too."

"Did you tell them the name of your lover?"

"No I refused and don't ask me again because I won't tell you either," she says defiantly.

"Did they say they found your DNA in the townhouse?" I ask.

"Yes."

Stammo and I exchange looks. We're both thinking the same thing.

"Did they say where or what type of DNA evidence?"

"No. When I told them I'd never been there, they just said they didn't believe me and that DNA didn't lie."

Bob Pridmore chips in, "I've asked my client not to meet with the police without me being present."

Stammo and I both nod. "What else did they interrogate you about?" he asks.

"They wanted to know how much money I would be inheriting."

"And how much is that?"

"I don't know. I won't get to know until I meet with his lawyers."

Now to get to the question I wanted to ask last night. "Marly you said that you and Dale got married six years ago; that would be twenty-thirteen, right?"

"Yes, April twenty-eighth. The police asked me that too."

"Did you know Dale had twenty-thirteen branded on his stomach?"

Her eyes go wide. "No. Who would do such a thing?" Then she realizes. "Is that why they think I did it?"

"That, and the DNA evidence, and the fact that you have a lover."

Now she looks scared. "Mr. Rogan, Mr. Stammo, you have to find out who did this." She rummages in her purse and pulls out a cheque and pushes it across the table to Stammo. "Please, take this and say you'll take the case."

Any thought of not taking the case dissipates. I look at my partner and he says, "Sure. We'll do everything we can to find out who killed your husband." I note he makes no reference to handing over to her lawyer any of the VPD's evidence which we might find. And, surprisingly, Bob Pridmore doesn't bring up the subject.

I wonder why.

———

"WHAT IF *HE'S* HER LOVER?" Stammo is wondering the same thing that occurred to me in the conference room. The way she kept looking at Bob Pridmore might not have been to check for a lawyer's approval but for a lover's. I nod my agreement. He takes a bite of his beloved chocolate digestive cookie and I sense there's more to come. "I didn't really think it before, but what if we're being played? I didn't think she could have killed her husband, I still don't, but he's big enough and ugly enough to have done it. Maybe they're just hiring us for cover. Using us to find holes in their stories, holes they can fill in later. Or finding other possible suspects who their lawyers can point a jury at. It makes perfect sense." He's warming to his theme now. "For some reason we can't think of, a year ago Dale stops boinking her. Finally, out of frustration, she starts an affair with her lawyer, big Bob. They hit it off and decide they'd like to make it permanent. If she divorces him, at best she'll get half his money, a lot less if there's a prenup. So they decide to off him."

"Makes sense up to a point," I agree with him. "Except she said that at the time of Dale's death, she was home, in bed, alone. If they did it together she would have admitted he was her lover and that they were both in bed, thus giving each other an alibi."

Stammo grunts and I continue, "We need to find out about the prenup. It only makes sense if there was one. With no prenup, she could get half his money in a divorce, it would be enough to satisfy anyone. As an heir to the Summers' fortune, it would be millions."

"There's no accounting for greed," he says round another mouthful of cookie.

"True." I worry the idea for a bit. "There's another angle: what if big Bob did the murder without her knowing?"

"Oh. Yeah. Makes sense. I can't imagine her doing it."

"There's just one thing bothering me," I say. "Why brand him with twenty-thirteen, the year they got married? Isn't that a giveaway?"

"Good point. I hadn't thought of that."

"Unless..." I mull the idea for a bit.

"Unless what?"

"Well it's a bit convoluted but think about this. Big Bob starts an affair with Marly. It's going great and she falls in love with him. But he's got his beady eyes on the Summers' fortune. So he kills Dale, plants her DNA at the scene and brands him. Now he's got a hold over her. He can give her an alibi for the time of the murder just by saying they were together but he can threaten to recant the alibi at any time if she doesn't do exactly what he says and then the evidence is stacked against her." When I've said it, it doesn't sound as credible as when I thought it up.

"Convoluted is right," Stammo says, taking another cookie. "S'more like an episode of Law and Order." He thinks for a moment. "Actually it's more like CSI," he says. "You found Dale's body yesterday afternoon and VPD have DNA evidence this morning? Come on!"

"Yeah, I was thinking that too. I suppose it's possible. But why would she lie about it?" Stammo shrugs. "Anyway," I continue, "I'm still going to check out whether or not she and Dale had a prenup."

"Right. But if she or big Bob didn't do it, who the hell did?"

I think it over and suddenly it hits me. There's an obvious question we've only asked once but never really looked into.

19

CAL

I can kill several birds with one stone here. I'm surprised and suspicious at the same time. Surprised he agreed to see me again at such short notice especially on the day after the death of his brother. Suspicious as to why he's at work at all; shouldn't he be mourning or dealing with his brother's affairs? But then again, it won't be the first time I have failed to understand the motives and thinking of the very rich.

"Come in Mr. Rogan, have a seat."

"Thank you, Mr. Summers. May I say how sorry I am at the loss of your brother."

He nods. "Thank you."

I decline his offer of coffee—it's getting a bit late in the day for a shot of caffeine from his fancy espresso machine—and sink into one of the deep leather armchairs. He does the same.

"I was surprised to get your call. I thought your assignment to find my brother was a closed case at this point."

"Well it is, but I just want to tie up some loose ends."

"You can take the man out of the police force but not out of the police*man*," he says.

I don't know if I manage to conceal my shock that he must have checked me out fairly thoroughly since our last meeting. I wonder if he uses a private investigator. Maybe we should go after the business; Stammo would love that. "How may I help you?" he adds.

I take a breath and start the questioning I rehearsed in the car coming over here. "First, thank you for seeing me at such short notice. I was surprised." He just gives a nod of the head. "I'd like to ask you just a few questions. First, you indicated when we spoke on Tuesday that you ran some checks on Marly." He nods again. "Might I ask how extensive they were?"

"Very."

"Would you be prepared to give me a summary?"

He looks at me without blinking. It's uncomfortable but I can stare with the best of them. My phone rings. Without taking my eyes from his, I reach down and through the fabric of my pants, press the button that sends it to voicemail. We continue for a while until a small smile creases his face. "Yes." Seems I passed some sort of test. "We were suspicious of her at first. She was paying her way through medical school as a waitress at a nightclub. Her job was to encourage the patrons to maximize their spending on the house champagne. Nothing sleazy, you understand. It wasn't *that* kind of nightclub." He makes air-quotes around the last word. "That was where Dale met her. She obviously fit what he was looking for and I'm sure she was delighted to land him. They were married three months after they met."

"You think she was a gold-digger?" I ask.

"No. Not really. I'm sure she was delighted to be married to a rich man but I don't think money was her primary motive. I think she really loved him."

"You said you had never met her..." I leave the question hanging.

"True but the investigators I used got to know her well enough to make the judgement."

"When they got married was there a prenup?"

"No. I tried to convince Dale over the phone that he was crazy to marry without one but he wouldn't hear of it. That call did not go well."

Without a legal prenuptial agreement, Marly

would almost certainly have got fifty percent of Dale's fortune in a divorce. Was he worth murdering for the other fifty percent? Likely not. It blows the Marly and/or big Bob scenario out of the water.

"In the event, it didn't matter," he continues. "My father was still alive at the time and altered the terms of Dale's trust fund so that it would not revert to his wife on his death or divorce unless they had been married for seven years."

"Did Marly know about this?"

"I really don't know."

I can't help feeling relieved that if Marly knew about the terms of Dale's trust fund, it puts her out of the running as her husband's murderer. However, if she did know, maybe her lawyer didn't.

"Can you tell me more about the trust fund?" I ask.

He gives me the steady stare again. It lasts a long five seconds. "How is that relevant to 'tying up loose ends'? I think that's what you said."

This guy is too astute for me to try and B.S. him. I smile. "OK, I'll come clean. Marly has retained us to find out who killed Dale."

"Why is that? Doesn't she trust the capabilities of Vancouver's finest?" There is a joking tone in his voice.

"It's more that Vancouver's finest don't trust her." I say it without thinking and it's a major breach of client confidentiality. I have to watch myself with Luke Summers; not let myself be too charmed by his easy tone.

"Oh. That's the way the wind blows is it?"

It may have been a gaff on my part but I can use it. "That's why I wanted to know more about the details of the trust fund."

"OK." He looks at his watch. "The trust was set up for myself and Dale with some minor shares to my father's siblings and their progeny. The trust holds some dividend paying investments, the largest of which is Summers Holdings Inc. The beneficiaries of the trust draw a regular income from the trust and are able to draw on additional capital for major purchases, for example a purchase of property. In the event of the death of one of the beneficiaries, their share goes to their next of kin. It's all pretty straight-forward."

I have a trust fund from the estate of Mr. Wallace as a thank you for solving his son's murder so I understand the workings. "I have a couple of questions, the first one being what was Dale's income from the trust?"

He answers without hesitation, "Twenty-five thousand a month."

It's a hell of a lot more than mine; I try not to show my surprise.

"US dollars," he appends. That adds another

seven thousand Canadian. Definitely out of my league.

"He had houses in West Van, Salt Spring and Whistler and a townhouse in Kits. Are they owned by the trust?"

"Kitsilano?" he asks.

"Yes, he owned the townhouse where his body was found."

"Hm?" There is a tone of surprise in the short grunt, from which he quickly recovers. "No, he was able to draw down on his capital allowance to buy the properties. They were his."

"So, Marly would inherit those?" Upward of fifteen million bucks worth of property is a fair enough motive for murder.

"Depends on Dale's will, I suppose."

Now to ask the question that might well open up a new line of questioning. "Dale and Marly were going through a bad patch in their marriage. They hadn't been intimate in over a year. Do you happen to know if Dale was being unfaithful?"

"No, I'm sure he wasn't. Infidelity wasn't Dale's style. Our family has always held true to our religious convictions. Dale was no exception. He was still a regular attendee at church. He would no more be unfaithful than he would kill someone."

He says it quickly, with a deep and firm conviction.

And I don't believe a word of it.

———

THE WEDGEWOOD IS a boutique hotel on Hornby Street; its lounge looks out onto the Law Courts and it's a favourite hangout for trial lawyers. With most trials recessed for the day, it is humming with activity.

I'm trying to enjoy a Hophead IPA, a good old standby, while waiting for Jim Garry to appear. His voicemail did *not* sound very upbeat and I'm more than a little worried. It's a worry that stirs the Beast, the craving for the blissful peace only heroin can provide. As I progress in my recovery, the longing comes and goes but it's rarely as strong as this. A tiny part of my mind is picturing me walking down to Hastings and Main to buy a flap of heroin. The longing is balanced by the fear of getting a fentanyl substitute which could kill me in one last blissful high. People ask why would a junkie run the risk with fentanyl. They have no idea. When the Beast takes over your mind, you lose all choice in the matter. Everything is subsumed by the need for the high. I try not to dwell on it but I can feel my muscles twitching, trying to force me to my feet, out the door, to my car and away to the east side dealers.

"Hi Cal, sorry to keep you waiting." Jim Garry

drops into the chair opposite and signals the waiter over. He is still wearing his lawyer's collar and short jacket, an anachronistic holdover from the English Courts which are the foundation of Canada's justice system. Despite the formal attire, his warm smile and twinkling eye give me a respite from the calls of the Beast.

He orders a Pinot Noir and leans forward. "We have a problem." The four words nobody wants to hear from their lawyer or their doctor. The respite was fleeting. "I had a discussion with your partner this morning," he says. Why didn't Stammo tell me about this? Was that why he had a glass of whiskey in his hand when I walked in? "There is a possibility he won't testify on your behalf."

A cold dread washes over me. "Did he say he wouldn't testify?"

"No. He just said he would have to think about it."

"But why?"

"I don't know for sure Cal, but you have to remember that no matter what the provocation, you did kill his son."

"They weren't even that close. Nick hadn't seen him in years." As soon as I say it I realize how stupid that is. Matt was his son. Could I stand up for Stammo if he had killed Ellie, no matter how compelling the reason? I know the answer to that question.

"If Nick won't testify to his conversation with Matt on the walkie-talkie, what does that do to my defence?"

"They have your blood on Matt's clothing. When they searched your apartment, they took a lot of clothing. They may well have his blood on something of yours. They took the receipts you used to buy the equipment you used on the island. You can bet they have got a knife identical to the one you bought and matched it with the wound in Matt's chest. It's possible you left something else there which they can tie back to you. They may have more."

"But what about motive? What would my motive be for killing him?" I can hear the anxiety in my voice.

"By your own admission, you were there spying on his boss, looking for evidence the girl was there. In court they will imply you killed Santiago and Perot. They'll say he found you and you decided to silence him too."

"But he shot me; doesn't that prove self-defence?"

"Without your partner's evidence about the sequence of the shots and his conversation with Matt on the walkie-talkies, there's no proof he shot first.

As you didn't check into a hospital, there is no proof he shot you at all."

He's right. "How do you rate my chances if Nick doesn't testify?"

"Not better than fifty-fifty. I don't know what other evidence they may have dredged up. On top of that I'm wondering—and I don't want you to comment on what I'm about to say—but I'm wondering if during their searches they found any evidence, at either your's or Nick Stammo's home. If so, it could implicate you in the murders of Santiago and Perot and if that were the case, you could be re-charged with committing those murders and Nick could be charged with conspiracy to commit. If that happened and if he had a lawyer with any brains at all, Nick would turn Queen's evidence against you. That would *not* be good."

I can feel the blood drain from my face.

———

I TELL myself I'm here because I like the food and I need to treat myself to a late dinner. But the truth is the location itself. The Pourhouse Pub is on Water Street in Gastown and although the beer and the food there are wonderful, it's just a couple of blocks from that strip of Hastings between Main and Abbott; the jungle where just about any drug known to man is available.

I've been sitting in my car at a parking meter, balancing on the edge of a decision for almost half an hour. I'm held immobile by the perfectly balanced forces of my need for heroin and my fear of the consequences. Three and a half years back when I was still using regularly, fentanyl was an exception. Now it's a different story.

I watch the cars on Water Street, a distraction from the need to make a decision. The sidewalks are teeming with people heading to and from restaurants and bars to celebrate the approach of the weekend, less than twenty-four hours away. I long to be part of that throng, to share the camaraderie of old friends or fellow workers or lovers on a date. I miss it all. Especially being on a date with a lover. It is a long time since I had an actual date. Although Sam and I were reunited for a brief instant a couple of weeks ago, we never found time to actually go out together alone; just for a meal; just to sit in a restaurant; just to hold hands across a table and read the world in each other's eyes.

How can I live without thee, how forego
Thy sweet converse, and love so dearly joined,
To live again in these wild woods forlorn?

I think my paradise with Sam is lost to me for ever. The thought sharpens the longing for the sweet oblivion. Just a quick hit to soothe my troubled breast, to erase for an instant the loss I feel. I can hear the Beast inside. He's telling me I won't feel so alone, that sadness can be banished, that I can just take one hit. One hit isn't going to get me hooked again. It'll just be a one-off. Let's go.

Then the longing is tinged with an anger, an anger at myself. Get over yourself Rogan. Your life isn't over yet. Sam is maybe lost but perhaps there will be other lovers. As I mull over the thought, I can't help thinking of Em. She has a nice quality to her. She uses her Southern accent to give a tantalizing mocking tone to what she says, a tone that mocks herself as well as me. Maybe there is hope for me with Sam or if the fates decide, with someone else.

Maybe.

I can't decide. What the hell, why not?

Then a voice rings in my head. The voice is Ellie's. Words spoken three and a half years ago. *A junkie's a good thing, right Daddy?*

And so I decide. Not tonight. Maybe tomorrow but not tonight.

I get out of the Healey and lock the door, not that it is a deterrent to any half-competent thief but just to stop any street person from rummaging inside for whatever he or she might forage. I walk west on Water Street in the direction of the pub, thinking of the Welsh rarebit, steak and frites or house burger I will have to choose between. And will I have the Jongleur Wit or the Rye Stout?

A yellow cab passes me and splashes water from a puddle a few feet in front of me. I'm about to cross the street but get distracted by the laughter of an early spring party of Japanese tourists standing beside the steam clock. As I look toward them the cab pulls over to the curb and a man approaches it. A man I know. It's Sean O'Day, the Irishman from Galway who is Southbrook's project manager. He opens the cab door and an elegant leg emerges and places itself on the sidewalk. I feel two conflicting emotions: a heart-skip of pleasure that I'm about to run into Emily Audley and a wrench of jealousy that she is here with O'Day. Perhaps they're an item. Her slim hand emerges from the cab and O'Day takes it, helping her out. Except it's not Em. My pleasure and jealousy evaporate and are replaced by puzzlement and shock.

What is Marly Summers doing here with her late husband's client?

20

TOMÁS

I talked to our lawyer, Javier. He has a good contact in the VPD. It seems Rogan *was* on the island when my father was killed. Whoever we killed in that boat may or may not have been involved in their deaths. They are sure Rogan was the assassin but have no evidence."

"Do you want me to take him *Patrón*? Our people are following him. He just went into a restaurant in Gastown." I like the eagerness in Javier's eyes.

"Not yet. I want to take the wife and daughter first, then his partner and then him. I want him to witness their deaths before I put a bullet between his eyes." I savour the thought. "I think we will kill the partner first. Then I want you to enjoy yourself with the wife while he looks on." Javier likes that. It is a fitting reward for him. "Then I will kill the wife."

"What about the daughter?" he asks, his eyes gleaming.

"How old is she?"

"Eight or nine." Javier licks his lips and looks intently at me. Uh-ha. So… Javier shares Perot's perversion. Good to know.

"Maybe we'll bring her to say goodbye to her father and then you can lead her away. Before I kill him, I'll tell him what you are going to do to her. We'll let him think on that for a while before I finish him."

"Thank you *Patrón*."

Javier is fully motivated now.

"But first we need to find them," I tell him. "And I know you won't let me down."

21

CAL

My choices are different from my expectations, rather than Welsh rarebit, steak or burger I'm having to choose between osso buco, veal saltimbocca and rack of lamb. I have followed Marly and Sean O'Day into Al Porto, a very fine Italian restaurant which has been a Vancouver landmark for decades. I was lucky enough to walk in a few minutes after them and it's late enough that I got a table without a reservation. It's not the best table in the place but it serves my purpose; it is beside the pillar of one of the terracotta-coloured archways and partially conceals me. However, by leaning a little to my right I can see their table well. I can see most of her face but have only a quarter view of his.

I'm trying to read the dynamic. She looks relaxed and he is leaning forward and seems to be doing most of the talking. As he talks, I can see a small smile playing on her lips. I wonder what he has to say to her that she finds amusing.

"Can I bring you a cocktail, sir?" My waiter is tall and cadaverous with the frostiest of smiles. He reminds me of a restaurant manager I once had a disagreement with at the Lift.

"A glass of Chianti would be nice."

"Certainly sir." As he walks away, I focus my attention back. At their table the waiter has brought a bottle and is pouring glasses of white wine. He puts the bottle in a cooler on their table. They lift their glasses to each other, clink them and she smiles. I wish I could see more of his face. Do they look like lovers? Is Sean O'Day the man whose name she refused to reveal either to Stammo and me or to the VPD? And if so, why? Is it because she was seeing him, her husband's client, behind her husband's back?

As I watch them, I can't decide. I think back to my meeting with O'Day. He's one of those people whom it's difficult to read but Marly's another story. As I watch, she reminds me of my meeting at her house last night. She seems to be talking slowly and deliberately and she seems to be giving him the look she gave me just before running her fingers up my thigh. Although I can hardly see his face, I sense he's as uncomfortable as I was or maybe I'm just projecting that. She smiles at him and pulls a cellphone from her purse. Her face loses it's smile and takes on a look of puzzlement. She hangs up and says something to him. He leans forward, gets up from the table, says no more than three words to her and heads toward the men's room. Unfortunately, it brings him past my table. I put my nose down into the menu and massage my temples with my hand concealing my face as well as I can, but not before I get a glimpse of his face.

The stoicism has gone. Right now it's showing a mixture of confusion and fear.

When he's past me, I look back up toward their table. Marly doesn't look completely at ease and certainly not an iota like someone who can instill such fear into a grown man. There's something serious going on here and I'm betting it has something to do with her husband's murder. A part of me wants to go over and confront her but the sensible part tells me to hold back and watch things unfold.

The waiter places a glass of wine in front of me. "Have you decided what you would like to eat sir?" he asks.

"The saltimbocca, please," I say without being aware of consciously deciding.

"No appetizer, sir?" It sounds more like an accusation than a question.

Having checked the prices on the menu, I have no difficulty in saying "No, thank you."

I drink some of my Chianti and focus back on Marly, she has finished her first glass and is pouring herself a second. She looks up and I can't read her emotion but then her face lights up with a simulacrum of that amazing smile I first saw in our offices on Monday afternoon. I follow her gaze. She's looking at Bob Pridmore, her linebacker-sized lawyer. He's handing his coat to the hostess and is surveying the room. Before I can react, his eyes lock with mine. I can see the wheels turning. He knows it's not a coincidence I'm here and I can see he wants to know why and how.

He walks over to my table. "Mr. Rogan, what are you doing here?" he asks.

I could tell him it's just a coincidence I happened to see Marly and Sean O'Day and that curiosity got the better of me, but instead I say, "My job." I lift my glass and take a sip.

"What part of your job is following my client?" he asks.

"I wasn't following her," I say with some flippancy.

I can see the anger now. Mr. Pridmore is not a happy camper. I look over to the other table and lock eyes with Marly. Her smile has changed. Her face is fixed in a mask. It evokes the image of a

Roman patrician watching a Christian and a lion with me cast as the former. It's not a pretty sight. I look back at her lawyer and see that Sean O'Day is standing behind him. If I saw fear in his blue eyes before, it's doubled now. It's naked and unadulterated. He turns and heads for the door. Pridmore follows my gaze, takes a step toward O'Day, thinks better of it, turns back to me and after a momentary confusion stalks toward the table where Marly is still sitting with her wine and her smile.

Decision time... after a second, decision made. Staying and watching Marly and Big Bob is a losing game now they know I'm here. Talking to Sean O'Day is a much better plan. I get to my feet, pull out my wallet, reluctantly drop two twenties on the table—to partly cover the half drunk wine and the saltimbocca I ordered but will never get to see—and head for the door.

Out on the street, a drizzle of rain has started to fall. I look left and then right. Sean O'Day is waving. I follow his gaze and see a yellow cab, one of the many which cruise Water Street. I'm held by a momentary indecision. Should I run up and try to speak to him? I weigh the options and decide. I turn my back on him and run east toward my car. Right now he's probably still in the grip of his fear. If I try and talk to him now, he'll panic and force his way into the cab and will be lost. Better that I follow him so that I can try and approach him when he's far from the aura of Marly and Big Bob. That's the plan anyway.

I make it to the Healey in record time. It starts on the first try, thank heavens, and the puny windshield wipers whisk the film of rain away. A second cab, a blue one bearing the Maclure's logo passes me and way up ahead I can see Sean's cab take off. It's a good two hundred meters ahead. I pull away from the curb and follow the blue cab up Water street; it's dawdling along looking for a fare and the street is just too narrow for me to pass. I have to hold myself back from hitting my horn; that would likely trigger his cussedness gene and make him slow down even more.

The yellow cab has no such impediment and is accelerating away. I made the wrong decision; I should have approached O'Day when I had the chance. For an instant I get a whisper of hope as I see the traffic lights at Cordova are red but that slim hope is dashed as they change and the cab follows the green arrow on to Richards and out of my field of view.

I slam the wooden steering wheel with the palm of my hand and curse the driver of the blue cab. As if on cue, a young woman in the mini-est of miniskirts flags him down and he pulls over. I jab my foot down on the gas pedal and the Healey leaps forward, the three litre engine responding by doing what it loves best. I don't have much time. A frisson of worry bites me: I'm already going way too fast; the Healey's a bit skittish in the rain and if a careless pedestrian... The green arrow of the traffic signal blinks out and for a nanosecond I consider accelerating and jumping the lights but sense prevails and I hit the brakes bringing the car to a slippery halt.

I've lost him.

22

STAMMO

The Two Parrots is a cop hangout. Most mornings you'll see a line of Vancouver Police Department motorbikes parked on the sidewalk outside. The food's good, cheap and plentiful. It was Steve's idea to meet here this evening and it works for me. I was surprised he suggested getting together. He could have given me the info over the phone but face-to-face is always better; he's more likely to tell me more than I asked for.

I roll up to the door and meet the first obstacle. There's a small step up to a tiled area in front of the door. I don't remember it being there. All the times I've been here were before the accident; I probably never noticed it, why would I? Fortunately the step's only a couple of inches high and I easily back the wheelchair up it. I gotta say I'm getting pretty good with the chair. Then the sign on the door: 'Pull.' It's like the conference room door back at the office. I grab the door handle with my right hand and wheel backwards with my left and, of course, the door bangs up against the front wheels of the chair. I lean forward and a voice says, "Dj'a wanna hand?" Anger stirs. I turn to tell the good Samaritan I can do this myself goddamnit and see the speaker. Old, dirty, ragged and homeless, he smells of too many nights in shelters and too much cheap vodka. All the anger blows away. I'm a million times better off than this old guy but he's taking the time to help a fellow human.

I swallow my pride. "Thanks man, I appreciate it." I let go of the door and wheel back a foot. He drops his bulging garbage bag on the floor and opens the door for me. After I wheel forward far enough to keep the door open, I reach into my pocket and pull out my wallet. "Have one on me," I say as I hand him a twenty.

He runs a finger over his lips and takes the money. "I d'int do it fer money," he says, "but thanks anyway." The bill disappears into the pocket of his coat.

He starts to wander off but I call him back. "Don't forget your stuff." He turns and shrugs, walks back and grabs the garbage bag, which probably contains everything he owns in the world. He hoists it up onto his shoulder and walks off into the rain. Rogan always says giving money to the homeless doesn't do any good because they're just going to spend it on drugs or booze. He's right about this one. My twenty will almost certainly go to buying him some cheap vodka but what the heck, it'll numb the reality of his life for a few hours.

I roll into the Parrots. There's a group of uniforms over by the giant air conditioning unit, catching a couple of innings of a Blue Jay's game before they go back out onto the streets. I recognize a few of them but they're focused on the game and don't see me which is as well because I can't stand the pity I see in the eyes of former colleagues.

There are a few tables occupied by civilians enjoying a Thursday night out. My favourite table by the window's empty and I wheel over and grab the menu which I'm pleased to see hasn't changed since I used to come here regularly a few years back. The way Vancouver is growing, I wonder how long the Parrots will be able to stay in business; this location on Granville and Davie has gotta be primo real estate. The other great breakfast place down the street has just closed down, not that I would ever have gone there with my cop friends but that's another story.

The waitress comes over with a menu. She's a

new face, well actually an old face but she's new to me. "Hi," I say. "Where's Jeannie?"

"She retired, honey," she says. "I'm Sue. What can I get you?"

Just as I'm ordering a Lucky Lager—Rogan's trying to get me to love his craft ales and they're OK but I still like a regular beer—Steve walks in. He exchanges waves with one of the uniforms and makes his way over to my table. Seeing him brings back all the old memories. We were teamed up years ago just after Rogan was originally thrown out of the VPD and we worked well together right up until I ended up in this damn chair. Steve looks well; his promotion to Sergeant looks good on him. He's a bright guy, I'd be surprised if he didn't make Inspector in a couple of years.

We shake hands, he orders a Lucky, sits down and drops an envelope on the table.

His "How's it going Nick," gets us chatting about what we're each working on and he tells a couple of funny stories about guys in the Department we both know. I laugh but, to tell the truth, it just brings home the pain of losing out on not being a member any more.

I think he senses how I'm feeling and changes the subject. "Anyway, you wanted some info on the Dale Summers murder," he says.

"Yeah, how's the investigation going?"

"Not great. It was a pretty brutal murder so we don't think the wife did it but who knows? I guess Rogan told you about the brand on his stomach: two, oh one three. It was the year they got married, so it could be her or someone trying to frame her. She was having an affair but she refuses to tell us who with."

"Yeah, she won't tell us either," I say. "She says it's not possible for her lover to have been the killer but before we could press her on it, her lawyer shut us up and said to move on to something else."

"Ah yes, Bob Pridmore. What do you think about him? Do you think he might be the lover and/or killer?" he asks.

"It's possible. Only thing is, if he was her lover and he wanted Dale out of the picture, why would he brand Dale with the year of their marriage? It would just implicate her. On the other hand, he's big enough to be the killer. He could easily have subdued Dale and he feels to me like he's mean enough to have branded him."

"Size isn't a factor. Dale had been given a roofie. Anyone could have subdued him, tied him up and gagged him."

"Anything else come up in the autopsy?" I ask.

"Not a lot. COD was sharp force trauma from

the dagger in his chest. They think he was alive when he was branded." He shakes his head and continues, "He was gagged with a wad of J-cloths and tied with regular duct tape. The only thing odd was the dagger."

He opens the envelope and slides out a photo. The dagger has an ornate handle with what look like coloured jewels embedded in it. The blade's thirteen inches long according to the ruler placed beside it in the photo but only the bottom five inches are bloodied. It doesn't look like the sort of thing you could buy in a store. "It looks old fashioned, like something Robin Hood might have used," I say.

"Yeah, we had an expert on medieval weapons look at it and he said it was a style of dagger used by the Crusaders but it's a cheap knock-off."

"Weird."

"We've contacted a bunch of businesses which supply weapons for movie, TV and stage productions. Most of them have got back to us but none of them recognize it. One guy said he thought there was a manufacturer in the States who he thinks might have made it. He couldn't remember the name but said he would get back to us."

As he pauses I ask, "Marly Summers said you had DNA evidence that she was at the townhouse. What was it?"

"It was a bluff. I was with Eric Street and he thought it was a good idea to try and rattle her. He's an idiot."

"I didn't think you could get the DNA done that fast, nor did Rogan. She also told us he kept on about whether she had threatened her husband."

"Like I said, he's an idiot."

I let it drop but can't help wondering if he's being straight with me.

The waitress comes over with the beers and takes our food orders. When she leaves the table Steve takes a big drink of his beer and says, "We're getting a lot of pressure from on high about this case. The Summers family are a powerful bunch and they want answers, so anything you and Rogan can do to help out on this one would be great. In the envelope are copies of the autopsy, the key interviews and all the crime scene photos. Why don't you look over them while I go to the john." He gets up and heads toward the bamboo awning over the entrance to the washrooms and I envy his ability to just get up and go to the bathroom without thinking about it. As he passes the table with the VPD members, he stops and puts his hand on the shoulder of one of them. "Thanks for your help with that arrest on Monday Jed, you did a great job." Cops try and act casual about compliments but I can see he's pleased. Steve's a natural leader and it boosts my belief he's going to make Inspector soon.

As he disappears into the washroom, my eyes catch the old advert for 'Sailor Jerry Spiced Rum.' There's a good story behind that.

As I'm sliding the pictures out of the envelope, I hear a familiar sound. I look out the window. I was right. It's the growl of Rogan's English sports car, driving west on Davie. I wonder where he's going? Hopefully following a lead on the case. Just hanging out with Steve and working on a case has let me forget for a moment the big issue between me and him. Now it's back, front and centre in my mind and I just can't decide what to do.

To distract my thought away from the decision I know I'm going to have to make sooner or later, I start to go through the photos; they're all pretty gruesome. I'll read the autopsy and interviews later. For now, I move the picture of the dagger to the top of the pile. There's something familiar about it but I can't quite pin it down. I just stare at it and try and think where I've seen it before or at least something like it. It's going to bug me 'til I figure it out. I just keep staring.

Steve and the waitress arrive back at the same time.

When we've made some headway with our

burgers Steve says, "So Nick. There's another reason I wanted to talk to you." His face is deadly serious. OK. Whatever it is, *this* is the real reason he wanted to meet face-to-face.

"Uh-huh," I grunt.

"It's to do with what happened on Samuel Island."

Oh jeez, what's he gonna say now?

"Go on," I say. Even I can hear the wariness in my voice.

"There's a lot of pressure to re-charge and prosecute Rogan for the killing of Perot and Santiago. It's technically IHIT's case of course but they have asked for our assistance on it. The thing is, they've got a forensics team going over that island with a fine tooth comb. So far they haven't found any evidence there was a shooter on the island other than Rogan and they're sure the shots came from where Rogan was hiding. They're working hard to find something that connects him to the assassinations." He pauses, looking at me. it's a good interrogation technique to get me to fill the silence. I don't fall for it. He continues, "I got a call from their lead investigator and he indicated they may have found something."

I keep my poker face in place. Rogan's sure he didn't leave any evidence of the shooting on the island and even if one of Santiago's gang told them about shooting up the decoy boat with all the evidence, there's no way they would be able to find it under a hundred and fifty meters of the Georgia Strait. He's bluffing, at least I hope he is.

"The thing is Nick, if Rogan goes down for the killings, you'll be prosecuted for conspiracy to murder or at the very least aiding and abetting. Either way, you'll serve time." He stops to let that sink in and it does. A memory from my past with the Ontario Provincial Police jumps into my mind. I had to go interview a possible witness at the Millhaven Penitentiary. It scared the crap out of me. At the time, I swore to myself I would rather die than go there as a prisoner. Steve lets me chew on the thought for a bit before saying, "I've been authorized to offer you an assurance of immunity against future prosecution."

"Turn Queen's evidence?"

"Yeah. If you co-operate and tell us how Rogan did it and provide any and all evidence you have, you can walk away scot-free. We'll even make sure you get to keep your security business license so you can carry on working."

I look across the table at him.

He gives a grim smile. "But you've got to decide quickly. If IHIT come up with any solid evidence against Rogan, they won't need you anymore. They'll arrest him and likely you too." he says.

He can see the indecision on my face.

"It's the smart choice Nick."

And he's right. God help me, he's right.

23

CAL

After what seems an eon, the green filter light flicks on and I curve onto Richards Street. Way up ahead I see two yellow cabs. Mercifully the light at Pender is green and as I speed through it, it changes to red. It gives me a new hope; the traffic lights along Richards are synchronized and if I can keep up a steady sixty-five klicks I should be able to catch them.

I just make the green lights at Dunsmuir and then at Georgia and after another three blocks I'm behind the two yellow cabs. As they approach Davie the lights turn red. One cab moves into the right lane with his turn signal flashing. The other stays in the left lane. Which one to follow? Undecided I straddle the lanes earning an irritated honk from the driver behind me. I ignore it. Which way? In the rain I can just make out the backs of the heads of the passengers: both male, both hatless, both unidentifiable. As I look back and forth between them, I get a break. The passenger in the cab on the left turns his head so that it's in profile, I can't be sure about identifying him but don't need to. There's a second passenger with him. She was obscured from view by the back pillar of the cab but I can now see her clearly through the back window as she leans over and kisses her companion.

The cab on the right is the one containing Sean O'Day... probably.

The cab makes the right turn and I follow him along Davie, past the good old Two Parrots at Granville and for three more blocks until he crosses Burrard and pulls over beside the community gardens. I can't stop behind him—it will be too obvious I've been following him—so I pass the cab and pull into a parking spot outside a computer store.

I get out of the car and stand under the awning outside the store. O'Day is just getting out of the taxi, at least I think it's him but can't be sure because he has turned away from me and is walking back toward Burrard. I start to follow but stop immediately. He has taken a right turn and is crossing to the south side of Davie. I pull out my phone and pretend to be texting while keeping an eye on him; on a rainy night he's not likely to spot me but I don't want to take that chance just yet. He turns right again and walks along the sidewalk then into the first building past the gas station. It's a Vancouver icon: Celebrities Nightclub.

He has opened up a whole new vista of possibilities in the murder of Dale Summers.

———

I KNOW I shouldn't but I feel uncomfortable here. It's not the loud music or the flashing blue, purple and pink lights shining down from the vaulted ceiling, itself alive with light. It's not that I feel uncomfortable with the clientele. I just feel like a fraud, like I don't belong here.

I make my way through the throng toward the longest bar I have ever seen. I find a gap between a man in the leathers of a biker and a tall, stunning brunette in a slinky red dress, with a blue martini and a large Adam's apple. I order a Black Russian from one of the bartenders and while she's making it I look to my right. Sean O'Day is a few feet away from me with what looks like a triple Bourbon on the rocks. It makes me think of Stammo; he would hate it here in Vancouver's best known gay nightclub.

O'Day looks a lot more at ease than he did in Al Porto. His normally expressionless mask is gone and he looks like someone who has just got home from a stressful day at work and is washing away the last of the tension with a favourite beverage. I suspect he feels safe here, safe enough to talk to me perhaps. I take my drink from the bartender, ease away from the bar and go over to him.

"Hi Sean."

He turns toward me and, for an instant, a volley of questions fire from his eyes until they are subsumed by his poker face. "What are you doing here?" he asks, neither aggressive nor pleasant.

"I followed you."

"Might I ask why?" His Irish accent seems stronger.

"I want to find out who killed Dale."

"And why are you following *me* then?"

Time for a little lie to get him on side. "Originally I wasn't following you, I was following Marly Summers."

A look of discomfort breaks through the poker face. "Marly?" he says. "Do you think *she* killed Dale?" There's a tone of incredulity in his voice.

"Maybe. Or maybe someone close to her..." I leave it hanging. He mulls it over but says nothing. I remember my conversation with the barman at the Railway Club. "You and Dale were in the Railway Club last Friday." I say.

Finally, he nods. "You know that's correct, we've

already talked about it."

"After you left, did you come here together?"

There's an even longer pause. He's probably wondering how much he can trust me. I feel a *quid pro quo* coming.

"If I tell you..." There it is. "Would you keep the information private?"

"I can't promise I won't share something you tell me with the Vancouver Police Department but only them and only if it turns out to be relevant to Dale's murder."

"Fair enough. But I really don't want my boss to know, she wouldn't approve."

"You have my word," I say. If what I suspect is true, maybe she wouldn't. Then I realize I might have just walked into a conflict of interest. Maybe this is what Em meant about negative publicity. No. Being gay isn't negative, not even in corporate America. What the hell. "Were you and Dale lovers?"

He just nods, not trusting himself to speak. Time for me to build some rapport. "I certainly won't tell Em about your affair. I can understand any boss would disapprove of an employee sleeping with one of your company's trusted advisors."

He nods again. "If she knew, it could ruin my career. If Dale was still alive, maybe it wouldn't matter so much but now my career's all I have."

The volume of the music ramps up a notch. "I'd like to talk to you some more. Do you think we could go somewhere quieter?"

He takes in a deep breath and exhales. "Sure," he says with a shrug.

For the second time this evening, I see his raw emotions unhidden by his usual poker face. The first time was the fear when he saw Marly's lawyer in Al Porto and this time it's just an infinite sadness.

And I need to find out about both.

———

THE PLACE COULD NOT BE MORE different. After the glitz and noise of Celebrities, Denny's is an ocean of calm, an old-style, twenty-four hour diner in the same block. It's the perfect place to sit in a booth and have a quiet chat. Sean O'Day, having taken the decision to trust me, is unburdening himself.

"In the first meeting we ever had, we both knew. Em had sent me up here to work with our CA firm Beloff and Plasker negotiating the lease on the building. Dale and his boss were in one of the meetings and he and I were tasked with working on some Canadian tax issues relating to the leasing of the building. After the meeting we went out to dinner and well, you know..."

"Did Marly know about the affair?"

"No. Dale never told her and we were really discreet. We would meet either at my hotel or at his townhouse in Kits. If we went out to dinner or for a drink, we would always act like it was a business meeting. That said, if she was suspicious, I suppose she could have found out."

"Did you ever go to Celebrities together?"

"God, no. That would have been a dead giveaway," he chuckles. "Dale was very much in the closet."

"Why? It's twenty-nineteen not nineteen-twenty."

"His family."

"He didn't want them to know?"

"Oh, they knew all right but they definitely did not approve. His ogre of a father put a rider on his trust fund that if his orientation ever became public, he would be cut off. When the old man died, Dale's brother Luke took over the administration of the trust and told him in no uncertain terms he would rigorously enforce the rider. Dale begged him but he was completely intransigent. He said that having a known homosexual in the family would disgrace them all, can you imagine that?" His Irish accent is becoming stronger as his anger at Dale's family shows though. "That was why he married Marly, to provide him cover; to help keep his secret. He always said when he made partner at Beloff and

Plasker he'd tell the family to shove their bloody inheritance where the sun doesn't shine."

I don't show the feeling of revulsion which is washing over me. Firstly at Dale's father and brother for treating him like that and then at Dale himself for using Marly in that way.

"How's it you know Marly?" I ask.

"I'd never met her before tonight," he says. "Dale was very fond of her and he felt really bad about using her as cover. I wanted to tell her that."

"I was watching you talk to her. She didn't register the sort of surprise I'd expect when she learned her husband had a gay lover."

"No she wouldn't. When I made the appointment to see her I told her then, on the phone."

"Did she seem surprised then?"

He bites his bottom lip and looks away. After a moment he says, "Not so much. It was difficult to read over the phone. I would have thought she'd be gobsmacked but no, she seemed to take it in her stride." His Irish accent's really strong right now. That may be a tell.

"Weren't you worried that by telling her, it might get back to your employer. You said you wanted to avoid that."

"I wasn't worried about her talking. She had as big a reason as me to keep it secret because of the clause in his trust fund. If it becomes public that

Dale was gay, his trust fund will be cancelled and she won't inherit a penny of it."

This all sounds very logical but I'm getting a nasty little feeling there's something rotten in the state of his answers.

I look him hard in the eye for a moment before asking, "When you came out of the washroom at Al Porto, you saw Marly's lawyer Bob Pridmore standing at my table talking to me. You looked terrified. Why was that?"

His face completely straight, he says, "Terrified? I think you misread me, Mr. Rogan. I had no idea Mr. Pridmore was Marly's lawyer. I had met him previously when we were interviewing law firms to represent Southbrook in Vancouver. I was just surprised to see him there and wondered why he was talking to you."

"So why did you dash out of the restaurant as soon as you had seen him?"

"I hardly think dash is the right word." His Irish accent seems even stronger now It's a tell that he's lying or maybe stressed. Good to know. "I just left. I had finished my conversation with Marly, gone to the washroom and then I left. It's as simple as that."

It's all very logical and reasonable but it has my B. S. meter registering off the scale.

24

CAL

Adry's on the phone as I walk into the office and she gives me a big smile. She's definitely becoming a big asset to the firm. Also she seems a lot happier than when she was working for that slime-bucket, porno movie-maker.

Stammo's absorbed in a bunch of photos arranged across his desk and looks vaguely irritated when he sees me. He doesn't like having his train of thought broken. As I sit down, I recognize the crime scene photos. "Where did you get those?" I ask.

"Steve. They're not doing that well with the case and thought we might be able to provide some input."

"Wow. That's not like the VPD to ask for assistance from anyone."

He grins. "We're not just anyone, Rogan." He

looks at me and then his expression changes. I can't quite read what he's thinking. "Did you get anything new?" he asks.

I tell him about my meeting yesterday afternoon with Luke Summers but skip the meeting with Jim Garry. I don't want to deal with the issue of him giving evidence in my flavor right now. I know I'm putting it off and I absolutely should talk to him about it right now but I guess I'm chickening out. Instead I tell him about the happenings in Al Porto and my conversation with Sean O'Day in Celebrities.

When he learns that Dale was gay, he nods his head and says. "When I first spoke to Marly I thought he might be."

"What made you think that?"

He shrugs. "Intuition."

I go on to the conversation in Denny's and finish with, "So the last person we know who saw him alive was also his lover."

"Holy crap. Do you think..."

But before he can finish his sentence, he stops and pushes all the photos into a pile and flips it face down on his desk. I follow his gaze and see that Adry has walked up beside me. "Secrets Nick?" she asks playfully.

"No. Crime scene photos, you don't want to see them," he grunts.

"I'm not squeamish. Let me have a look. Maybe I'll spot something you missed." She says it like she's teasing him but I can tell she really wants to see them. She holds out her hand and just leaves it there.

Nick looks conflicted and I can't help chuckling at him. "She's got you there," I say.

He shrugs and hands the photos over to her. We both watch her as she leafs through them. When she gets to the picture of the numbers two, oh, one, three branded on his stomach she asks, "What's the significance of that?"

"Twenty-thirteen was the year he married Marly," I say.

"Ahh. The pretty client you got all tongue-tied over Cal?"

"I didn't get tongue-tied," I say and immediately realize I shouldn't have spoken; it smacks of protesting too much.

"Now she got you too," Nick crows.

Adry's looking at the photo again. "If it's the year, why did the killer write the numbers like that, in a square with two zero on top and one three underneath?"

Nick says, "I dunno. Maybe he made the digits bigger to inflict more pain."

"Or she," Adry replies. "It could have been the lovely Marly." She thinks for a bit and adds, "Can I hold on to these for a while? I want to study them some more."

"Sure," Nick says. I can tell from his voice he's impressed.

"Anyhoo," she says in Canadian fashion, "I came in here to tell you boys we have a new client. I just got off the phone with them."

This is a shift in the dynamic of the office. Up until now, Adry would just pass the client queries to Nick. I look over at him to see if he approves of the role she has taken on unbidden. He seems cool with it.

"It's a couple in their seventies, claim they've been swindled. I spoke to the man but I could hear his wife in the background adding details. They seemed really sweet."

"Who do they say swindled them?" I ask. Like any other city there are a bunch of scammers in Vancouver who are happy to bilk innocent victims of their hard-earned savings. However these days the scammers could be anywhere in the world; I'm sure that with his growing computer skills Nick could track them down, but bringing them to justice or getting the mark's money back is next to impossible. They could be in Russia or Serbia or indeed anywhere.

"Their church," she says. "They say they were

cheated out of ten thousand dollars by the Church of the Pure Divine Light in Langley."

"Have they reported it to the Langley RCMP?" I ask.

"Well, that's what's funny. I asked them that but they said they didn't want to talk to the Mounties because one of the members of the church is an RCMP officer. So they called the Vancouver Police Department and asked for you, said they knew you. Whoever answered the phone at the VPD gave them our number."

A memory stirs from the past. "What are their names?" I ask.

"Phil and Florrie Franks."

I give a little smile. I remember them well. A cute little couple who had the license plates stolen from their truck and put on a similar vehicle which was used in the murder of a banker's wife a couple of years back.

Adry hands me a sheet with all the details on it. It's very organized and she clearly asked a lot of the right questions. "Good work," I tell her and get rewarded with a big smile before she heads back to her desk in the reception area.

"I'll check this out later," I say. Except I have to pick up Ellie from school today. Oh. The thought dies aborning. Ellie's not at school. She's hiding out with

Sam on Hardy Island. A maelstrom of thoughts and fears stir in my gut and I'm overcome by a burning desire to go there and see them. It's the weekend coming up. Why not? Hmmm. Let me count the ways.

Nick pulls me out of my thoughts. "Best thing we ever did was to hire that girl," he says quietly.

I nod and smile.

"So. Do you like him for the murder?" Nick asks.

"Sean O'Day? I'm not sure. I don't think so. He's one of those guys who doesn't show much. But I got the feeling he was hiding something from me. When he saw Marly's lawyer in Al Porto, his mask slipped and he looked terrified."

"Big Bob'd scare the crap out of me," he grunts.

"Me too." I can't resist a little chuckle at the thought of us being scared by Marly's lawyer. "But he tried to tell me it wasn't fear, just surprise."

"So what's the next step?" he asks.

"I told Emily Audley I would give her an update this morning then I'm going to go and grill Marly under the guise of giving her an update too. I want to know what her relationship is with Big Bob Pridmore and I want to find out what she was doing in Al Porto with her late husband's lover."

"Sounds good to me. I've got to catch up on some of our other cases while you're off doing the glamorous work."

I turn to go.

"Wait a minute, Cal."

I turn back. Stammo usually calls me by my last name.

"What is it Nick?"

He hesitates and looks like he's about to speak when Adry sweeps past me. She's holding the photo of Dale Summers' stomach. She walks over to Nick's desk and smacks it down on the surface. "Come and look at this Cal," she says. I walk over and look over her shoulder. She waits for a beat, getting our full attention, then says, "You see how he's burned the numbers in that square pattern and then has surrounded them with a square?" We both nod. "See between the zero and the edge of the square, there are two little burns?" She points with her finger. "That looks to me like a colon. What if it's not a year but a time?" She grabs a pen and writes *20:13* on a scrap of paper on Nick's desk. "That could be a time. Eight-thirteen in the evening. Maybe that's when he did it."

Nick grabs a file off his desk and pulls out the autopsy report. "Between six PM and midnight," he says.

"Yeah, but why would the killer brand the victim with the time of his death?" she asks.

"Beats the heck out of me," I say.

And I really want to know the answer to that question.

———

"How well did you know Dale?" I ask her.

"Not that well, socially; it was strictly business between us. Usually at his office or here at mine. We had lunch a couple of times and I learned he was married, no children and I even managed to drag out of him that he was from the family who owns the hotels. That's about all."

"Did you know he was gay?"

Em's eyebrow lifts a fraction; that's a tell, I just don't know what for. "I did not. Do you think that had anything to do with his death?"

"We're pursuing that line of inquiry?"

"Do the police know?"

"I'm not sure. My partner's the liaison with the VPD but he may not have updated them yet."

"It can be a dangerous lifestyle. I don't know about Canada but a lot of people in the States have a horrible hatred of gays."

"Knowing he was gay, is there anything you can think of that might be relevant."

She thinks for a bit then shrugs. "Not really. Did he have a lover?"

"Yes."

"Do you know who he was?" she asks and I wonder if she guesses. Maybe she already knows her project manager Sean O'Day is gay. Maybe now that she knows about Dale she may have spotted a pattern in Sean's past behaviour

"Not a clue," I lie. "Can you think of any candidates?"

"No. I don't think I know any gay men, not in Vancouver anyway."

That's feasible. She's only been here for a few months. Give her time. Everyone in Vancouver has at least one gay friend, even if they don't know it yet.

"What are your next steps?" she asks.

No harm in telling her. "Right after I leave here I'm meeting with Dale's wife. I want to see if she knew about her husband's orientation and if so, how she felt about it."

"That poor woman. Please give her my condolences."

"I will." Now I need to check something with her. "There's just one thing. You hired us to get ahead of any possible negative publicity. Would Dale's being gay count as negative for Southbrook."

"Heavens no," she laughs. "We're in the fashion business, half the people who work for us are gay."

I feel an internal sigh of relief. No need to worry about a conflict of interest between our client and the fact that Sean O'Day asked me to keep his orientation from her. However it makes me wonder why. If Southbrook is so gay-friendly a company why doesn't Sean want to be outed? Maybe I should ask him sometime.

I stand and grab my jacket from the back of the chair. For the first time I really take in the office. It's a very up-market shared office facility and is all very steel and glass. Her desk's very tidy having only a pen, a pad, a laptop and a framed photo on it. I find myself wanting to see the photo, wanting to know if there's a Mr. Audley waiting back home for her in Georgia or Alabama.

She sees the direction of my gaze and takes the frame, walks round the desk and stands closer to me than I was expecting. I can smell the subtle fragrance of her perfume. There are three people in the picture which was taken in what looks like a beautiful garden in the height of summer. There's an older couple who must be her parents; her mother is a very striking woman and I get an image of what Em will look like when she gets older. The third person in the picture is an amazingly beautiful young woman in a white summer dress with a blissful smile on her face. "These are my parents and my younger sister back home in Savannah." I was right about Georgia. "I must say I do miss them."

There's a sadness in her voice. "Are your parents still alive?" I ask.

"My mother is but sadly my father and my sister are not."

"I'm sorry to hear that. My condolences."

She returns the picture frame to her desk. "Thank you. I think of them every day."

She opens the door to her office. "Let me show you out," she says. We walk down a short hallway into an open office area with several lines of tables. Most of them have people working away on laptops of all types. "May I ask you if you're married Cal?"

I give her the technically correct answer. "I'm divorced."

We walk out of the office into the reception area. "I would really like to know how your meeting with Ms. Summers goes. Maybe you could pick me up here for dinner this evening, say seven o'clock?"

"I would love that Em," I say.

We stand in a companionable silence for a few seconds until the ding of the elevator intrudes. She extends her hand and I shake it, both of us holding on a little longer than would be considered necessary.

———

SHE LOOKS AT ME COLDLY. "Come in," she says without any preamble. As I walk through the door of the house she makes a bee-line for the living room, leaving me to close and lock the door and follow her.

When I catch up to her in the living room with the spectacular view of English Bay, she has already seated herself on the couch upon which she tried to seduce me. But there's no seduction in the air this morning. Standing, looking out the window, is Big Bob Pridmore.

He turns at the click of my heel on the parquet flooring. "What the fuck are you doing here?"

"Good morning Marly, Bobby," I say. That's me: Mr. Polite and Friendly. I smile warmly as I watch his anger ratchet up. I'm guessing Bobby is not his nickname of choice. "I'm here to give you an update on my investigation into Dale's murder."

"I want to know why you were following Ms. Summers last night," he says.

"Did I spoil your date?"

He takes a step toward me. "Cut the crap Rogan. Answer the goddamn question."

"As I told you last night I wasn't following Ms. Summers."

"Then what the fuck were you doing there?" he snaps.

I turn my gaze away from his and focus in on Marly. "I was following Sean O'Day, Ms. Summers' late husband's gay lover." There's no overt reaction from her except for a twitch in her jaw as she grinds her teeth together. "I'd be interested to know what was so amusing about their conversation."

Marly's forcing her composure. When she speaks there's an edge in her voice, "Sean O'Day was telling me that he—"

"Shut the fuck up Marly." Big Bob's voice is not loud but carries the fang of venom in its tone.

Marly shuts the fuck up.

I keep my eyes on her for a moment and can't help feeling sorry for her. I suspect she's an innocent caught up in the games of forces more powerful than her. Then I get a flash of intuition about those forces.

I turn and drill my gaze into Big Bob's eyes but I address her. "Correct me if I'm wrong Marly but Sean O'Day was blackmailing you, wasn't he. I was watching you." There's no reaction from Big Bob. Zero. None. Odd. "Sean told you he would out Dale's homosexuality in public which would give Luke Summers an excuse to trigger the clause in Dale's trust fund that cut him, and via inheritance *you*, out of the fund."

Marly's voice is only just loud enough to hear. "Sean wasn't even—"

"Marly!" Pridmore's voice is a growl. She shuts up again. "You're a smart man Rogan. I'm not sure how you figured it out but you're on the money. Right Marly?"

His eyes drill into hers. She just nods.

"Tell me what happened." I encourage her with a smile.

"She doesn't have anything more to say, do you Marly?"

That's it, I've had enough. He's big and he's strong but compared to Goliath, the gangbanger from my past, he's a babe-in-arms. And I bested Goliath three times out of three—well, three times out of four but he had help—I take two steps forward and lock Bob's eyes with mine. "Time for *you* to shut the fuck up Bobby-boy," I say.

He thinks about it for a second... and then thinks better of it. We both know he's done like dinner.

I turn my back on him with a measured deliberation. With every sense tuned to any movement Big Bob might make, I walk over to Marly and sit down on the couch beside her.

"Go on," I encourage her.

She looks up at Pridmore and holds his gaze for a long time. Something seems to pass between them. Then she drops her eyes on the coffee table in front of her. "Sean said that... well he said unless I agreed to pay him the income, I mean *half* of the income, from Dale's trust, he would send Dale's brother some pictures of him and Dale together. You know, explicit photos..." She pauses and I see a real pain in her eyes, or at least what I read as real pain. I don't know if I'm being a sucker for a pretty face or whether she's telling the truth. I lean toward the latter, but what do I know?

Big Bob's face is impassive. I don't think he's angry anymore but something bad is going on behind his eyes. Like a cobra getting ready to strike. Maybe I could get more from her with him out of the way.

"Would you feel safer if I threw this jerk out?" I ask her.

Her eyes are still drilled on the coffee table and with some relish I take this as tacit approval. I get up and walk toward him. "Easy or hard?" I say. But he's not looking at me; he's looking past me.

"No." Marly's voice sounds resigned. "I think *you* should go Mr. Rogan."

Bob Pridmore is smiling for the first time since I walked in. His hold over Marly is complete. I look from one to the other and wonder what that hold is.

25

TOMÁS

Javier looks very pleased with himself but the man with him looks a lot less happy to be here. I can sense his fear. Not a bad thing but, unlike my father, I do not want to rule by fear. "It's good to see you Victor," I say. "Thank you for coming." He looks relieved and surprised. I have made a point of learning the names and history of all our employees; it seems to be paying off already.

"Victor has some news *Patrón*."

I smile and nod.

"I have been following the girl on Instagram sir." Victor talks quickly, the words tumbling out of his mouth. "I went to her school's website and found their yearbook. I studied it for a while and then I set up a phony Instagram account in the name of one of the popular girls in the grade above Rogan's. She accepted my friend request in a heartbeat. She must have been flattered that a cool older girl wanted to follow her." He gives a very nasal snicker. He's an odious little worm but a brilliant coder and hacker and worth his weight in gold. "So I've been following her for a couple of days," he babbles on. "I asked her where she's staying but she says she's not allowed to say. I tried to get her to tell me but she wouldn't. Then she made a silly mistake. This morning she posted a photo of a lawn leading down to a beach. There was a dock with a boat moored to it. I downloaded the jpeg but there was no location information, she probably took it with an iPod or an iPad with the location services switched off. Her mother probably—"

"Cut out the details, Victor," Javier growls. "Tell the *Patrón* where they are."

Victor looks cowed. "No Javier," I say. "I want to hear what Victor has to say. He's one of our best people."

I can see from his face that I have a loyal employee for life now. "Thank you sir," he says. "Anyway, I couldn't track the location from the jpeg but I was able to enhance the image of the boat. It took a while, the pic wasn't very good, I had to try a number of times with different enhancement algorithms until I got enough of the letters in the name to make some intelligent guesses. I entered each guess into a search of the Canadian Register of Vessels and I finally got a hit. The boat's name is Sweetwater Rider. It's registered to a Mr. Neil Tapscott. Here's his address."

He hands over a tatty piece of paper. I look at it and pass it to Javier. "Unfortunately," Victor adds, "I can't search the land titles database by owner name but I can try to hack the database if you would like me to try."

"No need," Javier says. "I know the address. I can make a visit to this Mr. Tapscott and find out where the property is."

I mull over the idea. Javier's idea is a little heavy handed. I think this needs more finesse than he can apply.

"You have done well Victor. Javier will see to it that you have a nice little bonus for your excellent work."

"Thank you sir. Thank you. I really appreciate it."

I just nod magnanimously. "Excuse my rudeness but could you leave Javier and me alone for a moment?"

"Of course, sir. Of course." He scurries from the room.

"Tomorrow morning, you and I will deal with

this Javier. You too have done well. Your reward's one step closer."

Oh, Mr. California Rogan. You are going to suffer sorely for killing my father before I had the pleasure of doing so myself.

26

CAL

Three times in four days, Mr. Rogan. You're becoming a fixture here. Maybe I should offer you a job." His voice is convivial but I sense a certain irony. I don't want to wear out my welcome but I need to know something only he can tell me. I decide to play along.

"Maybe you should," I say, giving him a big, and I hope charming, smile. "Who do you currently use for investigations and security?"

Luke Summers' smile goes slip-sliding away as he says, "Cut to the chase Mr. Rogan, why are you here today?" Clearly the legendary Rogan charm's not working.

"The rider in the terms and conditions of your brother's trust fund." That's got his attention. "Why did your late father put it in and why haven't you taken it out?"

"Which rider would that be?" he asks just a bit too smoothly.

"OK, if you want me to spell it out, the rider that says if his homosexuality should ever become public, he's cut off. For heaven's sake it's twenty-nineteen." My anger's only partially faked.

"My father was an extremely religious man; he took the bible's prohibition of a man laying with a man *very* seriously."

"OK, I understand that, but do *you* take it seriously?"

"Yes Mr. Rogan, I do."

This is the question I came here to discover. And of course it begs another question but I need to approach it obliquely. "Might I ask why?" I ask in a gentle but puzzled tone designed to get him to talk.

He ponders that for a moment and I'm wondering if his next words will be to ask me to leave. Maybe gentle and puzzled aren't going to work.

"Have a seat Mr. Rogan," the urbanity is back on his face. I sink into one of his leather armchairs as he walks over to his precious coffee machine. "Would you like a coffee of some sort?"

Time to play ball. I need him relaxed if I'm going to get the answers I need. "I'd love an *Americano*, please." I wonder if I'll actually get to drink it this time.

He talks as he prepares the coffees. "My family have been members of the same church for four generations. Although the building has changed three times, the tenets of our faith remain the same." He tamps down coffee into the double-shot metal filters with a plastic tool. "In several places in the old testament homosexuality is clearly outlawed and nowhere in the new testament is that prohibition revoked. It's a sin under both the old and new covenants."

"I respect that," I lie, "but why should that cause you to cut Dale's trust fund if he were to make his homosexuality public. Surely to be consistent with your beliefs, you should have cut him out when you learned of his homosexuality."

He doesn't answer but clips the filters into the machine, places cups underneath them and presses a button. While the machine does its magic, he comes over and sits opposite me.

"Yes, I must admit you've caught me in a little bit of hypocrisy. My father always believed Dale was rebelling, that he would come around and renounce his homosexuality, but by the time Dale was twenty-three my father was ready to cut him off. That was when he announced his engagement to Marly. Father didn't approve of her but he took the engagement as a sign Dale had abandoned the gay lifestyle, so he never objected to Dale's choice of spouse.

"I, however, understand it's not a lifestyle choice. Like it or not, I know Dale was born the way he was."

"So why didn't you drop the rider after your father's death?" I ask, hoping my voice doesn't betray the condemnation I feel.

The silence is broken only by the hissing of the espresso machine. He gets up, walks to the window and looks out over Coal Harbour toward the mountains. Eventually he answers. "I should have done. But I guess I felt that if Dale came out, it would besmirch the family name and that it would spill over to the Hotels. We make a great deal of money from conventions run by people of faith. We host the Billy Graham Evangelistic Association whenever they hold their conventions in a city with a Summers Hotel. Will Graham's a personal friend. If my brother were to come out," he makes quotation marks with his fingers, "it would badly effect our reputation *and* our bottom line. Call me a hypocrite if you will but that's the way it is."

I rein in my feelings. It's not easy. Fortunately he goes from the window to the espresso machine and doesn't see my inner struggle. Two more questions now.

"How much would it impact the bottom line?

These days just about every family has a gay member. There are gay CEOs; Apple's stock isn't tanking under Tim Cook. Would it really matter that much?"

He turns. Physically and mentally. "Yes, Mr. Rogan it would." He looks at me and for the first time I see the hard inner core, the fierce determination which makes a successful CEO.

Now is the time for the final question.

"So how far would you go to keep it a secret?"

———

THE HUM of the Healey's engine is soothing and I'm looking forward to seeing the Franks; they're a lovely couple and I will do everything I can to help them out. Before I set out on this trip to Langley I looked up the Church of the Pure Divine Light. Their website looks like a scam waiting for marks. It promises to connect members with their loved ones who have 'passed on to the other side.' It will make a nice change from all the people I've met as part of the investigation into Dale Summers' murder. They all have a dark side. I'm starting to sound cynical, a hazard of the job.

I turn off the highway at the last exit before the US border and make my way eastward. I go over in my head Luke Summers' reaction to my final question. I couldn't tell if his anger was righteous indignation or guilty coverup. Either way, I never did get to try the delights of his fancy espresso machine; I was dismissed in no uncertain tone. I called Stammo and got him to do a deep plunge into Luke's background. If he's as religious as he claims, it's unlikely he killed his brother. But people do wildly out-of-character things when large sums of money are concerned; if Dale's coming out could have impacted the bottom line, who knows what Luke may have done, or have had someone else do, to his brother.

I pull up onto the Franks' property and see their immaculate, old, powder-blue Ford pickup truck parked in the large paved area behind the house.

As I get out of the car, the front door opens and Philip Franks is standing there with a broad smile on his face. "Come on in Detective Rogan," he yells. "We've got the coffee on."

My stomach reacts to the memory of Florrie Franks' coffee, without doubt the worst I have ever tasted. I walk through the door and he ushers me into the huge farm kitchen at the back of the house, where, alas, Florrie's pouring me a huge mug of the toxic brew.

"Here you are Detective Rogan," she hands it to me and I think with regret about Luke Summers' Americano. "Sit down, dear."

I do as she says and put the mug down. Philip sits down in his chair and starts to fill his pipe.

"First thing, I need to tell you I'm not with the Vancouver Police Department any more."

"I know that son, they told me but I still wanted you on the case. When your secretary called me this morning to tell me you would be here this afternoon, I was as pleased as Punch."

"He was," agrees Florrie. "Happiest I've seen him since..." She stops and a sombre look comes over her face. She takes a sip of her coffee and looks like she's going to cry. "Tell him Phil." she says.

He lights his pipe and when he's got it going, he starts to speak. "Last time you were here asking about my truck, I mentioned we had a daughter." Despite his years, there's nothing wrong with his memory. I nod. "Well about ten months ago, she died."

"I am so sorry to hear that," I say and they both nod. "No child should die before their parents." I know where this is going but I need to ask, "Were there suspicious circumstances?"

"Oh no, nothing like that," he says.

"It was the cancer," Florrie adds in her English accent.

There's a somber pause.

"Anyhoo," he sighs. "We were grief-stricken. It took a real toll on us didn't it Flo?"

She nods and takes a handkerchief from her apron pocket and dabs her eyes. I can feel an anger building at what I know is coming.

"So a friend of Florrie's tells us about this Church of the Pure Divine Light." He takes another puff on his pipe and continues through the cloud of smoke, "So we went to one of their services and there was a point where the preacher looked out at the congregation and he was looking straight at us, wasn't he Flo?" She nods her head furiously. "'You've lost a loved one,' he said. 'A daughter is it?' Well we were amazed. He asked us to stand up and he asked us some questions and we just knew he was in contact with Jan, he even knew she lived in Winnipeg and died of cancer. Then he said, 'She wants to communicate with you, there's something she needs to say. Something that you both need to know but she can't do it here.' There was a big pause and then he said, 'She's gone. I'm sorry.'"

"I still don't know how he could have known so much," Florrie adds. "He knew things not even my friend knew. I'm sure he's truly psychic. He can talk to the dead, I know that, but he didn't have to take all that money from us. He took advantage."

"I don't doubt his powers either," agrees Phil. "But he took ten grand from us because we were desperate to have some contact with Jan. We needed the comfort of knowing she was happy."

"We don't want to stop his work," says Florrie. "He helps a lot of people with his powers. But ten thousand dollars is a lot of money for some talking and for one trip to Winnipeg to communicate more closely with Jan. We don't want it all back. He can keep what's fair. That's all we want, what's fair."

It's the oldest and most insidious con in the book and I'm going to see to it that Phil and Florrie get back every penny.

I take a deep breath to calm the anger at the con artist who bilked these lovely people. The aroma of Phil's pipe tobacco enters my nose and it has an aromatic quality which I'm surprised I like.

"I've encountered people like this before," I tell them. "Anyone can speak to the dead but there are two types of people who claim the dead speak back: the deluded and the criminal. The pastor of that church is the latter."

"But how could he know so much about Jan if she wasn't speaking to him?" Florrie asks.

"I'll show you. Come and sit over here next to your husband."

She comes over and pulls a chair from the dining table over beside him and sits down. Now that I can see them both I can show them how they were conned.

"You said a friend of yours introduced you to the church?" They give tiny nods. "I'm thinking it's a woman." Again the micro movements of the heads. "Is it possible she told the pastor all the details of Jan's death?"

"No," they say in unison. Phil's head gives a slight move to his right and Florrie gives a quick double-blink. They're a con-artist's dream.

"All Ethel told Pastor Kilman was that our daughter had died, nothing more she swears."

I look at them. "Jan had blond hair," I say. The both nod furiously. "Her cancer, I'm getting that it was breast..." I catch Florrie's double blink. "No, not breast cancer, something to do with..." I pause and look like I'm concentrating and Phil rubs his thigh. "Was it bone cancer?"

"How did you know that?" he asks and Florrie looks amazed.

I ignore his question and go on, "I'm getting an idea about her work." I focus on them. "She took care of people." They give me their *no* tells. "Not in the way you would usually think, like health care, but more in business..." *no* "or education..." *yes* "Yes, that's it, she was in education."

Phil burst out with, "How the heck did you know that? She did admissions at a university."

"It's called cold reading. It's how con-men like Pastor Kilman fool you. I bet he told you Jan had blond hair." They nod. "Although you both have grey hair, you both have blue eyes. It was almost a certainty that Jan's hair was blond or at least light-coloured" I go on and explain how I established their tells and used those to guide me from general questions to specific ones.

"We've been had, Florrie," he says.

Florrie's not convinced. "But he even knew where she lived."

"I'll show you how," I tell her. "Jan was close to here…" I say it like it's a question and get Florrie's *no* tell. "No, I mean now, right now she's close to here in the spirit, but when she was alive… Canada…" *yes* "back east…" *no* "but east of here…" It's almost a certainty, most of Canada is east of Vancouver, but I still get the *yes* tell. In Canada, 'back east' is Ontario, Québec and the Maritime Provinces so there are three other Provinces to pick from, I choose the middle and smallest one. I speak slowly, "Not Saskatchewan, but west," *no* "no, no, she was from Manitoba." I remember Phil said she did admissions at a University. "She lived in Winnipeg," I say.

"That's how he did it," says Florrie, "not exactly the same questions, but like that. You're right Phil, we *have* been had."

"And remember how he got some of the things wrong but then went on to something else right away," Phil adds.

"That's how the con works," I tell them. "You remember the hits and forget the misses. I'll tell you something else. I bet after the service he asked you things like your daughter's last name and where she worked and where in Winnipeg she lived." They nod. "Well he used that to find out all sorts of other information about Jan that he could use on you later. By doing a few Google searches, digging around on Facebook and making some phone calls, he probably knew things about Jan even you didn't."

They nod some more and Phil grunts, "That son-of-a..."

"Tell me how he conned the money out of you."

"Well he charged us for private sessions where he gave us so-called messages from Jan. We had three sessions at a thousand bucks a pop. Then he said Jan had something vital to tell us but something was holding her soul back in Winnipeg and the only way was for him to go there. He said he needed money to go there and commune with her so he could free her soul and she could come back to us. Said he needed ten grand for the air fare and hotel and that it might take some time. We told him we only had seven thousand more in our savings and he said he would make an exception for us because Jan was such a lovely soul."

"What happened next?"

"He contacted us a few weeks later. Said he'd freed her soul and we should come to the church to meet with her again. When we got there he said Jan wanted to speak through him. He went into some sort of trance and we believed Jan was talking to us. He said a whole bunch of things we thought only Jan would know, then she thanked us for getting him to set her soul free and that she was passing over to the other side and would give us messages from time to time. It sounds foolish now but we really believed it was her talking. We kept on going to the church and every so often he would give us a message from Jan. We got one two weeks ago."

"So why did you call my office this morning?" I ask.

"We were doing some shopping in White Rock yesterday afternoon when we ran into a woman we'd met at the church. We asked her how she was and she said she was so happy because her husband was finally free. She said her husband was an American and that he'd fought in the Viet Nam war and that something was holding his soul in Viet Nam until Pastor Kilman went over there and freed him. We asked her when this was and when she told us the dates you could have knocked us down with a feather, eh Flo?" Florrie nods and her face is dark.

"Don't tell me," I say. "He was in Viet Nam and Winnipeg at the same time."

They both nod.

"I promise you Mr. and Mrs. Franks, I'm going to do everything I can to get your money back and the money of anyone else who has been bilked by this phony preacher."

"Thank you Detective Rogan. We really do appreciate it don't we Flo?"

She nods vigorously. "Yes dear, we do." I can tell her words are heartfelt.

"You told our office manager you didn't want to go to the Langley RCMP detachment because one of the members of the church is an RCMP officer, is that right?"

"Yes. We were worried he might be in on it."

"OK. Leave it with me. I'll look into it. But first I need you both to tell me everything you can remember about the meetings you went to at the church."

We spend a good half-hour going over the details of the con that was perpetrated on them and I'm starting to get a good idea of how it was done.

When I've got all they can remember, Phil says, "Now, I understand you need to be paid for this. How much do we need to give you as a retainer?"

Stammo won't like my answer. "Nothing. I'm going to collect my fee from Pastor Kilman. I don't know how yet, but I will."

But I need to go and make a purchase before my dinner with Em.

———

I DIDN'T EXPECT to be back here so soon but I thought it would be a nice place to bring Em. It's expensive but not too expensive and I really want to try the food I didn't get to try when I was here observing Marly Summers, Sean O'Day and Big Bob Pridmore. Fortunately the waiter who was here last night is not in evidence.

Em looks stunning. She's not wearing the same clothes she was wearing when I saw her this morning at her office. I'm wondering if she went home and changed. I kind of hope she did. I wonder where she lives.

The waiter pours our Chianti and we clink glasses. It goes down well.

"So tell me Cal, how did your meeting with Ms. Summers go?"

"It was interesting. She had her lawyer present." I describe Big Bob to her and give a summary of the meeting. "There's some sort of Svengali/Trilby dynamic going on there."

"Ahh," she says archly. "She's under his sway."

"I think so. I think either or both of them could have killed Dale."

"Really? Do you think she's the sort of person who could commit such a gruesome crime?"

"No. I think if either of them did it, it would be the lawyer."

"So he's your prime suspect?" She takes a sip of

her wine and I can tell she's enjoying it; she has a cat-like sensuality to her which I feel myself reacting to.

Trying to keep on subject, I say, "Maybe. However I had an interesting meeting with Luke Summers."

I give her a blow-by-blow of my meeting with the coffee-loving CEO.

"So he's a suspect too?" she asks. I nod. "How very Cain and Abel." She enjoys another mouthful of wine. "It has been my experience that a very small percentage of very highly religious people can be capable of the most horrendous crimes."

"A lot of people from your part of the world are very religious," I say. "Are you?"

"I was religious as a child but when I lost my sister, I'm afraid I also lost my faith."

She shifts her position and leans forward planting her elbows together on the table and putting her chin in her hands. I rein in a strong desire to lean forward and kiss her, although I don't think she'd object if I did. "Tell me about the rest of your day," she says.

"Talking about religions, I have an interesting new case centring on one."

I take her through the details of my afternoon with Phil and Florrie Franks, then she tells me about her job and how she has become pretty much of a nomad and then something spurs me to tell her about my heroin addiction. It's as if I want to get this issue out in the open before we go any further. If it's going to be a roadblock to a relationship I want to know sooner rather than later. Happily she seems to take it in her stride and we find all sorts of things to talk and laugh about through the antipasto della casa, the main course—cioppino for her, veal saltimboca for me—and the shared chocolate ganache torte.

Twenty-four hours ago I was sitting in my car just a hundred yards from here, whining about the fact I hadn't been on a date in ages and trying to decide whether to go and buy a flap of heroin and shoot myself into oblivion. Now here I am on a date, just twenty-four hours later, and not just a date but a great date. I take a sip of the cognac before me and ask, "Where do you live Em?"

"Why ever do you ask, sir?" she says in an over-the-top Southern drawl. Busted! I can feel myself blushing. "I'm sorry Cal, I didn't mean to embarrass you. My home is in Atlanta but for the past two-and-a-half years, I have moved between four different cities managing Southbrook's expansion. Right now, I'm staying at the Waterfront. If it's not raining again perhaps you could walk me home."

"I would love that Em."

We finish our coffee and cognacs chatting companionably until I call over the waiter and pay the bill.

We collect our coats and just as I'm helping her into hers, my phone buzzes and does the popcorn ringtone. It's a text from Stammo; he showed me how to set up ringtones for different people's calls and texts. Sorry Nick, you are not going to intrude onto my evening with Em. I ignore it and open the door for her. As we head toward her hotel, she links her arm in mine and I feel a lump in my throat and a frisson of pleasure mixed with a little bit of fear of where this might go.

Not ten yards along Water Street the popcorn ringtone summons me again. One hundred more yards of companionable silence and Stammo texts again. Em senses my agitation. "Why don't you answer it and get it over with?"

"Are you sure?"

She squeezes my arm and nods.

I pull out my phone. The three texts from Stammo read:

Google 20:13

Google 20:13 right now

Google 20:13 right now then call me.

"Sorry Em, if I don't do this my partner's never going to stop."

She gives me a warm smile and I have an overwhelming desire to kiss her but instead I Google 20:13.

Holy crap!

Now there's only one suspect in the murder of Dale Summers.

27

ELLIE
SATURDAY

I love the smell of bacon and Mommy cooks it just right. Daddy's a good cook too but his bacon isn't crispy enough. You have to pick up Mommy's bacon with your fingers because it just breaks up if you try and put a fork in it. Mommy puts my breakfast in front of me and sits next to me at the table. We always have breakfast sitting next to each other like this because we can look through the glass doors and see the beach and the water and Grandpa's boat. I wish Grandpa and Grandma were here.

"Are Grandma and Grandpa coming to see us?"

"Not this weekend sweetie."

"Why not?"

"They have a party to go to at Grandpa's yacht club."

Oh. That's a shame. Grandpa always makes me laugh. He pretends to box with me and gives me what he calls the Tapscott Tap. "Mommy?"

"Yes sweetie."

"My name's Rogan because Daddy's name's Rogan. Your name's Cullen but Grandpa's name's Tapscott. Why?"

"Don't you remember? I told you this before, when you were younger. When I was a little girl my daddy died. After a while Grandma met Grandpa and married him but I kept my daddy's last name."

"Daddy's daddy died too. I remember going to the funeral."

I wish Daddy was here. I really wish that.

"Mommy, can Daddy come and visit us?"

Mommy looks at me and she smiles but I think it's a sad smile. How can you be sad and happy at the same time?

"I don't think so sweetie. He's very busy with his work."

Mommy's busy with her work too but she has her computer here and works a little bit every day. "Is that really true?" I ask her.

She looks at me again and this time her smile isn't sad. She gives a little laugh. "You're just too clever for me El," she says and laughs again. "OK, I'm going to tell you the truth." Now she looks serious... and sad too. "Daddy did something and I'm very worried that the criminals he did it to will try and hurt him and us."

"Why would the bad people want to hurt us? We didn't do anything to them."

"They know Daddy loves us very much and that hurting us would hurt Daddy."

"That's like so mean," I say. "What did Daddy *do* to them?"

She looks at me again. I know that look. She's trying to decide whether to tell me the truth. "You can tell me, Mommy."

She leans over and kisses the top of my head. "No sweetie, I can't tell you the details. But I know it would make them very angry."

"How do you know they're trying to hurt us?"

"I don't."

"Then why are we staying on Grandpa's island?"

"Because I can't take the risk they might be trying to find us."

"How long are we going to stay here?"

"Until..." She stops suddenly and bites her lip. "I don't know El. I just don't know."

As I look at her, I can see a tear forming in the corner of her eye. It gets bigger and runs down her cheek. Poor Mommy; she misses Daddy as well. I give her a big hug and it makes me start crying too.

28

TOMÁS

I give her my most charming smile. I'm wearing a conservative suit and look as non-threatening as I can. "Good morning, Ma'am" I say. "I wonder if you can help me. I'm looking for Mr. Tapscott."

She returns the smile. "Oh, you have the wrong house, Mr. Tapscott lives next door."

"Yes, I know," I say, then add the lie, "I was just there but he seems to be out, nobody's home."

"That's funny, I saw him last night. Maybe they've gone shopping."

"I was wondering about that but it seems a bit early for shopping."

"Yes, it does. I don't know what to tell you."

"I need to get an important message to Mr. Tapscott. I work with his son-in-law. I'm afraid Cal had a very bad accident last night and I can't find his ex-wife. I really need to talk to her. I was wondering if she might be staying with Mr. and Mrs. Tapscott?"

"Oh dear." The old bat puts her hands to her mouth. Good. Her distress will put her in a frame of mind to be helpful. "I haven't seen Sam around but maybe she's there."

"Is there anywhere else they might be? Could they have gone away for the weekend?"

"They might have gone to their place on Hardy Island but there's no phone service there. I think cell phones *might* work up there. I'll go and get Neil's cell number for you if you'd like."

"That would be so kind of you," I say.

She turns and walks down the hallway to the back of her house. Silently, I step inside and close the door behind me. She doesn't hear me follow her into the kitchen. There's no one else here. I need to be sure. I step up behind her and clamp my hand over her mouth. She screams but the sound's too muted for anyone to hear.

"I'm going to let go of your mouth now. If you make a sound, I will kill you."

She nods.

I turn her round to face me. "Where's your husband?"

"He's dead," she says, puzzlement joining the fear on her face.

I step back and pull the silenced Colt from the holster under my jacket.

"Say hi to him for me."

———

As I GET into the back of the Escalade, Javier can see the look on my face in the rearview mirror. "Success *Patrón*?" he asks.

"Success Javier. I want you to get Victor to check out every parcel of land on a place called Hardy Island and get me the details of the one owned by Mr. Neil Tapscott."

"*Sí, Patrón.*"

I pull out my phone and open Google Maps. Hardy Island is about a hundred kilometres north of Gibsons. There are no ferries to it. It just keeps getting better.

"We will need the boat, Javier." I'm grateful for the thousandth time I had the good sense to leave Samuel Island on the cigarette boat immediately after my father's assassination. I look at his reflection in the mirror. "Your reward is near at hand my friend."

He licks his lips and smiles.

29

CAL

Nick has a big grin on his face. "I don't know why I didn't see it before. It was so obvious. I even remember my father quoting it to me. And it was all because of you, Adry. You are amazing." She gives a big grin that matches his and then some.

"Fantastic work you guys," I say. "I would never have guessed. Who thought to Google it?"

Neither of them speaks for a moment until Nick says, "Go on."

"It was me... well actually, my brother," she says shyly. "I was thinking about it at home last night. What if it wasn't the time of death? I thought it was a bit odd to be a time. Why would thirteen minutes past eight be significant to anyone? Unless it might be a scheduled time for a train or a plane or something. I racked my brains for what it could be. I thought it might be a ratio, twenty to thirteen—which incidentally is one point five, three, eight, four something, in case you're interested—or maybe part of a chemical formula. I called my brother, he's a chemist and I asked him about it but he said they don't usually use colons in Chemical formulas. He asked me if I'd Googled it. So I did."

"That's when she called me," Nick chimes in, "and so I texted you."

"I almost fell over when I saw it." I say, laughing again. "What you guys don't know is that I met with Luke Summers yesterday. I found out in the meeting he's very religious. He even referred to the bible in the meeting. I'm surprised he didn't quote Leviticus at me."

Nick turns to his screen. "I got this from biblegateway.com: *Leviticus 20:13. If a man has sexual relations with a man as one does with a woman, both of them have done what is detestable. They are to be put to death; their blood will be on their own heads.* It couldn't be much clearer than that could it?"

"So Cal," says Adry. "Do you think Luke Summers killed his brother?"

I don't want to dampen her enthusiasm but I don't want to get completely carried away with the idea. "It's looking that way, but let's play devil's advocate," I say. "The only thing we have is the fact that there *seems* to be a colon after the twenty in the autopsy photos. What if it isn't a colon, what if the killer's hand slipped while he was drawing the square around the numbers. Or what if Dale writhed in pain as he was doing it. That would rule out the Leviticus verse; there would be no religious angle to the crime."

Nick reluctantly agrees with me. Also, there's a part of me that doesn't want to think a religious person could do something like this. We look at each other. The laughter has gone from both our faces; I can see he feels as let down as I do. We had high hopes for a moment but my words have dashed them. I hope after all her hard work on this Adry doesn't feel crushed. I look at her and she's grinning broadly. "There *is* one other thing," she says.

She walks back to the reception area and returns with her iPad in hand. She holds it facing us. On the screen is the picture of a crucifix. The crossbar and the part above it are ornately carved and encrusted with jewels. It looks familiar; I think I know what's coming. "This is a picture of a cross from a cathedral in Cefalù, Sicily," she says. She scrolls the screen. Bingo! It's a crime scene photo, the photo of the dagger stuck in Dale Summers' chest. They are almost identical.

"Of course, a crucifix. I knew there was something about that dagger as soon as I saw the picture. It's because it looked like a crucifix. That cannot be a coincidence," Stammo says. "I've got to hand it to you Adry, you spotted something that Rogan and me and the VPD all missed. There's something else, Steve told me these may be manufactured by a company in the States. They're replicas of the daggers used by the Crusaders; that's another religious angle. As we're helping them on this case I can ask him for the name of the manufacturer if he's found it out yet."

"Fantastic work Adry," I say. "You've put us one step ahead of the game." I look back at Stammo, the question on my face. He knows what he should do here but I'm guessing he can feel the thrill of the chase too.

Five long seconds. "OK, Rogan," he says. "I've gotta tell Steve about this but I don't have to do it right away. I'm sure it can wait 'til Monday, I wouldn't want to spoil his weekend." His grin is back; we both know with a high profile murder case like this, the guys at VPD are working round the clock; everyone's weekend's already spoiled. "What you've gotta do is go see Luke Summers again and question him some more."

"Yeah, I might have blown that." I tell them about my meeting with Luke Summers yesterday morning and add, "When I asked him if it would have been worth killing his brother to keep their re-ligious customers, he pretty much chucked me out."

"A guilty man would do that," says Adry.

"Any man would do that," growls Stammo. "Why would you want to alienate him like that?"

"When I walked into his office, he made the point it was the third visit in four days. He wasn't going to see me again in a hurry, so I wanted to check his reaction." My words sound suspiciously like a rationalization, even to me. "I couldn't get a read on him. Either he was an innocent man feeling affronted or a guilty man pretending to be."

"Anyway," Nick says, "I wanted us to meet here at the office so that we could thank Adry for her work on this. Let's all go for a big, expensive break-fast over at the Pan Pacific; great food, great view and, seeing that despite everything we had our best ever month in March, the company can pick up the bill."

I had kind of decided to take the trip to Hardy Island and see Sam and Ellie. I really want to see them but I'm a little scared of how Sam might react to me turning up there unannounced. Not only that but, for some reason, I'm starving.

"I'm in. Let's do it. There's something else I want to talk to you guys about as well." I say.

I'll go see Sam and El tomorrow instead.

———

OUR PLATES HEAPED with breakfast goodies, the only sound is chewing and the occasional appreciative comment. Despite the rain, we can still see across Coal Harbour to the North Shore mountains, their peaks wreathed in cloud.

Stammo and I are eating like condemned men at our final meal. If I look back toward the waterfront, I can just see the hotel where Em's staying. It churns up mixed feelings. Despite the distraction of Stammo's texts we had a wonderful time. She was fascinated by the twenty-thirteen connection. Brought up in Georgia, she was raised in a religious family and immediately got the allusion. We drank cocktails in the hotel's bar until midnight. Then got to that awkward moment. Will she invite me up to her room or will she be too embarrassed to? Should I suggest it or would that be too much for a first date? My feelings were in a turmoil so I took the honesty-is-the-best policy route. I told her truthfully that I hadn't really sorted out my relationship with Sam but that I would really like to see her again. She responded by giving me a gentle kiss and saying she would really like that too. All-in-all, a great evening.

"Penny for your thoughts," Adry says.

I don't want to share those particular thoughts

so I say, "I was just thinking what a great decision it was to hire you."

"Liar, liar, pants on fire" she says with a grin.

"No it's true. Not only have you got the office humming along but you're also a real asset on the detective side of the business."

"That's for sure," says Stammo around a mouthful of Cumberland sausage.

"Thanks guys," her grin's even broader. "Here's to Stammo Rogan Investigations Inc." She lifts her mimosa and we all clink glasses.

"So Rogan," Stammo says. "You said you had something else to talk about."

"Yes. I'm pretty sure we're onto something with this religious angle and on the face of it, Luke Summers looks like suspect numero uno. But there's something going on between Marly Summers, her lawyer Bob Pridmore, and Sean O'Day, her husband's lover." I tell them about my meeting with Marly and Big Bob and her claim of being blackmailed by Sean, then finish with, "I get the impression Pridmore has some sort of hold over her. I think we owe it to her to find out what it is and see if we can help her."

"Except for one thing," says Adry. "Nick knows this Cal but I didn't get a chance to tell you. Late yesterday afternoon a courier arrived with a letter from Pridmore's firm ending our association with his client and there was a cheque for ten grand as final payment. So she's not our client anymore."

"Good money for not a lot of work. We should have a few more clients like her," adds Stammo.

I mull it over for a moment. "Who signed the letter?"

"Some paralegal 'on behalf of' Robert X. Pridmore," Adry replies. "The cheque was drawn on his firm's trust account."

"So, not from her."

Stammo puts down a forkful of mushrooms. "So you're thinking we should continue to investigate this?"

"Yes. Starting with a one-on-one meeting with Marly and without Pridmore. I'll set it up later," I say.

"Y'know what? Why don't I take a shot at her. A change of face might get her talking."

"Boys, boys," says Adry with what is becoming her signature grin. "No need to fight over her. Are you sure you're not interested in this case because she's... just... so... pretty?"

"No, I'm—" Stammo and I both say. I cut myself off from saying 'still married.' Funny, that's not even true, but my former marriage to Sam came to mind before how I feel about Em. I wonder what Stammo was going to say.

Adry giggles. "OK."

"Good idea Nick." I get the conversation back on track. "Go and see her and see what Big Bob has over her."

"Any idea what it might be?" he asks.

"Before, I thought that maybe Marly killed her husband, Bob knew about it and was blackmailing her. Or, Bob killed Dale and was threatening Marly in order to keep her quiet about it. But given what we know now about twenty-thirteen both of those are less likely."

Nick chews on this for a while, then says, "Unless one of them was the killer and knew Dale was gay and branded him with the twenty-thirteen to put us off the track."

"Maybe they were trying to implicate Luke Summers," Adry suggests.

A gloom descends upon us. We just went from one suspect back to three.

30

STAMMO

This is not the best way to do a stakeout. Apart from anything else, I'm still a bit buzzed from the five mimosas I had at brunch; I shouldn't have driven here at all but after sitting for three hours it's starting to wear off. Normally, I'd have left my meeting with Marly Summers until Monday—when Big Bob Pridmore is likely to be at his law office making himself rich—but I've got nothing else to do with myself so I might as well be here as anywhere.

I almost let it slip at brunch too. I need to be more careful. Then again, maybe Rogan *should* know, Adry too. I'll have to think on that.

I look across at the house again. I'm betting the blue F-Type Jag is hers and the fucking great matt-black Hummer belongs to Big Bob. I would like to have been here early this morning, to see if Prid-more spent the night. Rogan reckons they're having an affair and he's probably right except that he just doesn't seem like her type.

The front door just opened. It's Pridmore. As I guessed, it's the Hummer he gets into. He backs out the driveway and peels off in the direction of Marine Drive. I'll give it a minute, just in case he comes back for anything and then I'll—

Wait a minute. The door opens again and Marly steps out of the house. She locks up behind her and then looks down the road in the direction Pridmore drove off. She stands for a second staring then walks over to the Jag, gets in and takes off down the road. I fire up the van and follow her.

———

HAVING FOLLOWED her at a discreet distance from West Van to Vancouver, I'm right behind her in the line for the Hotel Vancouver's valet parking and I've got a good idea who she's here to see. She gets out of the Jag and walks behind it, passing inches in front of my van. I shrink back in the seat out of reflex. If she looks through the windshield she'll see me any-way... but she doesn't. She walks into the hotel and disappears from view. As one valet drives her car off, another one opens my door, "Good afternoon, sir

—" His greeting is cut off when he sees my chair. "Oh, sorry sir," he stammers. Poor kid, he's embarrassed. Why do people have to feel embarrassed by people in wheelchairs? It just makes matters worse. He looks like a nice kid; I can't get mad at him. I explain the hand-operated brake and gas controls to him, back my chair up, rotate a one-eighty and operate the buttons to open the back door and put down the ramp. Within two minutes of Marly entering the hotel, I'm wheeling through the door held open by the valet.

As I move forward I see Marly sitting at a table in the bar area and, no surprises, she's talking to a man who fits Rogan's description of Sean O'Day to a tee: black hair, blue eyes and good-looking. I stop and try and size them up. They're at a round table and are sitting next to each other rather than opposite so I can see both their faces. She's talking quite quickly, explaining something it looks like, and he's listening but also he's darting glances here and there as if looking for enemies. At one point he looks straight at me but only for an instant. He's never seen me before and anyway I'm just a guy in a wheelchair, no threat to him.

Now he's talking to her. It seems like a tense conversation on his part but she's just sitting there with that tiny smile on her face that cleverly hides what she's thinking.

I wheel over to the table, push the third chair out of the way and maneuver myself into its place.

"Good afternoon Marly." I extend my hand and she calmly shakes it, showing no surprise that I'm here.

"Hello Mr. Stammo."

I offer my hand to her companion. "Nick Stammo. You must be Sean O'Day." He looks confused, first at me then at Marly.

She comes to his rescue. "Mr. Stammo's a private detective, I believe you've met his partner Mr. Rogan."

Without a word he takes my hand but the mask has come down: his expression gives no indication of how he's feeling about my appearance at the table.

With the little smile playing on her face, she says, "Unlike your partner, I don't think you can claim not to have been following me Mr. Stammo."

I look from one to the other, his handsome face is completely expressionless and hers has that silly little smile, what they call supercilious I think. Time for me to rock their boat a little bit and, in a flash, I know how to do it.

"Cut the crap Marly. You two are up shit creek without a paddle and you both need my help to get you out of whatever trouble you're in. So stop trying to be a smart-ass and tell me what's going on and this time I want the truth from both of you."

Her smile's gone and so has his poker face. They look at each other and they both look relieved. I think I might get to some truth now.

31

CAL

I'm on the dock in the tiny village of Saltery Bay. For the tenth time since I left the ferry terminal at Gibsons, I have called Sam. After brunch with Nick and Adry, I decided to escape the frustration of the Dale Summers case and just come up here and see my girls. The problem is there's no ferry or water taxi to Hardy Island. The residents and their guests have to come or go by boat. I don't know if Sam's out with Ellie on her step-father's boat, or if they have gone for a walk in the rain, or if her phone's off, or if she's just ignoring me. I stopped leaving voicemails after the fifth call. There are a number of boats tied up at the dock but on a rainy day most of them are empty, their owners probably sitting by a cozy fire warming their toes.

I walk up to a Sea Ray. It's bobbing in the swell

left by the departing ferry and I can see someone in the wheel house. I walk into his field of view. He's an older man and he seems to be working on the boat's instrument panel.

"Excuse me sir," I call. He looks up and smiles.

"Hello, what can I do for you?" His accent is very British. It's not like Florrie Franks' accent; it sounds more upper-class.

"I need to get over to Hardy Island, it's an emergency. Could you possible ferry me over there? I'd be happy to pay you for your time and for gas."

"I'm awfully sorry," he says, "I'm afraid I can't. I'm having a spot of bother with the electrics. I can't even get the old girl started."

"Thanks anyway," I say. I look down the dock. There's one other boat which might have someone aboard so I start in it's direction.

"Wait a minute old boy. It's an emergency you say?"

I turn back. "Yes. My wife and daughter are over there and they're not answering my calls. I'm worried sick something might be wrong."

"Never let it be said that I left another human being in distress." He goes back into the wheelhouse and comes out holding a key on a chain attached to a yellow float about the size of a tennis ball.

"We'll take my pal's boat. He's a weekend sailor but he's not coming up until the end of the month. I keep a key in case of emergencies and this qualifies as one don't you think?" He sets off down the dock at a brisk pace and I follow on, effusive in my thanks.

We come to a rather luxurious motor yacht which looks to be forty feet or more.

"Hop aboard," my saviour says. "We'll be over there in a trice in this baby."

———

THE SMALL DOCK at Sam's father's property is empty. I don't know whether to be relieved or more worried. Maybe they've gone back to Vancouver but if so, why didn't Sam pick up my call? Surely after five calls she would have known it was important.

With great skill my newfound friend reverses the boat up to the dock. "Looks like nobody's here," he says. "Why don't you hop ashore and I'll wait while you check the house."

I step off the swim-grid onto the dock and jog through the little copse and the hundred-and-fifty yards or so to the house. It stands grey and grim in the rain. I walk up the steps to the patio, the third one creaks as I step on it. I look through the window to the right of the door. The dining table is in the foreground but it's overcast and getting dark so I can't make out any details of the room. It certainly looks deserted. I walk to the door and rap three times to no avail. I try the handle but it's locked. However the handle feels slightly sticky. I look at my hand.

It's blood.

32

STAMMO

She takes a deep breath and looks questioningly at Sean O'Day. He nods. She looks at me and she's different. I can see why. Before, she always looked like she was hiding something. Now, it's like I'm seeing her without makeup. I'm seeing the real Marly Summers. Behind the beautiful mask. Or maybe I'm fooling myself. We'll see.

"Bob Pridmore has been my lawyer since before I met Dale. One day, a few months after Dale and I had stopped having relations, I was feeling particularly down so I contacted Bob to find out what would be the situation if I were to separate or maybe even divorce. I gave him a copy of Dale's trust agreement. He was so nice to me. He was very supportive at a time when I needed someone's support. I don't want to seem like I'm making excuses for what I did, but I was very vulnerable and... well, I ended up having an affair with him. I wasn't in love with him but he was really nice to me and made me feel good about myself. I *really* needed that."

"Hi, what can I get you today?" Damn. The waiter has broken the flow of her conversation. We all order coffees of various types and he disappears to get them.

"Go on," I say gently, praying she doesn't change her mind about coming clean.

She pauses and looks at Sean again. Please don't stop! He nods encouragement.

She turns back to me.

"We had been seeing each other for a couple of months, when Bob started to make some, uh, suggestions about, you know, things he wanted to do in the bedroom. I'm not a prude Mr. Stammo, I went along for a while but then his requests started to get more and more creepy. So the next time he called me to get together, I told him it was over between us. He just said, 'We'll see about that,' and hung up on me.

"The next day, I got an email. There were attachments. Movies he'd taken with a hidden camera in his bedroom. Movies of the nastier things he likes doing to me. He was clever too. He never faced the camera and he blurred some of the images of himself where he might have been identifiable. The email said that unless I continued the affair, he would make them public, put them up on a website and send links to Dale and his brother Luke."

She hangs her head and looks at her hands clasped in her lap.

I feel rage and sympathy brewing in about equal amounts.

"Did you?" I ask.

"Continue the affair? Yes." The last word is little more than a whisper.

Sean reaches out and squeezes her forearm.

"You see," she continues, "I didn't know then that Dale was gay. I didn't want to hurt him and I knew if those pictures became public, he would lose his trust fund. I couldn't do that to him."

"Wait a minute," I say. "Why would he lose his trust fund? I thought he would only lose it if his homosexuality was made public."

"The trust fund also has a moral turpitude clause. Apparently his brother's does too. Basically it says if the recipient of the fund, or his immediate family, does anything that brings 'ill repute to the family name' I think the phrase was, then the trust could be folded."

"Pridmore had seen the trust fund documents and he knew that," I say. I can feel my anger ratcheting up.

She just nods.

My phone chirps: a text from Rogan. I ignore it; I don't want to break the flow.

"When my partner visited you yesterday morning, you told him it was Mr. O'Day here who was blackmailing you."

"I know, I'm sorry. When Mr. Rogan suggested the idea, Bob immediately latched onto it and agreed with him that it was true. When he looked at me I knew he wanted me to confirm it. I had to say what I said to Mr. Rogan. I'm sorry I lied. I'm sorry to you too Sean."

"Don't be," he says and squeezes her arm again. She looks at him and smiles her gratitude. I really like this guy. Dale was a lucky man to have him. He turns to me and asks, "Do you think Pridmore killed Dale?"

As I toss the idea around in my head, they both look at me hopefully. I hate to disappoint them. "I can't be sure but probably not. Part of his hold on you, Marly, was that he knew you didn't want to hurt Dale. Why would he kill Dale if it would weaken his hold over you?"

"You're right," she says. "Since Dale's death I have been thinking of telling Bob to go to hell. I don't care that much about the trust fund money; I supported myself before I met Dale and I can do it again."

I find myself liking the real Marly a lot more than the person she seemed to be before today.

"No need," I say.

They both give me questioning looks as my phone chirps again.

I don't want to break the rhythm of the interrogation, if I can call it that. I'm pretty sure she's being straight with me and the answer to my next question may settle the matter either way.

"Can you explain what happened in Al Porto on Thursday night? My partner saw the two of you there with Bob Pridmore."

"What I told your partner was the truth up to a point," O'Day says. "I had called Marly that morning. I wanted to offer her my condolences. I have to admit I broke down over the phone." I can see his eyes shining with the start of tears. "It all came out. My relationship with Dale, everything." He takes a handkerchief out of his pocket and dries the tear which has made its way down his nose.

Marly takes up the story. "We made a real connection over the phone, our shared grief I suppose. We must have talked for more than an hour. I told him everything including about Bob. He suggested we get together for dinner."

O'day blows his nose. "It would have been a lovely dinner but Pridmore showed up."

"Why did you tell him you'd be there?" I ask Marly.

"I didn't. While Sean and I were chatting, I got a phone call from him. He just said to stay where I was and that he would be right over."

"That's all?" I ask.

Her nod sets my internal lie-detector twitching. "How could he know you'd be there?"

"I don't know. Maybe he had me followed." She says it without any hesitation. I believe her.

"Marly told me I should go before he got there. I'll admit I was scared. I went to the washroom and when I came back, I saw the man talking to Mr. Rogan and I just knew it was Pridmore, so I high-tailed it out of there."

"What happened then." I ask Marly.

"Bob asked me who Sean was. I didn't have time to make up a lie so I told him the truth. He was happy with my answer especially after he learned about Dale's orientation."

The server arrives with our coffees and fusses with spoons and sugar and honey and napkins until I want to scream at him. When he finally leaves, I ask, "Do you have a lot of apps on your phone?"

"Why?"

"Because you're going to have to download them all again after you reset it to factory condition. I'll bet money Pridmore has installed a tracking app on it."

She looks devastated. And then angry. And then more angry.

"I feel violated," she says.

"So you should. The man's an animal," Sean adds.

Her anger morphs into a look of determination.

"Mr. Stammo, Nick, when I said I would give up all the money from Dale's trust fund, you said, 'No need.' What did you mean by that?"

Before I can tell her, my phone chirps again. Rogan. He must have something urgent.

I'll call him as soon as I give Marly the answer to her question.

33

CAL

"My dear chap, you look like you've seen a ghost." My rescuer has concern written all over his face. Using only my left hand I hold onto the side of the boat as I step onto the swim-grid. His sharp eyes notice my awkwardness. "Are you hurt?" he asks.

"No, but do you have a first aid kit aboard?"

"I'm sure there must be one. Do you want me to find it for you?"

"Please."

Looking a little like he may doubt my sanity he goes below decks and quickly returns with the kit. "Here we go," he says, opening the kit on the table behind the pilot seat.

"That's great. Would you help me with something? I have some blood on this hand. Can you first put on a surgical glove then take a gauze pad and wipe the blood onto it?"

"Evidence eh?" His mind's as sharp as his eyes. I just nod. "Just like on CSI." I smile at his reference to that most outlandish portrayal of the life of crime scene investigators.

He does the job efficiently and puts the bloodied gauze into the plastic pouch from which it came. I take it, make sure it's sealed and put it in my jacket pocket.

"Your emergency seems to be more urgent than I thought. How can I help?"

"I left my car at Earl's Cove and walked onto the ferry to Saltery Bay. Could you take me to my car please. I'd be more than happy to pay you for the fuel and for your time."

He deftly backs the boat away from the dock. "I'd be more than happy to and don't even think of payment. As far as the fuel goes, my pal's as rich as Croessus, he won't notice a few gallons. As for my time, I'm retired and my time's my own. However, if you tell me a little of what this is about, I think it will be a wonderful story to tell my grandchildren and will earn me a round or two of drinks next time I meet my pals at the pub."

As he pulls away from the dock, Sam's mother's words keep echoing in my head. *The gang will know you're the one who killed their leader. Samantha's petri-*

fied they'll try and extract vengeance on you and maybe on her and Ellie.

———

AFTER I TOLD my new friend an expurgated version of the reason for my visit to his neck of the woods, I tried to contact Stammo but he has answered none of my texts. As I get into the Healey, I try once more but to no avail. I toy with the idea of calling Steve at VPD but he'll just say they need to be gone for forty-eight hours to qualify as missing persons and I'm sure he's not about to bend the rules for me.

Driving fast on the Sunshine Coast Highway is not a good practice. In an Austin Healey three thousand, in the dark and in the wet, it's madness. I manage to restrain myself. The sound of the wiper blades is somehow soothing and calms me enough to let me think. Maybe I'm overreacting. Surely the remnants of Carlos Santiago's gang are too concerned with keeping his business empire going. They probably think a rival gang did it. Except for the fact they knew about me from before. They knew Stammo and I were on the Ariel Bradbury case. If they have someone in the courts or in the VPD, they'll know I have been charged with the killings. I have to assume the threat to Sam and Ellie is real.

If they hurt one hair on Ellie's head, I'll—

My thoughts are curtailed by the ring of my phone sitting on the passenger seat. Please be Sam! I grab it and take my eyes off the road for an instant. Not Sam but Stammo. I press accept and then the speaker option.

"Nick, thank God it's you."

"What's up?"

I tell him everything.

"Have you alerted Steve or better yet talked to the RCMP? The Mounties have jurisdiction up there."

"No. They'll just tell me to wait forty-eight hours."

He grunts. *"You really think Santiago's gang have taken them?"*

"I don't know. Maybe... Probably... I don't know what to think."

"OK. Stay calm and keep your eyes on that road. I'm going to talk to a friend who's with the Mounties. Do you know what car Sam drives and what's the registration? Also do you remember the name of the boat they use to get to and from the island?"

I give him the details and he hangs up.

Having him on it helps.

But what can we do if they've been taken?

34

MAX

He's 'sharing'. God I hate that word. Who gives a damn about his father's disapproval or his mother's overbearing love? My father never wanted me and my mother was useless. It's what makes me strong. He's whining on about how he got married just because his mother pressured him into it. This gutless worm is my next one. My number two. Number one was a huge mistake in some ways but I just had to do him and knowing him did add an extra pleasure, especially at the very end. I will remember that for a while. But I've got to be careful. No more rash moves. Stick to the plan. I'll have to think up something extra to do to number two just to ramp up the climax.

He's stopped and the other pathetic losers are all

clapping. I join in. How nice of them to have a support group for me to mine.

"Thanks for your share, Paul," the master of ceremonies says. "We'll take a coffee break and then our new member, Max, will be sharing." He smiles and nods in my direction. I return the gesture.

As we head to the coffee table, I intercept Paul. "Thanks for sharing, that was really inspirational." That's the type of garbage they like to hear.

"Thanks, Max. I'm looking forward to hearing your story. I'm betting it will be really inspirational too." He lays his hand on my forearm as he speaks and I have to work hard not to cringe at his touch; I need to take advantage of the move. I put my hand on his and give a little squeeze while suppressing the desire to scream at him. I savour the thought of watching him die and that brings a natural smile to my face which he translates as support. His weakness will make his death even better for me. Maybe I'll take a little longer with this one, really stretch it out over a few hours.

God, I love this game.

35

SAM

"Mommy, I'm sure that was Daddy's car." Ellie can be really insistent when she wants to be. She was quiet all the way back from Sechelt hospital but when we turned off the Sunshine Coast Highway to our marina at Madeira Park she saw Cal driving in the opposite direction.

"I told you sweetie, it must have been a car like Daddy's. He doesn't even know we're up here."

I navigate a bump in the road and find a parking spot. We get out of the car and she starts in again. "There aren't a lot of Austin Healeys. Daddy said so. And it was the same colour It must be him."

Without thinking, I take her hand and feel a sharp pain in mine. Wrong hand. For the hundredth time I berate myself for being so careless. What was

I thinking leaving that kitchen knife on the counter like that? With my MS, stumbling is almost a daily thing now and when I grabbed the corner of the counter, I cut myself really badly. The trip from the island to the hospital was a nightmare. I'm going to have to spend Sunday cleaning the blood out of Daddy's boat. I'm wondering if we should just go back to town. Maybe I'm just being paranoid, thinking that a vengeful gang's going to come after Ellie and me.

"Why don't you phone him Mommy. Get him to turn round and come back. We could wait for him here. He can come to the island with us."

"Don't you remember sweetie? In all the panic, I left my phone in the house. I can't call him until we get back to the island."

She descends into silence.

As we step onto the dock, I see an unusual boat moored one slip over from Daddy's Boston Whaler. It looks a bit out of place here. It's long and sleek and expensive and in the dim of the marina's lights it looks to be yellow. Most of the boats here are working boats or runabouts. That rich man's toy's really out of place.

"Look at that boat Ellie."

"Wow," she bounces back from her mood. "That's a really pretty boat."

What do they call those? Cigarette boats, I think.

I help Ellie aboard, undo the mooring ropes and hop aboard myself. The engine starts on the first try. I nose out of our spot and start the short trip to the safety of Hardy Island.

36

CAL

I t doesn't feel quite right being here. We should be at the office but Stammo insisted we meet here; I'm not sure why. I haven't been to the Yaletown Pub in ages. I think the last time was with Roy. It feels like a lifetime ago and in a way, it is. I'm drinking their Loading Dock IPA. It's good but not as good as the IPA their former brewmaster brewed before he started his own brewery. It's busy with the Saturday night crowd but Stammo has got us a table right up against the glass wall between the pub and the brewery.

"I talked to my buddy Greg MacKay at the RCMP detachment in Sechelt," he says, raising his voice against the noise. "Greg's a good guy. He's going to check out all the Marinas which Sam's parents might use, to see if he can spot their boat or

Sam's car. He's going to talk to the marina owners too. I'm sure you don't need to worry."

"I hope you're right. But what if Santiago's gang knew she was there and have taken her?"

"How could they?"

I just shake my head.

"Listen, Greg said he'd get back to me as soon as he heard anything. Why don't we take your mind off it and let's talk about our cases."

"Is there anything new since we had brunch this morning?"

"Oh yes indeedy. After brunch I went back to the office and created some Google alerts."

"What are they?" I ask.

"You choose a search term and Google will email you an alert every time a new webpage appears on the net which uses the term. I set up alerts for *Luke Summers, 20:13, bible gay* and *kill gays*. I've already got some hits on Summers but they're just news articles about his brother's funeral, which is on Tuesday by the way. I'll let you know if anything interesting turns up."

"So where do we go from here?" I ask.

"Well, seeing as how you burned your bridges with Luke Summers, I thought I'd better step up. I checked out the websites of all the more fundamentalist churches around Vancouver and found the one Luke Summers goes to. It's called the Baptist

Church of the Savior. He's in the 'About' section of the website as a 'Benefactor and Lay Preacher.' I dug around the website and they seem pretty fundamentalist; there's lots of Old Testament stuff. So I'm planning to go there tomorrow morning and check it out. He doesn't know me and I won't use my real name but I'll see what I can find out."

"Do you want me to come with you?"

"No. Looks like you've alienated Luke Summers enough."

The thought of going to the church prods my memory. I agree with Nick about Luke's church but there's another one I can visit.

"You've been busy for a Saturday," I tell him.

He gives a curtailed laugh, more of a grunt really. "That's not the half of it."

He tells me about his meeting with Marly Summers and Sean O'Day and their story of Big Bob Pridmore's blackmail.

"You believe them," I ask.

"A hundred percent."

"You look like you've got an idea."

He smiles. "I do. What if we turn the tables on him?"

"How?"

"Let's order a pizza and I'll tell you."

He signals the waiter over and my phone rings.

Sam.

"Are you and Ellie alright?" I shout above the noise of the pub.

I can only just hear her answer. *"Yes we are, no thanks to you."*

"What do you mean?"

I press the phone closer to my ear; I can hardly make out the words. *"Don't try and come up to see us again, Cal. Not ever!"*

"How did you know—?"

"Ellie saw your car. What if you'd been followed?"

"Sam, there's no way I was followed. I wanted to see you and—"

"It's over Cal. Do you understand? Do not contact us again! Not ever!"

Beep-beep-beep. She's hung up.

I feel a mixture of relief and pain. Both are extreme.

37

TOMÁS

The girls' eyes have that cocaine shine. They both have a certain wantonness I find appealing. They're following my instructions to the letter: pleasuring each other before they pleasure me. It's exciting watching each of them explore the other's body. One of them looks admiringly at me standing naked at the foot of the bed. It increases my excitement. This is going to be so good.

The vibration of the phone on the minibar drags my attention away from the beautiful bodies. It's the one phone I must answer. Only Javier has the number. I put it on speakerphone.

"Yes, Javier."

"*Good evening* Patrón. *The wife and child are on the island. They left for a couple of hours and went to the hospital in Sechelt but they're back now.*"

"Good, I was worried they might have left. That island's the perfect place for the last act of our little tragedy."

"*Should we move in on them now?*" Poor Javier. He's too eager to get his hands on the wife and the girl.

"Not yet. We stick with the plan. Get Ernesto to keep watch on them. I need you here to execute the next step."

"*Si* Patrón. *I will be there tomorrow.*"

"No rush, *mi amigo*. I don't plan to make a move until Monday, or Tuesday at the latest. Have yourself some fun. But just not with the woman on Hardy Island. You will have her soon enough."

"*Si, Patrón.*"

I hang up. Looking down I see my excitement has not abated. It's time to let the whores do their job.

38

CAL

SUNDAY

If you looked up the word scam in an encyclopedia, there would be a picture of the Church of the Pure Divine Light. I know how Phil and Florrie Franks fell for it. The church is in a building in New Westminster which used to be a theatre. The doors to the auditorium are not yet open and there's a throng of people in the large lobby area which is adorned with pictures of angelic and saintlike figures. On either side of the entry doors there are faux-gold bowls with the words 'Contribute what you can!' on them. Looking around, I can see there are quite a few people who look like they can afford quite big donations. There are even some statues which give the place an amazing aura. But I have spotted the real giveaways.

I find myself with a group of people who clearly

all know each other and who have welcomed me into their midst.

"You'll love Pastor Kilman," Milly, a white-haired woman in a purple hat tells me. "He has brought such peace of mind to me."

"He has dear," her friend Edna agrees. "And for us too. He put us in contact with Dan's late brother," she gestures toward her husband, a ramrod-straight middle-aged man in a blazer with the Masonic crest on it. He nods in agreement.

"Why are you here, Cal?" another woman asks me.

I opted to use my real first name and a fictitious surname and, fortunately, I have a cover story. "My wife Elizabeth passed on. It was very sudden, a car accident, and apart from our insurance policies, we had never discussed death or things like funeral arrangements. I want to know if she wants to be buried or cremated and if she wants her final resting place to be in Vancouver or at our house in Whistler or on Salt Spring. She loved the mountains but our place on Salt Spring has some very special memories." That's established some *bona fides*.

"If you come here often enough," says Edna, "I'm sure Pastor Kilman will be able to make a connection for you."

I plant another little seed. "I hope so. I would give *anything* to hear her voice again."

Another woman in the group whose name I didn't catch and the oldest by far, takes my hand in hers. "I'm going to pray Pastor Kilman helps you soon," she says, her voice trembling with age and emotion.

They all seem so nice and I have to work hard to hide my anger at the con-man who's bilking them of their hard-earned money.

I look around and hear other conversations of the same ilk. All good grist for the Pastor's mill.

The auditorium doors into the theatre open by themselves with no physical person in evidence; it's a cheap trick to support the ethos of divine intervention. As we move inside, people drop banknotes or envelopes into the faux-gold bowls. I take two fifty-dollar bills from my wallet and drop them in, knowing the bright red colour will be noticeable.

As I walk through the doors I see Pastor Kilman standing silently in the middle of the stage in a two-thousand-dollar-plus suit, his head bowed, hands clasped in front of him. On the curtains behind him is embroidered the crest of the Church. How much did that cost? More than his suit I'm guessing.

Milly and Edna usher me into the fifth row and sit me down between them. Before I do anything, I maneuver the 'man-purse' onto my lap and, without revealing the contents which I purchased after my meeting with Phil and Florrie, I slide my hand inside and do what I have been instructed by the helpful salesman. I look down to ensure that the microphone, disguised as a Rotary Club lapel-badge, is still in place.

While we wait for all the congregants to enter, I scan the space and do an estimate of the capacity. There are thirty-two rows of seats in three banks of twelve seats each. I turn to Milly. "How many services are there?" I ask.

"Tuesday to Friday, there's a service every evening," she says, "and there are two on Saturday and three today. You're lucky it's Pastor Kilman. He's been away for a week and one of the associate Ministers has been doing the services; he's very good but Pastor Kilman is special."

I look around again and see the seats will likely all be full. "Are they always as full as this?"

"During the week there are sometimes some seats available but not on the weekends. I always come early on Sunday to make sure I get a seat. On Wednesdays we can usually get a seat without a problem, can't we Edna?"

"Yes. Wednesdays are always good," Edna adds.

I do the math. Pastor Kilman's getting about nine thousand people through his doors every week. From my observation, the average donation dropped in the bowls at the door was at least ten dollars. From those donations alone he's making four to five million a year, let alone what additional monies he cons from people like Phil and Florrie. I'm hoping my two fifty-buck notes will do the trick.

I settle in to enjoy the show.

As the last of the congregants are searching for seats, Pastor Kilman looks up. His brown hair's perfectly sculpted and shows not a sign of grey despite his obvious age. A closer look reveals a certain shininess to the skin often exhibited by the clients of plastic surgeons. He has small, deep set, beady eyes and a smile which cost more than his suit. His hands unclasp and slowly circle away from his body until they're stretched out so that his body makes the shape of a letter Y.

The congregants all stand, some of the older ones being helped to their feet by their younger neighbours

"Brothers and sisters!" His voice is deep and rich and fills the auditorium without the need of a microphone. "Please bow your heads and silently ask the souls of the departed to join us in our fellowship."

Again the flock obey in unison.

After a full minute he speaks again. "Please be seated." He pauses, nodding his head as if hearing something interesting. "Your spirits are strong. There are many souls here today."

He pauses again and cocks his head to one side.

He's holding his audience in the palm of his hand. I have to admire his showmanship.

"Alexander," he says. "Jessie's here."

"Oh yes! Yes!" The speaker is a man about my age, three rows back and to my right. He's leaping to his feet.

"She says she's free now. She can cross over in peace."

"Oh thank you, thank you," Alexander says.

"She gives her thanks to you for setting her free."

The mark has tears streaming down his face. He tries to speak but is unable to. He collapses back into his seat and my stomach turns.

After two more similar displays, the huckster gives a startled look and surveys the audience. He walks in our direction to the front of the stage and looks me in the eye.

"Are you Cal?" he asks.

Careful not to overact, I nod.

"Elizabeth is here."

I gasp, stand up and lean toward him. It seems to be what's expected.

"She says you have a dilemma."

"Yes. Yes," I say.

"The island she says." He shakes his head and smiles. "She says you'll know what she means. Ahh, yes. She's asking that you spread her ashes on Salt Spring. You'll know where."

I nod enthusiastically.

His smile disappears and a look of pain comes onto his face.

"She needs your help. Oh no." Tears come to his face. Can he be that good an actor? "She's gone."

"What happened?" I ask. "Where did she go?"

He just shakes his head, his body like that of a man exhausted. He looks me in the eye and manages a wan smile. "Later," he says.

He turns and drags himself toward the centre of the stage and then stops.

"Poor man. It takes so much out of him," Milly whispers in my ear.

On the other side of her, the lady whose name I don't know says, "I prayed for Elizabeth to come." She reaches over and pats me on the arm.

On the stage Kilman seems miraculously to regain his energy. He straightens up and makes a bee-line for the other side of the stage.

"Donald," he says. "Bethany's here."

An elderly man struggles to his feet and I start to feel physically sick.

———

THE SHOW IS over and the Pastor has exited the stage through the curtains at the back only to be replaced by a well-dressed woman in her thirties with a pearl necklace and shoes worth a devil's ransom.

Nobody stirs.

She waits a beat and then speaks. She has one of the most vibrant voices I have ever heard. "While Pastor Kilman recovers from his work, is there anyone who wants to share?"

Share? Now it sounds like an AA meeting.

A woman holds up her hand. "I just want to say how grateful I am for Pastor Kilman's help. Thanks to him my husband's now at peace in the world beyond." My cynical side asks how much that cost her. It's hard to keep the rage out of my face. I just try to smile placidly. I keep the plastic smile in place through four more people sharing their gratitude to Kilman, peppered with supporting comments from Milly and Edna. I want to scream 'Fraud!' at the top of my lungs but somehow manage to restrain myself.

Finally the sharing comes to an end and the woman leaves the stage through the curtain behind her. "She's Pastor Kilman's wife. Isn't she wonderful?" Milly says squeezing my arm. I just nod.

We wait while the people in the rows behind us make their exits. When our turn comes I see into the lobby. Kilman's there and so is his wife. He's deep in conversation with a man in an ugly red sweater and she's smiling and shaking hands with people and ushering them through the doors which lead outside onto Columbia Street. I look at her and can see the crowd-control job is not what she's there for. She's scanning the congregation looking for specific people and I'm betting I'm one of them. Her eyes lock with mine and she smiles.

Milly and Edna steer me in her direction. She smiles and shakes hands with each of them but it's as sincere as a junkie's promise. When my turn comes she shakes my hand but does not let go. "My husband would like to meet with you. He's quite exhausted but needs to give you a private message from Elizabeth." I nod eagerly and she gestures with her head. "Just go over and talk to him." She releases my hand and turns her attention to the next person in line.

I say my goodbyes to Milly and Edna and promise to see them again next week before heading over to the small crowd gathered around Kilman. He catches my eye and says, "I'll be with you in a minute Cal."

I smile and nod then take the time to act like an overawed tourist and take photos of the lobby. I snap the pictures: the statues, the crowd and most importantly—not to mention covertly—the ceiling. He finishes talking to the man in the sweater and, ignoring the adoring fans around him, he locks his deep-set eyes with mine. "Cal," he says. "I'm so glad you have joined our little congregation; it could not have been more timely." He reaches out and takes my hand. "I'm so, so glad." Words from Henry IV spring into my mind. *Suppos'd sincere and holy in his thoughts.*

"I need to speak with you at your earliest convenience," he says. "It's about Elizabeth."

"I'm available any time," I say eagerly.

"I would speak to you right now but the service takes so much out of me. Could you come by tomorrow at around two?"

"Absolutely," I say.

"When you arrive, just ring the doorbell to the right of the main door."

"Absolutely," I say again. "Tomorrow at two."

He just nods and pats my shoulder, the very epitome of the righteous man exhausted by his labours

He has set his hook. He thinks into a mackerel, but he's snagged a great white.

———

THE FLAVOR of the lemon chicken and the Whistler Chestnut Ale go a long way toward washing away the taste of the Church of the Pure Divine Light. "So how was *your* visit to church this morning?" I ask.

"Good," says Stammo wiping away a piece of

noodle from the side of his mouth. "It's a long time since I've been to church. To tell you the truth, I enjoyed it; singing hymns, listening to the sermon and all that. It was nice." He pops some lemon chicken into his mouth.

"Anyway, they're a pretty fundamentalist bunch, especially by Canadian standards. There were a lot of readings from the old testament and the minister, the Reverend Joseph Mueller, was a regular fire and brimstone type but there was nothing specifically about gays. Luke Summers read a couple of the passages, he was pretty impressive. I talked to him after the service too and I gotta say, I find it hard to think he killed his own brother to cover up the fact he was gay. A bit too Cain and Abel." He chuckles and drinks some of his beer.

I chuckle too, remembering that Em used exactly the same words.

"Did he know who you were?" I ask.

"Nah. I just said I was visiting some friends in Langley and thought I'd drop into the church."

I reach across his desk and take the last piece of beef in black bean sauce. "If Luke's off our list, we don't really have a viable suspect for Dale's murder do we?"

"We don't," he sighs. "Although God knows I'd like to pin it on Big Bob Pridmore."

"Was Marly on board with the plan to deal with him?"

"One hundred and ten percent," he gives a big grin. "We've got it set up for tomorrow morning at his office. Do you want to come?"

I don't but I doubt Big Bob's going to *go gentle into that good night*. He's going to *rage, rage against the dying of* his hold over Marly. "Sure," I say. "Wouldn't miss it for the world. Has she got the stuff?"

"Yes. I couriered it over to her." He chuckles.

We finish our late lunch in a companionable silence. But it's a silence which gives me time to think. And not good thoughts. I've had time to digest last night's phone call from Sam.

It's over Cal. The words keep running through my head. Is it really over? And what about Ellie? Sam divorced me when I was still a junkie. Because of that fact, she was able to get sole custody and guardianship of Ellie. I have no legal way of making sure I get to see my daughter again. For the hundredth time, I toy with the idea of going up to Hardy Island again. Maybe I can persuade my English friend to ferry me over there, except that there's little likelihood of him being on the dock at Saltery Bay two evenings in a row. And what reception would I get if I turned up on the island?

Is it really over with Sam?

She's probably right. I count the times I have put

her and/or Ellie in danger in the last few years. They just don't deserve it. Maybe they *are* better off without me.

"OK, Rogan. Back to work." Stammo's words pull me out of the pit of self-pity I've been digging for myself. I remember the rule: when you're in a hole, stop digging.

He loads the empty food containers, paper plates and beer bottles on to his lap and wheels into the office's little kitchen. He's been in that wheelchair for a couple of years now and he's become pretty damned efficient in operating it.

He comes back out and wheels up to his desk. "You can clean up the kitchen before you go tonight, meanwhile don't you have to plug in that gizmo you bought to see if it worked?"

He's right. I pull the device out of the 'manpurse' and plug it into my computer. It takes me about five minutes to verify that it worked and worked perfectly at that. I got everything I need to get Phil and Florrie's money back from Pastor Kilman.

"It worked, I was right," I whoop.

He turns round and faces me. Through his shocked look he says, "But I was righter. Come and see what I got."

Somehow I know his news is bigger than mine. I walk over and stand beside him. "You remember how I told you I set up Google alerts?" he says. "Well I got a hit on the 20:13 search. Take a look at this."

My mouth falls open. I was right. His news *is* bigger than mine. There it is, on his screen: *twenty-thirteen.com*. A website with a scrolling banner across the top that reads: *Leviticus 20:13 says, 'If a man has sexual relations with a man as one does with a woman, both of them have done what is detestable. They are to be put to death; their blood will be on their own heads.'* Underneath the banner is a picture. One that I have seen before but taken from a slightly different angle. It's Dale Summers' tortured, naked, mutilated and murdered body, the dagger sticking out of his chest like a crucifix.

"You realize what this means?" I say.

"Well yeah! It means we've got a new lead on this case," he replies.

"Apart from that."

"What?"

"It says '*they* are to be put to death.' It means Sean O'Day is probably the next victim."

———

I HAVE MIXED feelings about making this next call. Sean O'Day isn't answering his cell. We tried calling his room at the Hotel Van, but there was no reply there either. Marly has no idea where he is. The obvious next choice is to call his boss, Em. Except I have to be careful. He specifically said he didn't want to be outed to his employer so I can't tell Em that we need to get hold of him because his life's in danger; she's way too smart, she might well figure out why. On the other hand I'm happy to have an excuse to call her.

"Hello Cal Rogan." She's accentuating her Southern drawl; it draws a big smile onto my face.

"Hi Em, I need to ask Sean O'Day something, do you know how I could get hold of him?"

"And here was I, hoping you were calling to ask a girl out for dinner again."

"Well I was." I say it before thinking about it. "But at the same time I'd like to get hold of Sean. He worked closely with Dale and I have a couple of follow up questions for him. I can't get him on his cell or at the hotel."

"Working on a Sunday. You are very diligent." There's laughter in her voice. *"Did you try my office number? Sean has the office next door to mine. He might be there. He's very diligent too."*

"Thanks Em, I'll call him there right away."

"But not before you ask me for dinner, I hope."

Oops. "Oh... no... Sorry, well—"

The tinkle of her laughter comes over the phone. *"Why don't I make it easy for you. Cal Rogan would you honour me with the presence of your company for dinner tonight?"*

"Thank you Em, I would like that very much."

"Eight o'clock at Tojo's on Broadway; I'll meet you there. My treat."

"Thank you, I'll see you then." There's a broad grin on my face as I hang up. Stammo picks up on it. "Another date with the client eh, Rogan?" I can't tell if he approves or disapproves.

"Yeah, no big deal."

To cover further questioning, I dial the number of Em's shared office space. Voicemail. The warm feelings of my interaction with Em are pushed out by my worry for the safety of Sean O'Day.

———

THE DRIVE from our office to West Broadway has helped a little. The frustration in the office has been high all afternoon. Despite trying all ways he knows how, Stammo has been unable to find out anything about the *twenty-thirteen.com* website. He even contacted a hacker he knows, a miscreant who goes by the name Drake. When Stammo was back east working for the OPP, he busted Drake—whose real name, believe it or not, is Justin Tyme—for hacking into the Royal Bank's servers. After he'd served his time, Stammo helped get him a job. Drake is one of the many who owe Stammo a favour However, even he was unable to find anything useful. The site is hosted on a Russian server, which means that not even a warrant will be of any use in finding out who owns the site. After he had found out everything he could, he turned the details over to VPD and went home in disgust.

My efforts to track down Sean O'Day have been equally stymied. Maybe Em will have heard from him.

The only bright spot in the afternoon was that the device I smuggled into the Church of the Pure Divine Light worked like a charm. I spent a couple of hours downloading the recordings and ended up with everything on a cheap digital recorder. I used some editing software to overlay some recorded tracks and got just what I needed. It will make an interesting item for dinner conversation with Em.

I luck into a parking meter right in front of Tojo's. I'm looking forward to eating here; it's the best—even if the most expensive—Japanese restaurant in Canada and the owner, Tojo, is a great character. My mouth has been watering all afternoon thinking about his signature dish, Tojo's Tuna.

As I get out of the car, I see Em is standing on the sidewalk by the front door. She looks amazing. The expensive Cordovan leather jacket makes her short blond hair look stunning. She's wearing a beige roll-neck sweater with tight beige pants and boots to match the jacket. She smiles and walks over and my heart skips a beat.

As I step onto the sidewalk, she stands on tiptoes and kisses me on the cheek. "I messed up," she chuckles. "Tojo's is closed on Sundays." My disappointment at the loss of Tojo's Tuna is more than compensated for by the kiss.

"I'll take a rain-check," I say. "There's a good Indian restaurant in this block. My treat."

"Well, alright." She takes my arm and we walk the fifty yards to Raga.

As soon as we are seated and have ordered the food, she asks, "Did you manage to get hold of Sean? I tried but he didn't answer."

"No," I admit, "I'm afraid not."

"What did you want to ask him? Maybe I might know."

I can't tell her that I want to tell him that as Dale's lover he might be in danger but fortunately, I'm prepared for the question. "He had a drink with Dale and some of his colleagues on the Friday evening before Dale's death; he may have been the last person to talk to Dale. I was wondering if Dale had said anything that might give some sort of clue or if Sean remembers anything unusual about Dale's colleagues."

"Oh, I see. Why don't you bring me up-to-date

on the case, that way you can claim this meal as a business expense."

For a moment, I had forgotten she was a client and that I need to keep her informed. "Yes, I'm sorry, I should have given you an update yesterday. Quite a lot has happened in the last forty-eight hours." I pause to take a draft of my Kingfisher then tell her about the significance of twenty-thirteen and the website Stammo unearthed.

"Can you track down who owns the website?" she asks.

"No. My partner tried and even had an expert hacker take a shot at it but no luck."

She mulls it over and I keep quiet, enjoying watching her.

"It seems to me there are two possibilities here: either someone who knew Dale killed him and then created the website to draw attention away from himself, or..." She pauses for a second. "There's a religious group who have taken to killing gay men."

I just nod. She's a very smart woman, if I let her think it through without interruption, maybe she can come up with something Stammo and I haven't thought of.

"If it's the latter, why would a religious group choose Dale? I knew Dale fairly well and I had no idea he was gay. I'm sure he was deep in the closet. How would they even know about him? Unless..."

she pauses again. "Unless both possibilities are true."

"Hold that thought," I say. "My partner, Nick, went out this morning to the Baptist Church of the Savior where Dale Summers' brother, Luke, is a lay preacher. He described them as a fire and brimstone type of church. Although there was no reference to gays during the service, homophobia is never far from the surface with fundamentalists."

"So you suspect Luke Summers?" she asks.

"Well that's just it, I don't. There's no way Luke would kill his brother and then create a website to out him to the world. Luke was, and is, all about treating Dale's orientation as a family secret. Plus when I talked to him about it, he seemed more liberal than I expected."

"Well, as you know, I'm from Georgia," with a broad grin she emphasizes her southern accent, "and down there we know a thing or two about religion." Her face becomes more serious. "Don't rule out Luke Summers just yet."

Maybe she's right.

"Then again," she adds. "Maybe there's some crazy out there who has decided he likes killing gay men. Maybe there will be more pictures appearing on that website before too long."

Her words lance a frisson of fear through me. I

remember Leviticus *'They are to be put to death'* and wonder again where Sean O'Day is right now.

"You look worried, Cal," she says softly.

Feeling guilty I can't tell her about my fears for O'Day, I say, "Just the thought that we may be seeing the genesis of a serial killer." For a moment, I want to come clean about O'Day; I realize that I don't want to lie to this woman, not even with a lie of omission. I look into her eyes and smile. "Let's change the subject," I say. "I went to church this morning."

I tell her about my visit to the Church of the Pure Divine Light and my plans to get back the money for Phil and Florrie Franks. It lightens the mood and she's delighted with my plan; she even claps her hands when I tell her about the device I took to the 'church' this morning and how it works.

We continue our meal swapping stories about various con-men famous and not so famous. She tells me about one who scammed Southbrook for over a million dollars. From there we go on to talk about friends and former lovers. As she tells me about her first high-school boyfriend, I feel a little pang of jealousy worm it's way into my consciousness.

She reaches across the table and puts her hand on mine. "Tell me about Sam."

I try to hide the turmoil of emotions which are

stirred up at the mention of Sam's name. "She told me it's over between us." The words are out of my mouth before I can stop them but, to my surprise, saying them makes me feel better for some reason. She doesn't say anything but just nods and gives my hand a gentle squeeze. I bring my other hand over to cover hers.

I look into her eyes and in them I see warmth and understanding. I feel the prickle of tears in my eyes. I don't know if they are tears of loss or of relief.

39

CAL

MONDAY

B ig Bob Pridmore's office is reflective of its tenant: flashy and ugly. It's downtown but in one of the older and slightly shabbier buildings. As Nick and I exit the elevator, I look round the walls at the garish pieces of art interspersed with photos of the great man posed with a slimy grin beside various supposed dignitaries, only two of whom do I recognize as minor city officials. Even the receptionist looks like she has retired from a less than lucrative career selling her favours on the streets of the downtown east side. Stammo wheels up to her desk and gives her a cheery smile. I remember back when Stammo's smiles were mostly creepy.

"Dick Butcher to see Mr. Pridmore," he says. I grin. When Stammo made the appointment, we borrowed the pseudonym from Henry VI Part II after the character who says, *The first thing we do, let's kill all the lawyers.* I think it's appropriate.

We have spent the last few hours preparing for this meeting with the help of Marly. She's waiting back at our office with a promise that if this works, she's going to take Stammo, Adry and me out for the best lunch we've ever had.

The receptionist asks us to take a seat and rings through to announce us.

"He'll be with you in a moment," she says in what sounds like a Russian accent. She doesn't offer us coffee.

The 'moment' passes, followed by a further ten minutes worth of moments.

I feel the buzz of my phone.

"Cal Rogan."

"It's Sean O'Day. Em said you wanted to talk to me."

I breath a sign of relief. "Where are you?"

"At work."

"I need to meet with you as soon as possible."

"OK." He says it slowly, a hint of suspicion in his voice. *"Can you tell me what this is about?"*

"It would be better if we spoke face-to-face."

After a brief pause, he agrees to meet this after-noon and we hang up.

As I give Nick the good news that Sean O'Day is still

breathing, Big Bob Pridmore lumbers into the reception area. He takes a look at us and his eyes narrow. He flashes an angry glance at the receptionist then turns back to us. "What the hell are you two doing here?"

"We didn't think you'd see us if we gave our own names," Stammo says cheerily.

"You're damned right. What makes you think I'll see you now?"

"Because if you don't, our next stop will be the Law Society offices. When they see what we have, *these* charming offices will be closed before the end of the day." Stammo's in fine form.

"What do you mean?" he snarls.

"I don't think you want to discuss that here." Stammo says and inclines his head toward the reception desk. "Let's talk in your office."

Bob stands there and stares at us, the enmity flowing off him. Finally, "OK."

He turns, heads down the corridor and takes the first office on the right. We follow and I take the precaution of closing the door behind us.

His office has all the charm of a mortuary. He flops down in his oversized faux-leather chair behind his oversized faux-teak desk. "So what the fuck do you want?" he growls.

I make a point of standing by the door but Stammo wheels up to the desk and nods toward the computer on the credenza behind it. "Go to stammorogan.com slash pridmore."

For the first time a sliver of uncertainty appears in his eye. He rotates his chair, opens a browser window and enters the URL, taking three tries to get it right. The page is empty but for a video. He clicks the start icon.

The scene is a bedroom. Marly's bedroom. "What the—" His expletive is deleted by the sound of his own voice. *What the fuck d'you mean you stupid bitch.* Into the frame of the video appears Bob dragging Marly by her arm. He pushes her toward the bed and she sits down on it awkwardly, her back toward the camera. Her voice has a catch in it, she's frightened but she says the words Stammo wrote for her. *I don't want to be with you any more.* He laughs. *You know what will happen to you if you don't.* The catch is gone from her voice, *What Bob? What will happen to me?* She's defiant but he just laughs again. *I will send that video of you enthusiastically fucking me to prissy Mr. Luke Summers and tell him unless he cuts you off from your trust fund, I'll post it online and I'll send a link to everyone he knows* and *to everyone you know too.* Marly plays her part to perfection. She says, *Please Bob, please don't do that.* The excitement of the sadist shows on his face. He says, *Take your clothes off, whore.* As she unbuttons her blouse the Bob on the screen starts to tear off his clothes.

The Bob across the desk from us stops the video before we get to see the horrible sacrifice Marly Summers had to make to get this slime out of her life. He stands and turns toward us. The anger's there but it's diluted by fear. "What do you want?"

"As of right now," Stammo says, "you never see or contact Marly Summers ever again, in any way. You pack all the files you have on her into a box and courier it to her home. You never do anything that would be detrimental to her or to the memory of her late husband. If you do anything, any little thing I don't like, a link to this video will be sent to the Law Society of BC and the Vancouver Police Department and to every one of those big clients you used to brag to Marly about. And, as a little bonus, I know some pretty sketchy thugs, from when I was a cop. For a very reasonable fee, they will track you down and beat the snot out of you. Clear?"

Bob just stands there grinding his teeth, a vein throbbing in his temple. I feel myself switch into combat mode, up on the balls on my feet, ready to move in an instant. If he's going to get physical, now's the time.

But he doesn't.

"I said, IS THAT CLEAR?" Stammo roars at him.

Options writhe over his face but he can't see his way out.

He just deflates.

Then grunts.

"So... that's clear?" Stammo says with a smile.

"YES," he yells then deflates again. "Get out of my office." The voice of a beaten man.

Without taking my eyes off him, I open the door for Nick who wheels out. I follow.

It's not every morning I love my job, but this is definitely one of them. Plus we get to have an expensive lunch on Marly.

40

SAM

The day is brilliant. The rain's gone and it's the first truly hot day of the year. I don't feel one bit of guilt about having taken the morning off from doing any work and just lounging in the sun in my most skimpy of bikinis. It's so private here on Hardy that I don't have to worry about anyone seeing me. I glance over at Ellie on the patio; she has finished the school work her teacher at St. Cecelia's gave me for her to do every day. Now she has her nose in a book. She looks so cute in shorts and t-shirt, so much better than having to wear the school uniform.

My skin feels warm under the sunscreen; I've probably had enough sun. As a prelude to getting out of the lounger, I take a long, luxurious stretch. It feels good. I do it again. It makes me feel like a cat, a sexy cat. Unbidden, thoughts of Cal come to mind and thoughts of our lovemaking on the night before Matt Stammo's funeral. It was unbelievably good. I indulge myself in a little bit of fantasy, reliving the moments: the gentle touches, the whispered words, the rising passion, the kisses, the joining and the incredible waves of bliss. It makes me aroused and I let the pent up feelings wash over me. I can feel my heart beat and the breath catch in my throat. I have an overwhelming need to—

"Mommy, can we have lunch?"

The words are the proverbial bucket of cold water. I clear my throat. "Good idea, sweetie. What would you like?"

"Well, I was thinking about grilled cheese sandwiches but then I remembered those oysters we got from the beach on Thursday. You remember? You fried them and they were yummy. Could we have those again? Please."

I check to see if the tide's out. "OK. Get the bucket and the screwdriver." I push myself up and out of the lounger chuckling at my daughter's sophisticated tastes.

As we walk down to our beach, she tells me about the book she's reading, it's about a Gecko who's a detective, and as she chatters on, my thoughts turn to Cal. For the hundredth time I question my shouted words of Saturday night. My good sense tells me it's over between us but I still have such powerful feelings for him; and not just the sexy ones, although they *are* pretty powerful.

"So that's why I want to be a detective like Daddy," she says.

"That's good sweetie," I say, having missed most of what she said. "But there are a lot of other jobs you should think about. For example, you would be a great—"

"Mommy, you know I've already decided. I want to be a policewoman."

Rather than fight it—I really don't want her in a job where she risks her life every day—I just say, "OK."

We head for the big rock formation which stands like a sentinel in the middle of the beach; it's covered in oysters. Putting on the work gloves, I pry off about ten big ones and drop them into the bucket showing her how to do it; then I spot one which is not too tightly attached and hand the gloves and screwdriver to Ellie. "Try that one sweetie."

She jams the screwdriver between the oyster and the rock and pushes. It pops off the rock and onto the sand at her feet. As she bends down to pick it up, I sing, "Eleanor Rogan, Picks up the oyster than no one—"

"Mommeeeeee. You know I don't like that," she

objects. She looks at me and gives me that you-think-you're-so-funny-but-you're-not look. I grin and point to another candidate, "Try that one... oh and that one right next to it."

As she applies the screwdriver, I stretch up and look out to sea. "Oh, look El," I say. She follows the direction of my finger.

"Oh yes," she says. "It's that pretty yellow boat we saw in the marina. I wish grandpa's boat was like that."

"It's probably a bit out of grandpa's budget," I grin.

We watch as the boat comes round the headland and turns toward us.

"Is it coming here?" she asks.

"I doubt it." But before the words are out of my mouth, it turns some more and is heading directly in our direction. "Oh, it is. Looks like we're going to have a visitor." It's not unusual for passing boaters to put into our little cove to ask a favour or even to ask if the house might be for sale. It will be nice to have adult company for a while. "Let's go and see what they want."

She drops her last oyster, together with the gloves and the screwdriver, into the bucket and we head across the beach toward the dock. Then I re-member I'm in my skimpiest of bikinis. I look to-ward the house. There's a beach towel draped over the patio balcony. Do I have time to get it? I look back to sea. Maybe.

"El, take the bucket of oysters back to the house and bring Mommy that beach towel on the patio. Quick like a bunny." She runs back, grabs the bucket and dashes toward the house.

Oh dear, the boat's faster than I thought, already it's entered the cove. Its prow is dropping as the driver throttles back. El won't be back in time with the towel, I'll just have to brazen it out.

I reach the dock just as the boat arrives. There are two men on board. The one at the helm maneuvers it expertly up to the dock as his companion gets up from his seat, steps up onto the sliver of decking beside him and jumps lithely onto the dock. He's wearing fashionable and expensive clothes which are a uniform for the richer members of the boating set but somehow they don't look right on him. And he's wearing leather gloves which is decidedly odd.

He smiles, looks me up and down and makes me wish Ellie would get here with that towel. His smile broadens but it makes me even more uncomfortable. It's not a nice smile, it doesn't reach his eyes which, incidentally, are now focused on my breasts.

"You must be Samantha," he says. The shock that he knows my name is increased exponentially by the hispanic accent with which he says it.

"My name is Javier," he says. "Mr. Santiago sent me."

I stifle a scream as Ellie runs up with the beach towel and, ominously, the driver reverses the boat away from the dock and heads back out toward the open water, leaving us alone with God knows who.

41

CAL

The office is very plush. It's behind the stage and was probably a dressing room when the building was a theatre. Pastor Kilman is sitting behind his desk dressed in slacks and a jacket. It's the same way I was dressed when I was here yesterday; he's even wearing a Rotary lapel-pin. The man has attention to detail, I have to admit; he knows how to imbue confidence.

He has used his cold reading techniques to impress me that he knows a lot about my supposed wife Elizabeth. He's good at it too. Despite myself, I can feel the rapport he has built. If we were talking about Sam, I'm not sure I wouldn't believe him. "Where was Elizabeth born?" He asks.

"Galway, in Ireland," I say without thinking. It's the first place that came into my mind.

"I thought so," he nods wisely. "There's something in her voice that reminds me of the emerald isle."

He's good. He doesn't say 'she has an Irish accent' in case she had moved here as a child. But if the mark's wife did have an Irish accent, or maybe just a hint of one, he has established he knows that.

"But that's the problem you see." His voice has taken on a grave tone. "Most people don't know this but when the soul leaves the body, it almost always heads to it's place of birth. It's part of the process of completing the circle of life. That is what Elizabeth has done."

"Why is that a problem," I ask, my voice laced with concern.

"Well on occasions, a soul can get stuck at their place of birth. They don't want to leave. They have too strong an attachment to the place. What's happening with Elizabeth is that she's staying in Galway because it's her place of birth, and there's something that's holding her there, but deep inside she longs to pass over to the other side. It's a rare condition and it's causing her great conflict and distress. The longer she stays there, the worse it gets until she comes to a point where she can no longer pass over to the bliss of the spirit world which awaits her. She would spend eternity as a lost soul. I sense she's very near to that point."

"Is there anything we can do?" I ask, leaning forward and injecting a note of desperation into my voice.

He reaches across the desk and pats my arm. "Don't worry, there is. If I can talk to her, I can lead her out of the conflict and over to the other side."

"Can you do it now? Please." I beg him.

"Unfortunately, no—"

"Why not?" I interrupt, adding a soupçon of anger to the mix.

"I can certainly help her but I would need to go to Galway to be able to communicate with her."

"Please Pastor, I'm begging you to do that," I say.

An undecided look moves on to his face. Man, he's good at this.

"I want to, but my flock here needs me—"

I interrupt with the magic words, "Please Pastor, I can make a significant donation to help the Church while you're away. Would twenty thousand dollars cover the costs?"

He looks like he's weighing the pros and cons. "It *would* help and I *do* want to help Elizabeth. If you can make that donation to cover the cost of keeping the Church running while I'm away in Ireland and add five thousand to cover travel expenses, I could leave tomorrow."

"I can do that," I say. I take out my cheque book. "Is a cheque OK?"

"Certainly," he says.

I write the cheque and hand it over to him. "Here it is."

He takes it and puts it in his inside pocket. "Thank you, my son," he says. "This money will ensure Elizabeth's safe transition to the spirit realm where she will wait until you are ready to join her there."

Gotcha!

"There's one other thing I want you to do Pastor," I say.

"Anything," he says magnanimously.

"I want you to listen to something." I take the digital recorder from my pocket. "Do you know what a police scanner is?"

His smiling mask is replaced by puzzlement. The first genuine emotion I have seen on his face. "It listens to police transmissions?"

"Not exactly. What it does is it scans the radio frequency spectrum and records any transmissions which are in progress at the time. When I was here yesterday, I brought a computerized scanner with me." It starts to dawn on his face. "Would you like to hear what I recorded?"

He stares at me in silence, not trusting himself to speak, I suspect.

I flip the playback switch and a woman's voice starts talking. The voice is rich, vibrant and playful.

"Hello Petey. I hope you can hear me. If you can't, you're in big trouble. I have a couple of hot ones for you. The first one's named Cal. I got everything. He was standing right under one of the microphones. He's sitting in the fifth row between Silly Millie and Edna. He's loaded. He even put a hundred bucks in the plate." There's a pause but I skip past it. *"His wife was Elizabeth. He doesn't know where to bury her ashes. Poor baby, like it matters. Ha ha. Tell him Salt Spring."* I skip by the second, longer pause. *"OK baby, the next one's a sap named Donald, his daughter's name was Bethany, she died of heart failure."*

I switch off the player.

His face is white. "What do you want?" he asks.

"I want the ten thousand dollars you scammed from Phil and Florrie Franks with an additional ten thousand dollars fee for me. I want it in cash and I want it now."

"Twenty thousand dollars? Are you serious?"

I chuckle at the hypocrisy. "I'm as serious as a heart attack. If I don't walk out of here with the cash in hand, this recording of your wife," I stand up and wave the digital recorder at him, "and the recording of the so-called service you conducted yesterday will go to the CBC, CTV and CityTV just in time for tomorrow's news cycle. Then tomorrow morning I will visit a friend in the RCMP fraud squad with copies and with the recording I just made of you accepting my cheque for twenty-five grand."

He stands up and madly tries to find a way out of the hole I've dug for him... but to no avail. He deflates. "How do I know these are the only recordings?" he asks.

"You don't." I put the recorder back in my pocket.

"So how do I know you won't—"

"Because I want to keep you in business Pastor. You didn't think twenty grand would buy me off did you? It's just a down payment."

He slumps back down into his chair and puts his head in his hands.

Finally he looks up. There's a slyness on his face. "OK," he says. He opens a drawer, pulls out two bundles of bank notes and pushes them across the desk to me. I can't help but wonder how much cash is in that desk.

"Thank you." I reach back into my pocket, take out the digital recorder and drop it on his desk. I turn and walk to the door, then do a 'Columbo'. "Oh, by the way, don't try and deposit that cheque I gave you, I already put a stop payment on it."

The sly look vanishes from his face.

"Get out!" he says as he picks up the digital recorder, the second one I had in my pocket, the one with no recordings on it.

"See you soon," I say as I leave.

The big grin on my face tells me this has been a great day; to add the icing on the cake, I just need to make some calls on the way to meet Sean O'Day.

———

"I SHOULDN'T HAVE CHOSEN this place," he says, sitting down opposite me. I thought he chose Bean Brothers in Kerrisdale because it was far enough away from downtown that it would ensure some privacy.

"Why," I ask.

O'Day looks around the place. "Dale and I would often come here on Sunday morning for breakfast." His face shows no sadness to match the words and again I wonder at how well he masks his emotions. "So what was so important that you couldn't talk about it over the phone."

I tell him about the twenty-thirteen-dot-com website and the bible quotation. "As it says '*they* are to be put to death,' I was worried for you."

O'Days inscrutability fields are still in place. I can't tell how he feels about this news. He looks at me for two or three seconds. "OK," he says. "Thanks for letting me know. I'll be careful."

He starts to get up from the table and a lightning

bolt of intuition tells me I need to keep him here. "There's more," I ad-lib. "Please, sit down."

Not taking his eyes off me, he complies.

"You don't look like someone whose life might be in danger," I say, to give myself some thinking time. However, he says nothing; just gives a small shrug.

My gut tells me there's something about him I need to find out. I just can't work out what. Maybe if I ask about Dale. "Dale was from a religious family, was he religious himself?" It's the first thing I can think to ask.

"Not as such. I'm sure he believed... but he couldn't stomach the religious views on his orientation. He blamed his family's church for causing the split with his father and brother."

"And you?"

"Me? I'm afraid the Catholic Church beat any belief I might have had out of me. I'm a fully paid-up atheist." His Irish accent is more in evidence.

"Did Dale go to a church?"

He gives a small laugh, more of a grunt really. "Only church basements," he says. "Why?"

I ignore his question. "His brother said he was a regular at church."

"Then he's a liar."

Why would Luke Summers lie about something

268

so easy to verify? I'll tuck that question away for later.

"What did you mean, church basements?" I ask.

He thinks for a while, weighing some decision probably, not that it shows on his face. "Have you ever heard of gamma?" he asks.

"Sure, it's the third letter of the greek alphabet."

"Yes, it's also an acronym for Gay And Married Men's Association. It's a self-help group for married men who are gay. Dale had been a member for years. To him it was the closest thing to a religious group. He went at least once a week. They held their meetings in a church basement downtown."

A self-help group to help married gays is hardly going to be involved in Dale's death. So I guess I've drawn a blank in my meeting with Sean O'Day.

Then it hits me.

Maybe I haven't drawn a blank.

———

"Have you ever heard of GAMMA?"

"Sure," Adry says with a giggle. "It's what I called my grandma when I was a kid. Why?"

"Nothing, where's Nick?"

"Don't know. A couple of hours ago, he got a phone call from his landlady and she seemed worried about something. Next thing I know, he's flying out the office saying he won't be back for the rest of the day. I asked him what the problem was but he just wheeled off into the elevator."

I head to my desk and take out my phone. Siri calls Nick for me but there's no reply. Oh well, I guess I won't get to run my theory past him after all.

42

STAMMO

The pain pushes through into my mind. Where the fuck am I? I hear a groan. It's me... I think. My head feels like it's going to explode. Through the throbbing, I can feel the hardness. I'm lying on something hard. Like a floor, except that it's bouncing. Why's it bouncing? Floors don't bounce. I try and get up but I can't. My legs won't... Of course they won't. I'd forgotten. Where's my wheelchair? I try and open my eyes. They won't open.

It's loud. The noise is familiar. I've heard it before. It's an engine. The floor gives a big bounce and throws me up. For a second I'm weightless until it slams me down again. I yell out in pain. But now I know where I am. I'm on a boat going fast through the water, bouncing on the wave crests.

But I still can't see.

What the fuck happened to me? I was at the office. What happened then? Oh yes, I got a call from Mrs. V saying I had to come home, there'd been a terrible accident. She was hysterical. I seem to remember going through the front door of the house. Then nothing until here.

Why can't I see? I try and reach up but my hands are tied. I can't move them.

Why am I on a boat? I haven't been on a boat since...

Oh no.

Oh no way.

43

CAL
TUESDAY

I feel like an outsider, twice over. I'm an outsider to this church; it didn't matter during the service when I sat at the back and stood when everyone else stood and kneeled when they kneeled and sat when they sat. But here at the cemetery I'm the person nobody knows. I'm an outsider as far as Luke Summers is concerned; his look made it quite clear I am not welcome. But that verse from Leviticus fits so well with the ethos of this church.

The minister officiating at the grave is a tall florid man with a huge head and small hands; he's definitely the fire and brimstone character Stammo described. I'm sure Dale Summers would have shuddered to think he was being buried at the church which would have condemned him. However, funerals are for the living not for the dead.

Two of the living are noticeable by their absence: Marly Summers and Sean O'Day.

My phone vibrates, thank heavens I remembered to turn the ringer off. I ignore it; pulling it out of my pocket and answering it would be the quintessence of gauche.

As the Minister drones on, I look around at the assembled congregation. They all look like upstanding citizens. But my experience tells me even the most solid citizens can commit the most heinous crimes. My gaze wanders and I do a half turn toward the limousines. Six black, stretched vehicles polished to a tee. Then out of the corner of my eye, I see something that doesn't fit. In fact two things: an RCMP cruiser and a black Chrysler without hubcaps which is almost certainly an unmarked police vehicle.

They drive slowly and quietly up behind the last limo in the line.

I look toward the grave. The congregation are facing away from the cemetery's roadway, so they are unaware of the new arrivals, but the minister's eye has caught them. He stumbles over a word and then regains his stride and continues.

I look back. Standing beside the unmarked car are two faces I recognize: Steve Waters, my former partner at VPD, and the odious young detective named Eric Street who should have been fired two years ago. The sight sends a frisson of fear dancing up my spine. The last time I saw Steve at a funeral he was arresting me. Have they found new evidence on Samuel Island? I can feel my heart beat in my chest. How did they know I'd be here. Maybe they called the office and Adry told them. They don't seem to have seen me yet and I wonder if I can sidle away and back to the main road where my car's parked. I look in that direction... not a chance. I am royally screwed.

At the grave the minister has finished and a line of relatives, led by Luke Summers and a woman who's probably his mother, walk to the grave side and, one by one, each casts a lone red rose into the grave.

As I try to guess what new evidence they may have found—which I have tried to do a thousand times before—the minister has a few words with Luke and his mother and turns to go but then stops. I follow his gaze and see that Steve and his sidekick are heading toward him followed by a uniformed RCMP member with Staff Sergeant chevrons.

I let out my breath. Maybe, just maybe, they're not here for me.

They have a brief conversation with the minister and then are joined by Luke Summers. It's clear no one's happy with what the police are talking about, especially Summers. He's running one hand through his blond crewcut and his voice is raised but I can't catch what he's saying. Then the RCMP officer says something and everyone seems to calm down.

Finally the Minister goes with Steve and gets into the back of his cruiser.

The congregation are agog. Some are aghast and some are bemused. This is the most exciting thing they have witnessed this century.

Luke Summers speaks quickly to the RCMP member and then heads over to a congregant in a two thousand dollar suit. I'm guessing he's a lawyer. After a brief conversation Luke scans the crowd until his eyes land on mine. He heads toward me and, taking me by the arm, leads me out of hearing distance of his fellows.

He says four words and when I agree, he shakes my hand.

———

I CAN'T WAIT to tell Stammo we have a new client in Luke Summers. I press and hold the button on my earpiece. "Call Nick Stammo." Pause. Voicemail. "Nick, call me as soon as you get this."

I accelerate along 200th Street toward the highway. Pastor Mueller has not been arrested but has been asked to 'help the VPD with their inquiries' into the death of Dale Summers. That was all Luke Summers could garner from Steve and the RCMP officer. He has hired us to try and find out what possible evidence there could be against the minister. As I mull it over, I'm betting the techies at the VPD, or maybe the RCMP, have traced the ownership of the *twenty-thirteen.com* site to Luke's church.

Steve won't take a call from me but he and Stammo are still buddies so Nick might be able to find out what's happening. Of course, Nick's going to say it's a conflict of interest but he'll come around when I tell him Luke Summers said he would send us a twenty-thousand dollar retainer.

I mentally review everything I know about Dale's murder. For Steve to have taken Pastor Mueller in for questioning, he must have a boatload of evidence.

As I reach the Trans-Canada, I press my earpiece again. "Call Office."

"Hi Cal."

"Hi Adry. Is Nick there?"

"No. He hasn't been in." Her voice sounds worried. *"Hasn't called either. It's not like him."*

"I'm on my way back. Can you try and get hold of him for me?"

"I've tried Cal. I even called his landlady Mrs. Van Vloten." Oh right, that's Mrs. V's name. *"But got no reply from her either."*

"OK, well, try him again please."

"Sure Cal."

"Thanks. See you in about half an hour."

"OK." I reach up to tap my earpiece but stop as she says, *"Did someone named Sam get hold of you? She phoned to say she tried your number but it went to voicemail."*

My heart's beating faster again but this time in a good way. "Thanks Adry, I'll call her right now."

I'm feeling like a love-sick schoolboy; this is the call to say all is forgiven. I feel excited at the thought of speaking with her... but scared too. Then I remember the call I missed at the cemetery; it must have been from Sam. I can get a preview of what the conversation is going to be about. Good or bad.

Tap. "Check voicemail."

"Cal, call me as soon as you can, it's urgent."

Not exactly what I was hoping for but... Tap. "Call Sam."

One ring. Two. Three. Four. Fi— *"Cal. I need you to come up to Hardy, right away."*

"Why? Are you OK? Is El?"

A pause. "Sam?"

"It's my MS, I've had a bad attack. Fortunately the doctor on the island was able to see me. But I need you here to take care of Eleanor. Please hurry Cal."

I process it for a second. "I understand. I'll be

there as soon as I can, it may take a few hours but hang in there. Stay safe."

The Healey leaps forward as I push the gas to the floor.

I have to get to Hardy as soon as possible and I know someone who can help.

If I can just remember his name.

44

CAL

As we come round the headland, the house comes into sight, looking peaceful in the lowering sun. The man at the helm brings the boat into the cove and expertly executes a one hundred-and-eighty degree turn, reversing gently and allowing me to step off the transom onto the dock. "Good luck Cal," he says, his voice reassuring.

"Thanks, you too," I say absently. I start out toward the house, wondering exactly what reception I will get. The boat's engines roar as it accelerates out of the cove.

I walk along the dock and onto the trail which leads to the house. As I come through the tiny copse, I focus on the house, its grey, weathered wood looking golden in the sun. The curtains are drawn which is unusual; they're reserved for keeping the sun out of the main floor in the hotter days of July and August. I try to remember the interior layout but it's so long since I've been here; it was when Ellie was a baby, about four months before that fateful night when, in an unholy show of machismo, I first took heroin. I shake off the memory as I cross the lawn and walk up the six steps to the patio, the third step creaking under my weight.

I pause at the front door and take a deep breath, open it and step inside.

Sam and Ellie are sitting cuddled together in the middle of a long couch to the left of the wood stove which is opposite the door. Sam's in my favourite bikini but is partly covered by a cushion which she has drawn into her lap. Ellie looks terrified.

Resisting the desire to go to them, I say, "Why are you sitting in the dark?"

I turn on the light, move quickly to my left and open the curtains.

"How nice of you to come Mr. Rogan, I'm delighted to meet you at last."

I spin toward the source of the voice. The speaker is a tall, good looking man, impeccably dressed, with a broad smile on his face. He's standing in front of the dining room table, like a soldier 'at ease', legs apart, hands behind back. Beside him is another whose most noticeable feature is the Uzi machine pistol in his left hand. Immediately in front of the speaker is a man gagged and secured in a dining chair, his head hanging down, face a mass of blood and bruises. It's Stammo.

"Who the hell are you two?" I ask, carefully backing away from them toward the far left of the room.

"Don't you recognize me? People say I resemble my father." His voice is educated, smooth as Devon cream. "Allow me to introduce myself." A pause, a smile. "I am Tomás Santiago. This is my colleague, Javier." He turns toward his sidekick. "Javier, please offer Mr. Rogan a seat."

I back further away, my eyes betraying my fear.

"Sit there." Javier indicates an upright wooden chair near the left hand end of the couch. I comply. Objective accomplished. Javier walks over, his pistol trained on my gut. "Hands behind." I do as he asks. I feel my body tense, ready to spring. Javier takes one step closer, two steps. Just one more...

"Don't do anything hasty Mr. Rogan." I look at Santiago. One of the hands that was behind his back is now in evidence. In it: an identical Uzi. It's pointed at Sam and Ellie. I don't move an inch as Javier goes behind me and none too gently cuffs my hands with cable ties. He uses three of them. "You might be able to break one but never three," Santiago assures me.

"No need for the Uzis," I say. "Why don't you put it down? Please."

Santiago shrugs and points the Uzi toward the floor away from Sam and Ellie. I breathe a sigh of relief as Javier secures my ankles to the legs of the chair and frisks me thoroughly: underarms, back, pockets, ankles and finally crotch. "Clean," he grunts.

"Good." Santiago says. He stays in the dining area behind Stammo's chair; the curtained windows to the right of the front door are at his back.

"First I would like to thank your daughter. Her photograph of the boat at the dock was all my people needed to track you down to this charming hideaway." He does a mock bow toward Ellie. "Now... Let me describe the evening's entertainment." I feel myself struggle against the ties as I'm overwhelmed by a desire to kick the confident smile off his face.

"First you are going to watch the execution of this one." With his free hand, he punches the side of Stammo's head. "But we are not going to do it quickly with a bullet. Oh no, that would be just too easy. You see, we know his part in the assassination of my father. So you will get to watch as Javier and I beat him to death. We even brought a baseball bat for the very purpose."

Sam has put her hands over Ellie's ears and pulls her closer. "You pig," she spits at Santiago.

He just laughs. "Then Mr. Rogan, Javier's going to get his first reward and you are going to watch him." I look toward Javier and his eyes are drilled on Sam. "Yes that's right. You and your brat are going to have ringside seats to Javier enjoying the pleasures of your wife's body. He has promised he will make sure you get to see every little detail."

"You bastard," I rage. "I swear to God if that animal touches a single—" My words are cut off by Javier's fist full in my face. As the pain surges through me I tell myself, keep calm. Don't let them rattle you. Your chance will come.

Santiago laughs long and cheerfully. "Just imagine her naked body writing under Javier's. She'll pretend she's not enjoying it but we both know she will secretly love it."

"Never," Sam chokes out. "NEVER." Tears are streaming down her face.

If I can just get Santiago closer... "Wow," I say, my voice matter-of-fact. "Despite your educated voice and nice clothes, you're just a degenerate thug like that useless sack-of-shit father of yours."

For the first time his urbane manner slips. He takes two furious steps toward me but catches himself. Damn. I need him closer. Way closer. He regains his composure. "Javier," he says and nods in my direction. My blood runs cold as Javier steps toward me and puts the end of the Uzi's barrel on my knee. He looks at Santiago who smiles.

I squeeze my eyes closed ready for the impact of the nine millimetre bullets.

But they don't come.

"Not yet," the smooth-as-cream voice says. I open my eyes and Javier steps back. "Not yet."

I try and get my breathing under control. I have to think of a way to get Santiago three or four steps closer.

"I have to go to the bathroom. Badly." Ellie's voice cuts through the thought.

Santiago looks at her, his face expressionless.

"Badly," she repeats.

"Go." He says. El scurries to the far end of the room and through to the bathroom behind the kitchen. "Perhaps it's better she doesn't hear what's next. You see, Mr. Rogan, after Javier has sated himself on your wife's body, you are going to watch while we kill her. Then I am going to break every bone in your hands, feet, arms and face and Javier will enjoy putting some of those nine mill bullets into your knees. We will then break as many ribs as we can without puncturing a lung. Then Javier and I will say goodbye to you and leave you to die a long, slow and painful death, with the bodies of your partner and your wife. You will be safe in the knowledge that your little girl will be in our care." He smiles expansively at me and my rage returns. "When we have enjoyed her company enough ... then we will sell her. You would be surprised what a child of her age will fetch on the dark web. You will have lots of time to imagine the buyer and what he will do to her." I struggle with all my might to control myself. I must keep calm. I must get Santiago to take two more steps in my direction. Just two.

Then I see our one chance. Now I *have* to keep Javier's attention on me. He's grinning down at me. Keeping my eyes locked on his, I say, "*Now* I see why your boss is happy for you to have Sam. He can't embarrass himself. He's not man enough to have her because he can only get it up for little girls."

Javier's hand snakes back. I turn my head to lessen the impact of the blow and in the millisecond before it strikes, I see that Santiago, his face contorted with rage, has taken a step forward and that our one chance, Ellie, is behind him holding what looks like a screwdriver in her hands.

Three seconds.

One. The back of Javier's hand connects with my face, I hear a yelp of pain and a clattering.

Two. As my vision clears, I see Santiago holding on to his right arm, the Uzi and the screwdriver at his feet. Ellie runs toward me and with a snarl Santiago follows her. I yell "Now!"

Three. Ellie slams into me.

Santiago, bathed in the last of the sunlight coming through the window, reaches out to grab her. His head explodes. There's a tinkling as a shower of glass hits the floor. Javier pitches forward and there's a second tinkling followed by the sound of Sam's scream.

"Both targets are down," I yell.

Suddenly silence. Five seconds of it. Then Sam's whispered, "Thank God. Thank God." She's trembling but she forces herself off the couch, stepping over Santiago's body, and envelops Ellie in a hug. "What just happened Cal?"

I start to laugh as Sam starts to sob: both normal reactions.

The front door slams open and an RCMP member in full swat gear steps inside and sweeps the room with his Smith and Wesson. He ignores us and checks the bodies. "Down and out," he says into the microphone attached to his helmet.

A little voice says, "I did good Daddy, didn't I?"

"You did sweetie, you really, really did."

My laughter takes on a hysterical overtone.

———

An RCMP Emergency Response Team member holds Sam's hand as she steps off the dock across the transom and onto the boat's deck. "Thank you," she says. "And thank you for what you did…" she looks toward the house, "back there."

"My pleasure," he says. She just keeps looking at the house until, with an air of finality, she turns away and takes a seat in the cabin.

Ellie's next. "How did you know the bad people were here?" she asks him. Her voice is excited. She's showing no sign of any trauma. I wonder if this is normal and worry how witnessing a double killing might affect her psychologically.

He smiles as he lifts her over the stern and puts her down on the deck. "Your daddy told me. He asked us to help him stop them from doing anything bad."

Ellie turns to me as I step aboard. "How did *you* know Daddy."

"It was Mommy who let me know. When I spoke to her on my phone, she said two things that let me know something was wrong."

"What did you say Mommy?" she asks as we step into the boat's cabin.

Sam doesn't answer. She's staring out the window across the water toward the last sliver of the descending sun.

"Mommy was very clever," I say. "She told me she had seen a doctor on the island but there's no doctor here; there are only five properties and I didn't remember any of the owners being doctors. Then she referred to you as Eleanor."

"But that's not my name. My name's Ellie. I don't like it when people call me Eleanor."

"I know. That's when I knew for sure that something was wrong. So I asked the Emergency Response Team people to help us." I remove the lapel pin from my jacket and hold it for her to see. "They gave me this tiny microphone so they could hear what was happening in the cabin. When I saw the bad men I said 'Who are you two?' so that he would know how many of them were inside."

The ERT member walks into the cabin and takes his place at the helm.

"I can refer you to a company which specializes in crime scene cleanups," he says to Sam. "No one will ever know what happened there."

"But we will," Ellie pipes up.

Sam grabs her and pulls her close. "Listen to me Ellie," her voice has a fierceness I have never heard from Sam before. "You must never, ever, speak about this to anybody. Do you understand?"

"Mommy, you're hurting me."

"Do. You. Understand?"

"Yes."

"Promise me you'll never talk about it."

"I promise."

"What do you promise?"

"I promise I'll never talk about it."

"Not to anyone!"

"OK, OK. I promise. I'll never talk about it to anyone."

After a beat, Sam's shoulders relax. She pulls Ellie into a hug on her lap and stares out over the water again, while I wonder if Ellie will ever need to talk about it to a shrink.

I want to talk to Sam but have absolutely no idea what to say.

The ERT member starts the engines. "There was a third one," he says. "He was in a yellow cigarette boat moored on the east side of the island. We arrested him." He points to the corner of the cabin. "That wheelchair was on board."

Greg MacKay, Stammo's buddy from Sechelt RCMP, whose name I managed to remember, steps into the cabin carrying Stammo like he weighs nothing and puts him gently into the wheelchair. His face has been cleaned up and he has been given basic first aid but he still looks a mess.

He looks around the cabin and his gaze settles on me. He smiles. "You know what Rogan?" he says, "If I live to be a hundred, I swear I'm never stepping on another boat." He gives a crooked smile and adds, "Unless it's a frickin' great cruise ship."

At least Stammo and I are OK.

45

CAL

WEDNESDAY

The atmosphere in the office is upbeat. Halfway home from Hardy Island Stammo had remembered how Santiago and his thug Javier had taken him. They had gone to his apartment and forced his landlady to call him and get him to come home. When he wheeled through the front door all he remembers was being knocked senseless. He was worried sick for the safety of Mrs.V. When we got back there last night, to our great relief, we found her trussed up in a chair, hungry, thirsty, indignant but unharmed. She fussed around Stammo and I left him to her ministrations knowing they were both in good hands.

In an attempt to put Hardy Island behind us, we are in early and focussing on our caseload. Just as I finish telling him about how it all worked out with the conman Pastor Kilman, Adry walks in.

"What are you early birds doing h—?" She sees Stammo's face. "My God Nick! What the hell happened to you?"

"I got mugged."

"How did—?"

"I don't want to talk about it, OK?"

"Sure... I guess." She doesn't sound too sure but she lets it drop until she sees my face. "What the... Have you boys been fighting?"

"Not with each other," is all I can think to say.

"So anything happen at the funeral?" Stammo cuts in, pointedly changing the subject..

"Oh yes indeed. Sit down Adry, you need to hear this too."

She gives a big smile.

"We have a new and, might I add, rich client."

Now Stammo gives a big smile. I notice he has a missing tooth, courtesy of either the late Tomás Santiago or his newly departed buddy, Javier.

I tell them about Steve showing up at Dale Summers' funeral and taking the pastor with him. And about Luke hiring us.

"So now we have three people paying us to find Dale's killer." There's glee in Stammo's voice. "Marly Summers, the Southbrook's VP—what's her name Cal?—and now Luke Summers. Go figure."

"It's Emily Audley," I say. I must call her. Maybe she'll be free for dinner tonight. "Nick, do you want to give Steve a call and see if you can find out why he showed up at the funeral and if he's got anything on the Pastor."

"Sure."

"There's another thing. I found out Dale Summers was a member of an organization called GAMMA."

"Oh yeah, the Gay and Married Men's Association. They've got chapters all over the place," Stammo says. "Makes sense that Dale would be a member."

"So I thought it might be worth checking out the Vancouver chapter. Someone might know something."

"Good thought." Stammo rotates his wheelchair and taps his keyboard. After a few keystrokes and a couple of clicks, he turns back. "They have meetings Wednesdays, Fridays and every other Saturday. I'll go tonight and check it out."

I feel an initial surge of irritation; I wanted to check out GAMMA myself. But then again, I'd rather have dinner with Em and let Stammo go.

"What time are the meetings?" I ask.

"Tonight's is at seven-thirty."

"The last time Dale was seen by anyone was at seven on Friday. He left the Railway Club with Sean

O'Day. Maybe he went from there to a meeting. I'll ask O'Day."

"Great and I'll ask around at the meeting."

"Anything I can do Cal?" Adry asks eagerly.

"Three things." I take one of the bundles of cash donated by 'Pastor' Kilman and hand it to her. Her eyes go wide. "You can deposit that in the bank. While you're out, buy about a thousand of the cheapest thumb drives you can find and I want you to copy a file onto each drive; I'll email it to you." She looks disappointed. "But before you do all that I want you to do some investigation for me." When I tell her, the disappointment disappears from her face.

———

As I PULL into the parking lot my phone rings. I tap the earpiece.

Stammo. *"I talked to Steve. He was a bit close-lipped but I found out one of the reasons they questioned Pastor Mueller."*

"Go on."

"After I told Steve about the twenty-thirteen.com website, he had his techies look at the site and in the metadata, they found a reference to Luke Summers' church."

"What's metadata?"

"It's like data on the site you don't see; it's used by search engines and stuff."

"So does that mean the site was created by someone from the church?"

"Not necessarily, but it could be. The thing is..." He's silent for a beat. *"The thing is I must have missed it when I looked at their site and... well I should'a spotted it."*

"Don't sweat it. Anyway, I'm there now, so it's good to know. I'll call and tell you if anything new comes up."

"OK." He hangs up. He's annoyed and I know why. Nick's getting to be pretty good with all this computer and internet stuff and he's just mad at himself that the VPD techies found something he missed. He'll get over it.

I get out of the Healey and walk over to the side door of the church. I'm surprised to find myself in a reception area pretty much like you would have in a regular office. There's even a receptionist: a lady in her fifties with glasses like my mother used to wear.

"Good morning," she smiles. "Are you Mr. Rogan?" When I say yes, she points to a door opposite her desk and says, "Pastor Mueller and Mr. Summers are expecting you."

Before I reach it, the door opens and Luke Summers ushers me in and introduces me to the florid pastor who has a thin sheen of perspiration on his forehead. He's not as impressive as he looked at the funeral yesterday morning. Was it only yesterday? It seems longer. He's dressed in chinos and a golf shirt but is wearing Nike's. I can't help noticing that although he's a good twenty kilos overweight, his arms are muscular and he's wearing three rings: a wedding ring, what looks like a fraternity ring and a large, ornate ring with a crucifix embossed on it.

"I'm so glad to meet you," he says as he shakes my hand. "Luke says you are one of the best private investigators in Vancouver." Interesting. Why would Luke say that? I got the distinct impression he didn't like me. Maybe he's done some digging. "Please, sit down, sit down." I sit at an impressive boardroom table; the church is clearly not short of cash. Pastor Mueller sits opposite me but Luke Summers stands by the floor-to-ceiling windows covered in sheer curtains, through which I can see the Healey.

"What happened with the police after the funeral?" I ask.

"It was very strange. Very strange indeed." He's speaking quickly. "They said they thought I could help them with their inquiries and they took me to the RCMP office just down the road from here. They asked me about a website, I'd never heard of it before, they asked if it belonged to the church. I told them the church only had one website and they asked me the name of the people who manage our site. They didn't tell me what it was about. It was quite distressing really." He pauses for breath.

"Was the website called *twenty-thirteen.com*?"

"Yes, I think it was. Yes, it was. What's it about?" I have an uneasy feeling about him. It feels like he's acting the part of an aggrieved and innocent man. I look over to Luke Summers but his face is impassive.

"How seriously do you take Leviticus 20:13?" I ask.

"Oh. *twenty-thirteen.com*. Oh, I see. Well, it *is* quite clear. We take it to mean that homosexuality is abhorrent to God. Is that what the website's about?"

"Yes. It has images of Dale's murder. Explicit pictures which were almost certainly taken by the murderer." I turn again to Luke. "I don't recommend you look at it," I say to him. He gives no noticeable reaction.

Pastor Mueller says, "And the police think the church had something to do with it? Why would they think that?"

Without taking my eyes off Luke I say, "Your church's name was in the metadata for the site." There's no reaction from Luke.

"How could that be? Just because we are opposed to homosexuality, it doesn't mean we would kill someone... well, gay." As I turn back to the good pastor the words *doth protest too much* come unbidden into my head. Or am I just being cynical? The line between skepticism and cynicism can be a fine one. Yet I can't shake the feeling this meeting was rehearsed.

"So how can Stammo Rogan Investigations help?" I ask.

For the first time since he made the introductions, Luke Summers speaks. "Quite simply. You are investigating the murder of my brother on behalf of his wife." There's venom in the final word. "I will pay you to do the same. By increasing your revenue, I will expect you to put more resources on the project and look at *all* possible suspects. Can you do that?"

"Yes."

"Good."

"And I'd like to start with the name of the people who manage your website."

The Pastor looks uncomfortable for a second or two then takes a pen and a business card from his pocket and scribbles a name and number which he hands over.

"Unless there's anything else you need...?" Summers leaves the question dangling. There are some things I'd like to ask the Pastor but I don't want to ask them with an audience present. I shake my head. "Good. There will be a retainer cheque at your office in the morning."

I get the feeling he's paying us to implicate Marly and, when I think about it, she may be paying us to implicate him. Well at least if one of them did it, the other will still be left standing to pay our final bill.

———

ALTHOUGH I USUALLY TAKE IT black, I add as much cream as I can—within the bounds of politeness—to Florrie's toxic coffee; I even add sugar in the vain hope it will make it drinkable. The cinnamon bun she has placed before me is fresh from the oven and smells sublime. I take a bite. "Mrs. Franks," I say in all truthfulness, "that's the best cinnamon bun I have ever tasted." She smiles broadly and there's even a hint of a blush in her cheeks.

I slide the envelope across the table. "There's ten thousand dollars in there, courtesy of the so-called 'pastor' Kilman."

Phil's face lights up. "Tell me you're not joking, son," he says. I shake my head. "You were right Florrie, we got our money back. I'd never have believed it." He opens the envelope and looks inside with a chuckle. "How did you persuade him to give us a refund?"

I pull the digital recorder out of my jacket pocket

and play them the recording of Kilman's wife telling him what the microphones in the lobby picked up.

"So that's how he did it. Well I'll be..." He chuckles again.

"Thank you so much Detective Rogan. You're a real hero," Florrie says. "But you must let us pay you for this. We'll share this money with you won't we Phil?"

"Absolutely," he concurs.

I tell them Kilman also covered my fee so there's no need for them to pay me. "However," I add, "a couple of cinnamon buns to take home would be OK."

As Florrie packs some buns in parchment paper and a Ziploc bag, Philip says, "We're real grateful you got our money back Cal but I don't like it that Pastor Kilman's still stealing money from good folks. I wish we could do something about it."

I finish my mouthful of cinnamon bun and say. "Funny you should say that."

They look at me and they're both all ears.

46

STAMMO

The guy speaking right now has one of those voices which make you want to drift off to sleep. I look around the circle and there's just about as big of a variety of men that you are going to see anywhere. Of the dozen or so, two are bikers in leathers and chains, one man who looks like he's close to homeless; in contrast there are a few businessmen in suits, one of them looks like he's worth a small fortune. There's an older guy named Jeb who looks like a rock 'n' roller from the nineteen-seventies and there's one well-dressed guy with a blond crewcut who's good looking, but a little bit too, I dunno, gay for my taste. He's sitting between a couple of jocks who look like they play for the NHL and overuse steroids.

I wonder if Rogan noticed I was a bit too eager to check out this meeting. I don't think I gave anything away. Then again, why not. Maybe he and Adry should know. I dunno. I'll have to think about it some more.

"Anyhoo," the speaker drones, "When I told her, she was OK with it. Said she thought I'd found another woman. It was like she was relieved I was gay." He smiles for a second and then gets serious. "Now I gotta tell my kids. It's gonna be tough on my oldest, he's made a few remarks about gay kids at school; said some ugly things. I dunno how he's gonna take it when he finds out his old man's gay." He pauses for a second. "So that's about it."

Everyone joins in an applause for him. A couple of people share their stories about coming out to their kids and one guy has some pretty good advice. It makes me think of my own kids. We've been pretty busy with work which has been good. It's kept me from thinking about Matt and how he died. I wonder how he would have reacted.

It gets me thinking again. If I admit Rogan was acting in self defence, I'm admitting my own son was a crook and a killer and he deserved to die. How can I do that? I let Matt down in life. Can I let him down in death? As I reach up to rub my eye, my hand brushes across the bruises; it reminds me I owe Rogan. If it weren't for him I'd likely be dead.

Hell, I'd definitely be dead. Then again maybe I'd be reunited with Matt somehow.

"Who's next?" The words snap me out of the darkness. Paul, the guy running the meeting, is tall and good looking with a small scar under his left eye shaped like the Nike swoosh. He catches me looking at him, "Nick, would you like to share something?"

I think about it for a bit. "Sure," I say. Why not? They seem like a pretty nice bunch of people.

I wheel up to the front, turn and face them. A couple of the guys smile encouragingly. I take a deep breath in.

"I've been in the closet my whole life. When I was a kid, I tried to tell my dad but he just quoted the bible at me. Leviticus twenty-thirteen." I look around the group but there's no reaction from anyone. "He said I should snap out of it or he'd beat it out of me. I lived back east and I always wanted to be a cop, so I joined the OPP, got married and had two kids but never said anything about how I felt... you know... about guys. The OPP was a pretty macho outfit; if I'd have come out it would'a been hell. The few times I actually got together with a guy, I was always scared someone would find out. If I got close to someone, I'd usually end up breaking it off.

"My wife knew something was up of course, but

like your wife," I nod toward the previous speaker, "she just assumed it was another woman. I never manned up and told her. After we got divorced I moved out here and joined the VPD and was with them until this." I tap the sides of my wheelchair. "So anyways, I'm still in the closet.

"My ex was out here a couple of weeks back, for the funeral of our son." I cough away the catch in my throat. "Listening to you guys, I wish I'd've come clean with her. I wish I could'a told my son before he... you know... before he died." A tear's running down my face and, when I brush it away, I realize I don't feel embarrassed with these guys.

"Thanks for sharing Nick," Paul says and there's applause from everyone. For the first time in my life, how I feel about men doesn't seem like such a burden. "Well I guess that's it for this evening. Max brought coffee and goodies."

"Atta boy Max," someone says and the blond guy with the crewcut gives a little wave.

Now to test Rogan's theory that Dale's murderer might be someone he met at GAMMA. I wheel over to Paul. "Thanks for letting me speak," I say. "You don't know how much it helped."

"It was great to hear your story, Nick." He gives me a big smile and I realize I'm attracted to him. Better be careful, I've kept it bottled up for so many years it may just be an overreaction. "How did you hear about GAMMA?" he asks. Perfect.

"My friend Dale Summers told me about it."

"Just a point Nick, we don't use last names here."

"OK. Sorry."

"No prob. There's a Dale who's a member but he hasn't been to a meeting for about, what...? ten days, I guess. It's not like him. He's a regular. He was all set to come out to his wife."

"Marly," I say.

"Yes. I wonder why he's not been around."

I shrug, feeling guilty for not coming clean with him.

"Anyway," he continues, "I've got to go." He gives a little smile. "On a date." I feel a little jab of jealousy that he has a date. He hustles off to get his coat and I wheel over to a group chatting and having coffee. I join them and they immediately welcome me. We spend some time chatting and once I feel I've got some rapport going, I ask them if they remember anything about Dale's last evening here. No one remembers anything unusual or seeing him leave with anyone. In fact they remember him as a bit of a loner who usually left the meetings right after they finished. Rogan's idea that someone here might have met up with Dale is a dud. But to tell the truth, I didn't put much faith in it. I've often thought about coming to their meetings and this was a good excuse.

I'm glad I came.

47

CAL

I walk up the steps to Sam's apartment, my Ziploc bag full of Florrie's cinnamon buns clutched under my arm. El is going to love them. Sam too... if she lets me in. On the boat from Hardy Island she was silent pretty much the whole time but when we got to the marina I walked her and Ellie to her car. Before she got in, she hugged me so tightly it hurt then whispered, "Thank you so much for saving us, Cal. I thought..." She stopped speaking, kissed me on the cheek, got in her car and drove off. I'm hoping that at least we can get back to talking.

I look through the stained glass in the front door. The apartment's in darkness but they're probably preparing dinner in the kitchen at the back. Maybe I'll get invited in to eat. I was hoping Em would be free for dinner but she has to have dinner with her boss, who's in from San Francisco for a flying visit. Thinking of Em while I'm standing on Sam's doorstep stirs up the emotional conflict again.

I ring the doorbell and it seems to echo in the apartment like it did when I was here ten days ago. There's no response. I ring again. I feel a thread of paranoia tug at me. Maybe I'll just check around the back. As I start down the steps I hear the front door open.

Great! They *are* in.

I turn back but Sam's door's still closed. It was the neighbour's door I heard. "Detective Rogan, hi."

"Hi, Mrs. Hunt. How are you?"

She looks embarrassed. "I'm fine. Thank you. I heard Sam's doorbell. I thought it might be you. Sam guessed you would be round soon. She, uh, asked me to give you something." She holds out an envelope. There's no way this can be good news. Part of me just wants to run away but instead I take it from her.

"Thank you Mrs. Hunt, I appreciate it." I get a strong premonition I won't ever see this good lady again. "And thank you for being such a good neighbour to Sam. I know she thought the world of you." I realize I just referred to Sam in the past tense. Is this some other nightmarish premonition.

I hurry down the steps and into the waiting

Healey. I fumble open the envelope and in the feeble glow of the interior light read the letter.

Dear Cal,

I want you to know I love you very much. I will never love anyone the same way I love you. But I just can't go on like this. Ellie and I were put in deadly danger again because of you. I know you had a good reason for killing those people but I can't live with the consequences of your actions anymore and I can't allow Ellie's life to be in danger. We are going away, far from Vancouver. When we get settled, I will let you know but for now I think it would be better if you don't try to contact us. I will arrange for you to message El and at some point talk to her by phone.

I would be happy if you gave up your career but I know that being a detective is in your soul, so I would never ask you to make that change.

All my love,

Sam

and Ellie xoxoxoxxxoo

I read it a second time, then rest my head on the steering wheel and try not to cry.

48

MAX

He fumbles with the key. That's good. The roofie's starting to take effect. Perfect timing. I'm getting good at this. So I should; I've had some practice. He finally gets the door open and stumbles into the entranceway. I slip off my backpack and as I place it on the floor the contents clink together. "What'ja got in there?" His voice is starting to acquire a slur. "A toolkit?"

I can't help laughing, he doesn't know how right he is. He takes my hand and I try not to flinch as he leads me into the living room. It's beautifully and expensively furnished with a spectacular view. As soon as we are inside, he grabs me and tries to kiss me. Degenerate! "Hold on tiger, hold on," I say, fending him off. "Let's take this slow and sexy." I try not to gag on the words. "Why don't you fix us a couple of drinks and we can, you know, get to know each other first."

"OK. Scotch?" Good, he's in the compliant phase. I nod. He walks over to a cabinet and takes out some glasses and a crystal decanter. "What made you decide to come to GAMMA?" he asks as he starts to pour unsteadily.

"Through a friend," I say and smile. I learned Dale's nasty little secret when I saw him heading for the GAMMA meeting just ahead of me. I often wonder what would have happened if I had got there first and *he'd* have seen *me*.

"Oh, who's that?" He hands me a glass and I catch the smell of peat.

"A guy named Dale," I say. No reason not to tell him. "Cheers," I say and take a sip of the single malt. Excellent. I must remember to take this glass with me.

"Cheers." His voice is becoming more slurred. Not long now. I feel the tingle of pleasure starting to build. "Yeah, I know Dale. Funny that you men... you mentioned him. D'you rem... remember the guy... the guy in the whee..." He starts to sway. "I feel a bit..."

"Why don't you lie down Paul. Let me take you into the bedroom."

"The bedroom. Yeah," he leers. "Thought you'd never..." He starts to sway.

I put my arm round him before he falls and help him into the bedroom. A quick push onto the bed and he's unconscious before his head hits the pillow.

I look around. The room's decorated in pink and purple and has a delicate smell of roses. The bed linen has patterns of tiny flowers on it. It brings memories flooding in.

———

HIS EYES FLICKER OPEN. The effects of the drug are wearing off. He looks around the room in puzzlement. He obviously knows he's in his own bedroom. He tries to roll off the bed but the ropes and the duct tape hold him in place. He starts to struggle. "Welcome back Paul," I say. He rolls his head in my direction and blinks, his eyes trying to focus. He recognizes me. He tries to speak but the sock in his mouth, secured by duct tape, mutes the sound. He looks puzzled. Now I get to play.

"Now for some fun." I say. His eyes widen but he doesn't object. He thinks I've tied him up so that I can fuck him. Fat chance, faggot. I take the tailor's shears out of my backpack. There's fear in his eyes. I feel the tingle through my body. Oh this is going to be good. Not yet, take your time, Max. I start at the bottom of his shirt and cut up to the right armpit and along the sleeve to the wrist. I do the same on the left side then throw the remains of his shirt on to the floor. I give him a big smile and he nods. He's enjoying the game.

I start to tell him the story.

There's a slick of sweat on his chest and belly. I run my gloved fingers across his belly just above his belt and I can see the swelling in his jeans. He's turned on. Disgusting!

With a smile I unbuckle his belt and pull it off. "Mmmm," he moans.

Still talking, I take a leisurely walk to the bottom of the bed and cut through the thick denim of his jeans. From ankle to waist, left leg then right. The rendered jeans join his shirt on the floor. Two more cuts and his underwear adds to the pile.

Now he's really turned on. I just stand and watch, savouring the moment, feeling the excitement growing inside me. I stop telling the story; this time it might spoil his reaction. He looks into my eyes and he knows I'm turned on too, he just doesn't know why. But he will in a moment. I'm still holding the shears. I put them on the bed between his legs. Oh yes, this is good. I've thought of a new addition to my routine. Oh my God yes, why did I not think of this before? My breath comes fast as the pleasure builds.

I take him in my left hand and gently massage

up and down; my anticipation drowning my disgust. He's moaning through the gag and nodding to me. His eyes lock on mine and I gently speed up the movements of my left hand. With my right hand I pick up the shears and spread the blades. He doesn't see the movement, he's too caught up in his own pleasure. My left hand pumps a little faster... and then faster still... and just as his moaning approaches its crescendo, my right hand jabs forward and snaps the blades closed. I lift up my left hand for him to see the trophy and reach down my body with my right hand.

His muted shrieks of pain trigger the ecstasy and I can hardly hear him over my own groans of pleasure.

49

CAL

I step off the elevator and stop. The doors close behind me. My mind's in turmoil. I just can't decide. It's not too late to turn back now but if I go forward there will be no turning back later. I want to take the dozen or so paces to the room but I'm wracked by indecision.

Ping. The elevator to my right stops at the floor, disgorging an elderly couple holding hands. They smile at me and I feel like a fool standing here. "Are you lost?" the lady asks.

"No," I smile embarrassedly. "Just lost in thought." Not wishing to seem a complete idiot, I walk to the door marked 803 and knock. Thus are decisions made: by embarrassment not by logic.

The door opens. "Cal, I'm so gla— Oh my god, what happened to your face?" The punch in the face from Javier has turned me into a trash panda. She steps back and lets me enter. I smother my shock that she's wearing a bathrobe and walk into the room. It turns out that it's a suite. Must be nice to be the VP of a large company like Southbrook.

"Oh it was nothing. One of the bad guys decided to take a shot at me."

"Are you all right?"

"Sure," I shrug it off. "I'm doing better than him." I try not to think about Hardy Island; it's a sure-fire mood destroyer.

"Well, I'm glad you came."

"Yes, well, to tell the truth, I was sitting at home feeling sorry for myself. So I was really happy to get your call."

"Do you mean you *wouldn't* have been happy to get my call if you *hadn't* been feeling sorry for yourself?" Her Southern accent is playful.

I can feel myself blushing. "No I didn't mean that, it's just that—" I stop in mid-sentence. I have an overwhelming desire to tell her about Sam and what happened and the letter she left for me but I don't know Em well enough yet. I search for the right words but her laughter saves me from saying anything more.

She lets the door close and slides her arm through mine. "I know," she says. "I was just joshing you." She leads me over to a beige sofa—why are hotel room sofas almost always beige?—and sits me down. "What would you like to drink?"

"Do you have the makings of a Black Russian?"

"I sure do." As she leans forward to open the door to the minibar, her robe slides to her shoulder and I see the rise of her breast. My breath catches in my throat. She takes out two little bottles of vodka and two of Kahlua. She drops ice into a glass and pours in all four bottles —vodka first, then Kahlua—picks up her glass of red wine and comes back to the sofa. She hands me my drink saying, "It's a double so you can catch up to me," and she sits down beside me, facing me, with her knees drawn up onto the couch between us.

"So tell me all about Calvin Rogan," she says brightly.

"Well first thing it's not Calvin, it's California. My mother had a thing about it; she always wanted to go there."

"That's a good start. California's a lot cheerier than Calvin."

I tell her everything: my childhood, university, my early days in the VPD, Sam and Ellie, the heroin, my years living on the streets, finding my father and finally how Stammo and I came to be partners. She's such a gentle and attentive listener—asking questions and offering supportive comments—that

I feel safe enough to tell her an edited version of the letter from Sam.

She doesn't comment, just reaches out and takes hold of my hand.

It feels good.

"Tell me about you," I say.

"I had an idyllic childhood growing up in the South. My parents were quite well-to-do and my younger sister and I wanted for nothing." She smiles as if savouring a memory.

"That picture in your office of your parents and your sister, did you take it?"

"I did. That was when I was home from college in the summer of two-thousand, remember Y2K? I had taken a course in photography and fancied myself as the Annie Leibovitz of Georgia. Silly really."

"No, it's a wonderful photo," I say. "You said your sister... passed away?"

"Yes, a year after I took the picture, almost to the day."

"How did she die?"

As I look into her eyes I see the sadness.

I give her hand a squeeze. "Sorry, I didn't mean to..."

She smiles. "That's fine Cal. I'll tell you about it some time. Soon. Not just now."

Instead she tells me some stories about her exploits as a Southern ingenue doing a business degree at Columbia. After a particularly hilarious one about how she paid back an overly flirtatious older professor, we both collapse in laughter.

As the laughter dies, our gazes entwine and as one, we lean forward until, with exquisite gentleness our lips meet in the lightest of kisses. The touch of her lips sends a sparkle of electricity up and down my spine as she draws me toward her.

———

THE JANGLING of an alarm kicks me into wakefulness. Disorientation. Dark. Where the— I roll over and feel the warmth. Oh. Em. I slide my arm round her and she rolls toward me. "Mmmm," she purrs. "Cal-if-or-ni-a." She kisses me gently and I run my fingernails softly down her back. "That's nice," she says. I bring my hand round and cup her breast and am rewarded with another kiss. I reach downwards.

"Oh no, Mr. Sexy," she says, arresting the progress of my hand. "I have work to go to." Before I can complain, she rolls out of the other side of the bed and walks into the bathroom.

I look at the green digits of the alarm clock. *6:32.* I have time. Time to think about last night. It was without doubt the most amazing experience. Somehow we... I don't know... we just fit. It was like we had known each other for years. We each seemed to know how to excite the other; her bound-aries were my boundaries, I was turned on doing the things that turned her on and vice-versa; we re-joiced in each other's body. We were perfectly syn-chronized. Three times. It was like we could reach into each other's mind. And the in-between times were wonderful too: we talked, we laughed, we even sang *We All Live in a Yellow Submarine* together. We talked sexily to each other until we were thrown into a renewed bout of passion. Everything worked.

I hear the sound of the shower and have an urge to go in there and make it a two-person sport but think better of it.

When she comes out of the bathroom she's naked. I smile at her and she looks sideways at me. Pause. "OK," she says. "You can watch me get dressed." Did it again: she read my mind.

When she leaves, I feel the loss and know our connection is more than just the sex.

50

CAL
THURSDAY

C al, I got something, and you are *not* going to believe it." The words tumble out of Adry's mouth before I'm halfway through the door of the office and the alarm has finished its triple beep. "I was waiting for you to get here so I could tell you and Nick together."

"OK, great." I give her a big thumbs-up. "Let me get a coffee and you can tell all."

"Already on your desk," she says, following me into the office.

Nick is at his desk. Some of the purple bruises are starting to take on a greenish hue. "Nice colour scheme," I say. "Very attractive."

"Don't be a smart-ass, Rogan. Did *you* look in the mirror this morning?"

I did. Not pretty.

Adry cuts through our less than witty repartee. "OK boys, settle down," she says. "Don't you want to hear what I found out?"

"Sure, have at it." I take a chocolate digestive from the plate on Stammo's desk and sit down.

"Cal, you asked me to do a deep dive into Pastor Mueller at Luke Summers' church. I did and I found some very interesting stuff." She pauses, savouring the moment I guess. "Have either of you heard of the Westboro Baptist Church in Topeka, Kansas?"

"I've never heard of Topeka, Kansas," Stammo grunts. "Is that where Dorothy came from?"

"Who?" she asks.

"Dorothy, Toto, you know."

"No." Adry looks annoyed at Stammo for breaking her rhythm.

"I feel old. Sorry. Go on," he says.

"So... the Westboro Baptist Church was this horrible, totally anti-gay church that would do things like picket the funerals of dead soldiers. They were disowned by the Southern Baptist Convention and just about every other church in the world. The guy who ran it died in twenty-fourteen, good riddance, but guess who used to be a member back in the nineties when it was at its height?"

I can guess, but after Stammo's interruption I don't want to steal her thunder.

She looks at me with a big smile on her face. "Pastor Joseph M. Mueller."

"Are you sure?" I ask. "I don't want to falsely accuse someone."

"I am. At first I thought it *might* have been a coincidence, you know, a different Joseph Mueller. But then I was able to find a few old videos on CNN's site showing some of Westboro's demonstrations and in one of them, he was right there, twenty years younger of course, holding a 'God Hates Fags' sign. It was definitely the same guy whose picture's on the website of Luke Summers' church, although his bio at the current church doesn't say anything about Westboro."

"I knew there was something wrong about Mueller. These Westboro people, was there any evidence of them doing physical violence?"

"Not that I could discover."

"I'm looking forward to seeing Mueller's reaction to this bit of info. I wonder if VPD knew about this. Did they say anything about it when you spoke to them Nick?" Stammo shakes his head, his mouth full of cookie. "That was really well done Adry. Did you discover anything else?"

"Nope."

"Yeah, Adry, well done," Stammo says. With a broad grin she heads toward her desk but Stammo calls her back. "Wait a minute, there's something I want to tell you guys."

Something seems to be bothering him. He takes a drink of his coffee and clears his throat. "I went to that GAMMA meeting. Dale was a member there. They didn't know about his death. One of the guys there said they were worried about him 'cos he hadn't shown up for meetings. Anyways, they seem like a good bunch of folk. I didn't see anyone who looked like they didn't belong."

"Shame. I just thought maybe Dale met someone there the night he was killed. Worth a try."

"Yeah, it was. Thing is..." he pauses and takes a deep breath. "I thought you guys should know and I hope it doesn't change anything but, uh, I never told you guys before that I'm gay. I've been in the closet my whole life so I thought it was about time to come out."

I wonder if I should tell him that I know.

Adry leans over his wheelchair and gives him a big hug. "Doesn't matter to me Nick," she says. "Half the members of my family are gay."

He gives her a hug but is looking over her shoulder, eyes drilled in on me.

I give him a big smile and a thumbs up. He looks relieved. Maybe, when we get a quiet moment together, I'll tell him it was an open secret at the VPD and no one had a problem with it.

"You guys finish your hug-a-thon; I've got phone calls to make."

———

THE OFFICES ARE NOT MUCH BIGGER than ours with eight people crammed in, all huddled over their computers. A skinny young guy who looks like he's not old enough to drink yet, looks up from his screen, "Are you Mr. Rogan?" he asks.

"Yes. Hi. Cal." I step over and extend my hand which he takes and shakes. His hand feels like a bag of bones but his grip's more than firm.

"Ronny Chu. Come and sit down." He pulls over a guest chair which just fits in between his desk and the desk of one of his colleagues, a young woman with her right arm covered in tats. "You said you were looking for someone to redesign your website?"

"Yes." I smile, trying to imagine the conniption Stammo would throw if I were serious about getting someone to redesign the site he so lovingly crafted.

"After you called, I took a look at it and it's already pretty good. What was it you wanted changed?"

"I like our site, it's just that I saw the website for the Baptist Church of the Savior and I really liked it and Pastor Mueller told me you did it."

"Oh," his eyebrows go up. "Are you a member there?" He's one of those people who wear their emotions on their sleeve. This emotion is hope.

"No, why?" I ask.

Hope dies. He bites his lip for a moment. "It's nothing." I just look at him with a questioning expression. It works. "It's just that they owe us money. Four months ago we did some changes to the site so their members could make donations by credit card and they haven't paid us yet."

"Sorry, I can't help," I say, suddenly glad Luke Summers is the client and that his cheque for our retainer arrived at the office just before I left for this meeting. "Did you do any other sites for Pastor Mueller?"

The hope which was on his face has been replaced with suspicion.

"Are you with the police?"

"No, why?"

"There was a detective here yesterday afternoon asking about the church's website."

I shrug. "Do you ever do websites to run on servers in Russia?"

"That was what the detective wanted to know too. I'll tell you what I told him, basically no, never. Why do *you* want to know?"

"It's just there's a Russian-hosted site where Pastor Mueller's name is in the site metadata and I was wondering if he had got you to put up the site for him."

"Oh. The detective didn't tell me that. But no." He shakes his head and looks at me. "You don't really want us to redesign your site do you?"

I feel a twinge of guilt. More than a twinge, in fact. Normal people don't use lies and subterfuge as part of their business model. This visit has drawn a big fat blank. Time to come clean.

"No, I'm sorry I deceived you, it's just that this Russian website has some pretty disgusting stuff on it and I wanted to find out if Pastor Mueller might have been implicated. When he told me you did website development for him, I just thought maybe you could cast some light on it."

"I told you." It's the girl with the tattoo at the next desk.

"I know Meghan, you were right," he sighs.

I look toward her, the question on my face. "I told Ronny not to do business with that church," she says.

"Why was that," I ask.

"We'd never done church websites before and the first one we did was just horrible; the client kept trying to tell us how to do our job and the stuff he wanted to do on the site was a design nightmare. It was horrible And it was *him* who referred us to Pastor Mueller and the Baptist Church of the Savior and then he didn't pay us our final payment, said it was his commission for the referral. Now *Mueller* owes us a ton of money *too*. No more churches, OK Ronny?"

"OK Meghan, OK... I get it." I feel like this is a familiar dynamic between them.

But she doesn't want to stop worrying this bone. "I ask you," she says, "what church would go by the name of the Church of the Pure Divine Light? It's got woo-woo written all over it."

The hair on the back of my neck stands to attention.

"You guys did the website for that shark Kilman?" I ask. Meghan grunts in the positive. "And Kilman referred you to Mueller?"

"Yes."

The fact that Kilman the conman and Mueller the gay hater, know each other cannot be a coincidence. I can't guess what it means but I just know it's germane to the case. I smile at the feeling of elation building inside me. I can't wait to talk to Stammo about this.

"Thank you both so much. You've been very helpful. One last thing, did you tell the detective about the connection between Kilman and Mueller?"

"No. It never came up."

Yes! It's always great to be one step ahead of the VPD.

My phone rings.

The caller ID is like a bucket of cold water.

It's the call I've been dreading.

51

STAMMO

The phone rings. Damn. Adry's out picking up lunch. Just when I don't need the distraction. Maybe I'll just let it go to voice mail. Then again maybe it's a client; maybe even a new client. Better make sure. I press the right buttons. "Stammo Rogan Investigations."

"Hello Nick, it's Steve." My former partner at VPD.

"Hey Steve, what's up?"

"I was just phoning to see how you're coming along with your investigation into the murder of Dale Summers."

My suspicion antennas are twitching. He's having trouble with his case. "I'll show you mine if you'll show me yours," I say.

Silence for a bit then, *"OK. You first."*

Luckily I can trust Steve. "Did you know your

suspect Mueller was once a member of a radical anti-gay church in Kansas."

"Yeah. It was the first thing that decided us to take him in for questioning. How did you know about that?"

"We have our ways." I must remember not to mention this to Adry, she was so proud of digging it up, and rightly so.

"Have you dug up anything else on him?"

I was right; his case against Mueller's weak. He's not going to be happy when he hears this. "I don't think Mueller did it."

"What d'you mean?"

"Rogan's out following up on a lead but I don't think he'll come up with anything. I just don't think Mueller did it."

"Why not?"

"You remember that website *twenty-thirteen.com*?"

"Yeah, what about it?"

"Your guys found Mueller's church's name in the metadata on the website."

He chuckles. *"Yes we beat you to it, eh."*

I ignore his little jeer. "There's two things wrong with it though. First, why would Mueller put their name, or have a website developer put their name, in the metadata in the first place?"

"Our techies say it was probably done in error by whoever developed it when he first set up the site. He

might have copied some data from Mueller's church's site."

"Possible. But I don't buy it. I told you about the site on Sunday. When did your guys find Mueller's name?"

"They told me Monday morning. It was the second thing that decided me to go and question Mueller the next day. Why?"

"I looked at the site after you told me about his name being in there. I found it, but I'm certain that when I looked the first time his name wasn't there. If I'm right it means Mueller's name was put into the metadata sometime after Sunday morning when I found the site and before Monday morning when your guys found it. That can't have been an accident."

"If you're right that it wasn't there originally."

"I'm sure Steve. Absolutely sure. Someone who knows Mueller put his name into the metadata of the *twenty-thirteen.com* site sometime after Sunday morning and before Monday morning. Someone's trying to frame him."

He's silent. Cops hate it when the case against a favourite suspect gets shaky. Now it's Steve's turn. "So what have you got for me?" I ask.

"Hang on." I hear some background noise and the sound of a door being closed. *"You didn't hear this from me, OK?"*

"OK."

"This morning there was a new booklet entered into VICLAS." I can guess what's coming. VICLAS is the Violent Crime Linkage System and a booklet's a file on a new crime; the name's a hangover from the days when it used to be a physical booklet. *"Murder in Burnaby. The body was found by his cleaning lady early this morning. It's just like Dale Summers; almost certainly the same killer. Twenty-thirteen branded on his stomach and death caused by the sword buried in his chest. There was one extra thing, his penis had been amputated. The killer's escalating."*

"Jeez... that's sick." The thought sends an unpleasant tingle worming through my gut. "Any indication he was gay?"

"No but I'm betting he was."

"What was the time of death?"

"Won't know 'til the autopsy but the booklet says probably late last night."

An uncomfortable thought worms into my gut. The words of the Leviticus verse: *and* they *shall be put to death.* "What was the vic's name?" I ask.

"Paul Beauchemin."

Thank God. It wasn't O'Day.

Then the worm bites down... hard. My relief vanishes. I try to focus my mind on last night. Paul.

"Did he have a small scar under his eye...?" I

focus on the memory, "left eye I think. Looked like the Nike logo."

Silence.

"Steve?"

"Hang on I'm checking the crime scene photos."

In the silence I can hear the clicking of his mouse.

There's a sharp intake of breath. *"Did you know this guy, Nick?"*

Oh Jeez!

"Yes. Well not really. I met him last night."

"How d'you meet him?"

"Rogan got this lead that Dale Summers was a member of an organization for gay married men. I went and checked 'em out last night. Paul was one of the guys in the meeting."

"Did he leave with anyone?"

"Not that I noticed. But he did say he had a date that night."

"I need to talk to these people. Can you give me the details of the group?"

I do as he asks and then he's silent for a second. *"I might need your help on something."*

"Sure," I say. "Anything."

"OK, I'll get back to you."

He hangs up.

I grab my mouse and click on a browser window.

New tab. Type *twenty-thirteen.com.*

Right there with Dale Summers' murder scene are the explicit photos of Paul Beauchemin's mutilated body.

I close the tab before I throw up and before Adry comes back to the office. No one should have to see that.

We are going to get this monster before he escalates again.

Wait a minute!

Escalating!

Yes. If he's escalating, I wonder if...

I grab my mouse and get to work.

52

CAL

It's not your typical lawyer's office. It looks more like someone's living room... someone's untidy living room. There are books and files everywhere but I get the distinct impression Jim Garry could lay his hand on any file or any book he wanted on the first try. Right now he's sitting opposite me with a worried look on his face.

"As I told you on the phone," he says, "we've got a court date for you. Six weeks from today."

"Is that good or bad?" I ask.

"Bad, I think. Normally it takes months but it's only a few weeks since they arrested and charged you, yet already they have a court date. It's so unusual it worries me."

"Do you have any idea why it was so fast?" My nervousness is chewing into my gut.

He just shakes his head and rubs his knuckles on his chin.

"But you still think I'll be found innocent right?" I can hear the pleading in my voice.

"No one is ever found innocent, only not guilty," he says. I know of course but I'm not thinking straight right now. "It depends on the testimony your partner gives. Do you have a read on that?"

"Well I think he's pretty conflicted about it. We haven't really had a good conversation about it. He cuts me off if I bring up the subject."

"Listen carefully Cal. You need to have that conversation. I have to know which way he's going to go. If we don't get this right you could spend a very long time in jail."

———

FOR THE SECOND time in as many days, I park the Healey in the lot of the Baptist Church of the Savior. If this goes as expected it will be my last visit here but we shall see. Armed with the shocking information from my long phone call from Stammo, I enter the offices.

The same lady with the glasses is behind the reception desk.

"Oh, hello," she says. "It's nice to see you again. Mr. Rogan isn't it? Do you have an appointment?"

"No. I was hoping Pastor Mueller was in and that he had a few minutes to talk. I have some good news for him." I know he's in. Adry called a couple of times and asked to speak to him and then hung up when he answered. I didn't make an appointment because I want to see the Pastor without the presence of Luke Summers.

"Let me see," she says. "Have a seat." She taps away at her keyboard for a second and announces, "He'll be right out."

While I wait, I re-run the conversation I had with Jim Garry. I can't imagine Stammo throwing me to the wolves but what if he does? The thought of being an ex-cop in a high-security prison frightens me. And I can't imagine Sam would let Ellie visit me. I worry this over in my mind until the Pastor arrives.

"Good afternoon Mr. Rogan. Please, come with me." He shakes my hand and leads me into the same conference room as before. After we are seated, without an offer of coffee or water, he asks, "How can I help you?"

"Can you tell me everything you did from about eight o'clock last night until eight this morning?"

He looks at me uncertainly but answers, "I gave a Bible class from seven-thirty to eight-thirty and then I had a meeting with the finance committee from nine until about eleven. Then, after a last prayer with my wife, we went to bed."

"That's good. I'm sure if the police ask you the same question you will be able to give them the names of the people you met with?"

"Why would the police ask me?" He looks uncertain now.

"Would those people verify you were with them?"

"Well... well, yes. Of course, yes. Why do you ask?"

I ignore the question. "Do you still believe God hates fags?" I ask.

His face goes pale. He starts to speak and then thinks better of it. He licks his lips. "How did you find out about that?"

"Quite easily, actually. So did the police. It was the main reason they took you in for questioning on Tuesday."

If anything, he goes a whiter shade of pale.

I press my advantage. "Do you think it's God's work to kill gay men Pastor?"

He pauses. I suspect it's in order to word his answer just right. "No. They will receive judgment at God's hands not mine."

"What about Paul Beauchemin?" I watch him with all my senses for any indication he might have known the second victim.

"Who?"

There was absolutely no reaction to the name that I could detect. I run it again. "You know... Paul Beauchemin."

"Sorry, I've never heard of him." I'm sure he's telling the truth. The good Pastor Mueller is very probably out of the frame. But there's still something I need to know.

"I spoke to the people who did your website. They told me you were referred to them by a Pastor Kilman. Is that correct?"

His guards come up. "Kilman gave them our name, that's true."

"How do you know him?"

"I met him at a conference about a year ago. He seemed like a nice enough guy. The conference was about uses of technology for churches. I mentioned we were looking to redo our website and he referred us to Ronny Chu."

"Was that your only contact with him?"

"No. He called me a couple of weeks after the conference and suggested we meet for lunch. I agreed at first but when I checked his website I saw immediately that he was a false prophet. I cancelled the lunch and never heard from him again."

"Did he say why he wanted to meet with you?"

"Yes, he did. He wanted to talk about a joint fundraising exercise. It sounded like a good idea on the face of it but it was likely some ploy of the devil."

Damn. More likely some ploy of Kilman to perpetrate a scam on Mueller's church. I was hoping for more. Now I only have one more thing to ask him.

"Does the bible say something about a workman worthy of his pay?"

"Indeed it does. First Timothy five-eighteen. *For the scripture saith, thou shalt not muzzle the ox that treadeth out the corn. And the labourer is worthy of his reward.*"

"Perhaps you should take that verse to heart and pay the money you owe to Ronny Chu and his company."

To give him his credit, he blushes. Then nods.

We both get to our feet and say our goodbyes and I leave in the hope I never have to return here.

————

I'M EARLY. The barman's different from the last time I was here but the tall cadaverous manager's the same; fortunately he doesn't recognize me. I sit at the bar with a cold glass of Trash Panda, an appropriate drink as my black eyes, courtesy of the late Javier, still make me look like the raccoon on the label. For what must be the tenth time I re-read the email from Sam. *Cal,* not dear Cal, *We are getting set-*

tled into our new life. I will contact you soon to arrange for you to have some contact with Ellie. She sends her love by the way. I just need to find a way for her to have a relationship with you that maintains the anonymity of our location. Bye, Sam.

I had Stammo look at the email. He dug into the metadata but was unable to work out where she was emailing from. 'I'm thinking somewhere in Canada,' was the only guess he would hazard.

I have to accept that my life with Sam is over but the thought that I won't see Ellie any time soon is a real physical pain, a gnawing deep in my gut. I long to hear her cheery little voice and the chime of her laughter. And it's all my fault. I order a second glass and think that if I weren't having dinner here with Em, I would go find a quiet bar and drink myself stupid; not the wisest of plans but infinitely better than heading to the downtown east side and finding some smack to shoot into a vein. The thought gets the old longing washing over me. In rehab they told me it would come and go but I've been pretty lucky it has never overwhelmed me yet. The thoughts get darker. I even think maybe I could—

"Why hello tall, dark and handsome."

The playful tone of Em's Southern lilt pulls me out of the darkness. I slide off the bar stool and she kisses me on the cheek. "This place is beautiful, I've never been here before."

The manager leads us to our table right by the window with a view across the sunny expanse of Coal Harbour and the Burrard Inlet. Vancouver at it's springtime best. The mood of mere seconds ago dissipates and I'm ready to enjoy our dinner at the Lift.

"How was your day?" I ask, unconcerned about the sheer banality of the question.

"It was fine. Meetings, meetings, meetings. Then I took my boss to the airport. Altogether a good day."

"When will the new store open?"

"It's scheduled for six months from now."

"Well that's good. I can look forwards to six months of your company," I raise my glass to her.

Before she can respond the server appears at our table, takes Em's order for a glass of Chardonnay and recites the specials of the day.

"I look forward to every minute of our time together," Em says. We hold each other's eyes for a moment. "Let's get business out of the way first. How's your investigation into Dale's murder going?"

"Not great. There's been another murder, another gay man. Like Dale's, the pictures have been posted to that *twenty-thirteen.com* website I told you about. By the way, don't go to the site. It's horrific. The second murder was even more gruesome than Dale's. He's clearly escalating. We had an idea that maybe the pastor of Dale's brother's church was the murderer, he's a rabid anti-gay—or at least he used to be—but he really didn't work out."

"Was the new victim connected to Dale in any way?"

"Yes, as a matter of fact he was. They were both members of a self help group for married gay men."

"So who are your suspects?"

"We're back to square one. Dale's wife, her lawyer, Dale's brother," I don't mention Sean O'Day because I promised to keep his orientation from his boss however, he's a possible I suppose.

"Good. Business over."

Feeling a sliver of guilt about withholding Sean's name, makes me want to give her some more details. "With two similar murders the Police will put an IHIT team together and my partner indicated they might want us to help them, though I don't know in what capacity. I've got to admit, I'm at a bit of a loss."

"What's an IHIT team?"

"Integrated Homicide Investigation Team. As the second murder was in Burnaby there will be VPD and RCMP members in the team."

Our server brings Em's wine and learns we haven't even looked at the menus yet.

Em raises her glass. "I have faith in you, Cal. I'm betting you find the person doing these horrible things before the IHIT people have even scratched the surface."

We chink glasses and she smiles deep into my eyes. I return her smile. It's nice to have someone have faith in me. Maybe I can find a new line of inquiry. Maybe there's some connection I'm missing.

53

MAX

It's all out of control this time. Not like before. It's all because of number one. The previous number ones were all anonymous. Why didn't I stick to the plan? If I'd have stuck to the plan... but I couldn't. It's all because of number one. Damn him! But knowing him did add that little bit of extra pleasure didn't it? Yes, number one was wonderful. In a way I'm glad it was him even if it did throw everything off.

And number two, oh number two was sublime. When I amputated his prick, I've never felt such pleasure. In the warm and the dark, I reach down and relive that moment. Within seconds the pleasure's building... building... and... Ooooooh. Ooooooooooh.

Frustratingly, it's not the same. Not like the real

thing. I need the real thing. I need it soon. For the next one, I want to add some nice little touch, I don't know what it is yet but I'll think of it. I really do need the next one soon. Number three is always the best. My usual method's blown; I can't go there again. That damn guy in the wheelchair, Nick Stammo. *He* was what Paul was mumbling about. But there's a golden lining, I can chose someone I know as my number three. And I know just who he'll be.

But this time I will have to leave everything behind. Everything. But it's worth it.

You will be avenged my love.

54

CAL
FRIDAY

I feel equal parts of glow and guilt. I'm basking in the glow of another wonderful night with Em and I'm feeling guilty because of my feeling I'm betraying Sam. It's not even three weeks since Matt's funeral and already I'm in another woman's arms. But what a wonderful woman. We are so good together and not just in bed. We talked for hours last night and we talked about so much. I can't help the feeling this could be huge.

As I go to insert my key, I see the office door's unlocked. Why the hell's it unlocked so early in the morning? Adry's really conscientious about locking up and Stammo would never leave without locking up and setting the alarm. I push the door open. The alarm gives its triple beep; it wasn't set last night.

I close and lock the door. If anyone's in here I don't want them to escape.

Silence.

I wait.

Nothing.

Quietly I step around the partition wall separating the reception area from the office. I don't spot anything. Then I see him, slumped over his desk. Oh God.

"Nick," I rush to his side. "Nick are you alright?"

I reach down to feel for breath.

I cannot lose this man.

"Nick!"

I shake him feverishly.

"NICK!"

"Wha...? Who...? Ooh. Jeez, Rogan... You scared the crap out of me."

I let out a long groan of relief. "*You* scared the crap out of *me*. I thought something had happened to you."

He straightens up with a sigh and stretches. "I was just taking a nap."

His hair looks like a spiky halo.

"Hell Nick, you look like something to hang on the front door at Halloween to scare the kids away. Were you here all night?"

He thinks about it and then something dawns on his face. "Rogan, you've gotta see this."

He shakes his mouse and logs into his computer.

"Yesterday afternoon, I got to thinking. Our killer's escalating right?"

"Yeah."

"Right. So I started to think, what if Dale wasn't his first. What if this guy's a serial killer. And what if Dale was also an escalation."

"Makes sense."

"Does it ever. The day after you found Dale's body, I did a bunch of searches for similar killings where the victim had been branded with twenty-thirteen. But I didn't find anything. But this time I thought, what if the branding was an escalation? So I spent a few hours trying to find murders where twenty-thirteen was written on the bodies rather than branded. I tried a whole bunch of different searches and then I found it by accident. I was getting a bit tired and I mistyped twenty-thirteen as twenty-*nine*-thirteen. As I went through the search results I saw a reference to the Quran. So I thought about it. The Bible doesn't have a monopoly on being anti-gay and I did a search of the Quran and found the main verse that condemns homosexuality. It was verse twenty-nine in book twenty-nine."

He grabs a stale glass of water from his desk and drinks it down before continuing. "So I redid all my searches and found this." He clicks on his browser and there's a website that looks very much like *twenty-thirteen.com* except that it's *twenty-nine-twenty-nine.com*. As Stammo scrolls down the page there are photos of the bodies of dead men in various stages of torture. Two of them have 29:29 written on them in what looks like marker pen and the third has the letters carved with a knife. All have identical daggers sticking up from their chests with a quarter moon on the handles, a symbol of Islam.

"Holy crap. When were *these* murders? I don't remember anything about them."

Stammo has a big smile on his face. "Seven months ago and you wouldn't remember them because they happened in Minneapolis. I checked the newspapers at the time and the murders were a big deal down there. Caused all sorts of crazies to come out of the closet. There were even anti-Muslim demonstrations by the local skinheads. There were only three murders, each one a bit worse than the previous." He finishes with an even broader smile.

"So the Christian thing is all a red herring. It's someone who hates gays and wants to blame it on religion. Who would be anti-religion and hating gays?"

"There isn't a religious angle," he has a smug look on his face now.

"But both the site are supposed—"

"Listen and learn," he grins. "It was about three in the morning when I found the Minneapolis murders. I knew if I went home I wouldn't be able to sleep, so I carried on trying to find other murders inspired by religion. I tried everything I could think of but I was out of luck. Then I remembered the skinhead riots and I added skinhead into the searches I'd been doing and look what I got."

Another click of the mouse and yet another familiar-looking website appears. Three bodies, all tortured, all with §175 written on them. "It stands for Paragraph 175 which was a section in the German criminal code from 1871 banning homosexual acts. It was used by the Nazis to justify sending gays to the death camps. This website was supposedly set up by a skinhead group with the dumb-assed name of *death4gays.com*."

"When and where?" I ask.

"Just over a year ago in Tallahassee, Florida. After this one I must'a fallen asleep."

"Do you think there might be others?"

"Maybe, I don't know. But three's enough to see the pattern, right? When I tell Steve, he can get his techies to see what they can find out about 'em or maybe find more. Let *them* work all night, eh."

"Nick, you are brilliant."

"Thanks, Rogan. Yes, I am."

A thought hits me. "Are there GAMMA chapters in Minneapolis and Tallahassee? Maybe that's how he finds his victims." Twenty seconds of keyboarding later I get an affirmative from Nick. "Was there a mention of GAMMA in any of the press coverage?"

"No." He thinks for a second. "Maybe the police never released that information to the press. I'll tell Steve and he can get his guys to find out." He picks up the phone and starts dialing.

As he starts talking to our former colleague, I suddenly deflate. Our job's over. The killer's some random guy who goes from town to town killing gays. Three in every town. I wonder why three. Maybe he's smart; knows that the more he does, the greater the chances of being caught. Three's the magic number. But he's only done two in Vancouver. Two down, one to go. Steve's going to have his job cut out for him if he's going to find an out-of-town serial killer before he kills again.

I've spent the last ten days or so on this one case. Although Adry and Stammo have been working on the rest of our caseload, I'd better get dug in and pull my weight.

I open the spreadsheet which we use to track our cases, an innovation made by Stammo when we first started the business. We've got a lot on board at the moment. I update myself on each case until I come to one I was involved in before the kidnapping of Ariel Bradbury and it was—

"Absolutely Steve, no problem." The excitement

in Stammo's voice breaks my concentration. I look up and he gives me the thumbs-up. He listens with a big grin on his face interjecting the occasional "Sure," and "Right" and "Got it" into the conversation.

He puts down the phone.

"You'll never guess what," he says.

"What?"

"The VPD have asked us to help 'em. Seems like they can't get along without us."

I chuckle at his enthusiasm. "What do they want us to do?"

"They want me to go undercover into the GAMMA meeting and see if I can sniff out any suspicious activity. They figure the people at the meeting have already met me, so they might open up about who Dale and Paul hung out with."

"Why don't they send one of their own people?"

"Steve said something about sensitivity to the gay community. Said it was the fiftieth anniversary of Stonewall, whatever that is."

"Do you want me to come with you? As backup? I mean it could be dangerous if there's a killer in the group."

"Good point but no. I'll be OK. Maybe I'll go home first and get my Glock. Put a blanket over my legs and hide it underneath. Just in case."

"Make sure the safety's on."

"Right," he chuckles.

A former thought runs through my mind. "When you're there Nick, ask if Sean O'Day was ever there?"

"I thought we'd ruled him out as a suspect."

"Yeah I guess so, but not as a possible victim."

"OK. Good point."

Now's the time.

I've avoided it for too long.

"Nick we need to talk."

"What about?"

"What happened on the island." Muscles in his jaws tighten as he clenches his teeth. "Jim Garry says they've got a court date for the trial. It's in six weeks."

"Uh-huh," he grunts.

"It's just that I need to know what you are going to say. Are you going to back me up? Tell them the sequence of events that show it was self-defence?"

He doesn't speak, biting his lip. He won't make eye contact.

I resist the temptation to ask again, to basically plead.

Finally. "They searched my apartment."

"Yes, sure. They searched mine too. They didn't find anything did they?"

"That's it. I don't know for sure. They took a lot

of stuff. There could be something that ties us to the murders of Santiago and Perot."

"If there was, they'd have filed charges by now, surely."

He shrugs and goes silent for a bit. Then his voice is little more than a whisper. "They offered me immunity."

A cold hand grips my gut. "In return for what?"

There's embarrassment all over his face. "Steve said they might have found evidence that you were the shooter."

"So you're going to turn Queen's evidence on me?"

An even longer silence. Then, "I can't go to jail like this." He thumps the arms of his wheelchair, the wheelchair he's in because of my negligence two years ago.

Before I can respond, Adry unlocks the office door and walks in with donuts. It may be a cliché that cops love donuts but it's definitely true in this office.

But Adry mustn't hear any of this. Stammo shrugs and mouthes the words, "I'm sorry," before wheeling past Adry and out the door.

―――

DESPITE MY CONVERSATION with Stammo weighing on my mind, it's been a productive day. I've discovered the identity of a cheating husband's girlfriend; between us, Adry and I have tracked down six former employees of a now bankrupt airline; and Workers' Comp has given us a list of people to check out for possibly faking or exaggerating their injuries. All pretty boring stuff but boring can be good. It's certainly better than the drama of the last few weeks.

Nick came back for a while but has now gone home to pick up his gun and go to the GAMMA meeting and Adry left an hour ago.

I stand up and stretch. Holy mackerel, it's eight-fifteen; I've been in the office for over thirteen hours. A new indoor record. Shame Em has meetings again tonight, I really would like to get together with her. I wonder if I dare tell her about Samuel Island. I need to tell someone and I can't think of anyone else I could talk to. My feelings for her are... well... amazing. Probably a bit too soon for the 'L' word but it's not off the table.

OK. Stop acting like a love-sick teenager Cal Rogan. I'm going to head over to Stormcrow and eat a plate or two of wings and sample their fine choice of ales.

As I head for the door, my eye's diverted to the Vancouver Sun lying on the coffee table in reception. Right there at the bottom right hand corner is a picture of Em. The headline reads Southbrook VP High on Vancouver. Em never mentioned she was going to be in the newspaper. It's probably no big deal for her. She's a Vice-President of a major corporation and probably appears in the press and on TV all the time. It makes me wonder if maybe she's a bit out of my league. I'd never really thought about that. It gives me an uncomfortable feeling. I pick up the paper and start reading.

Southbrook, the high-end US department store is opening its first location in Canada. Located in downtown Vancouver on the site of the now defunct Harrows store, Southbrook hope to capitalize on the growing number of successful residents our City boasts. Maxine Audley, Southbrook's VP of—

Maxine? Her name's Emily. At least I thought it was. Then I remember her saying 'Call me Em.' I just assumed it was short for Emily, not the letter em. I grin. I'm starting to fall for a woman and I don't even know her name.

As I read on, enjoying the warm glow that reading about her produces in me, I get to find out all sorts of interesting new stuff about Em the businesswoman and her history with the firm.

Suddenly two names jump off the page and smack me in the face. My mind races over the options and suddenly all the wheels click into place. Why didn't I spot it before? I know who the killer is.

Stammo's at the GAMMA meeting. I dial his number. After five excruciating rings it goes to voicemail. I retry. Same thing. "Nick, it's Cal. Call me *as soon as you get this*. Sean O'Day is the killer. I'm just reading an article in the Sun about South-brook." I grab the paper, "It says, 'Over the last fif-teen months, Ms. Audley's team have opened stores in Tallahassee and Minneapolis.' They're the cities where the other murders happened." Then another thought hits; I worry it for a few seconds and then I know I'm right. "Oh my God Nick, one of the rea-sons we ruled O'Day out as a suspect was because he was Dale's lover. But we only have *his* word for it. When I followed him to Celebrities, maybe he was there looking for his next victim. Telling me he was Dale's lover was probably the first thing that came into his head. Wait! It was *me* who suggested it. He just agreed." I stop to think about this. It fits. And... "He probably told Marly Summers the same thing. On top of that, he was insistent I didn't tell Em he was gay. It must be because she almost certainly knows he's not." I stop, take a couple of deep breaths and make a snap decision. "I'm going after him be-fore he kills again." I hang up.

Boring cases may feel good for a while but *this* is what I live for.

55

STAMMO

I turn off the sound at the first ring and do a guilty check of the caller ID. Rogan. He can wait until the break. This speaker's interesting. He's one of the guys who was here on Wednesday in a business suit but today he's dressed for casual Friday. His story's a bit like mine: married, kids, macho job—although his is in the Stock Exchange, not law enforcement—still in the closet. Except that I'm not any more, telling Rogan and Adry was a lot easier than I thought it would be; maybe I'll tell this guy about it.

He comes to the end of his talk and one of the bikers called Noah, who's running the meeting today, says, "Thanks Jeff, good share. We'll take a break now. After the break, yours truly will talk about how he broke the news to the wife and kids and the people at work." Good. I'll be interested to hear about that.

Noah seems like he's been coming here regularly for a while, so I wheel over to him at the coffee table. I introduce myself and say, "Paul's not here tonight." It's an OK opening remark, I suppose.

"No, he usually comes to all the meetings." His voice is either Irish or Newfie. "He's in a real difficult situation with his wife and I think it helps him a lot." He hands me a coffee and chuckles. "He had a date Wednesday night. Maybe he hasn't recovered yet."

"With anyone here?"

"No idea. But he was pretty excited about it, I can tell you."

I think I'll work the Irish angle. "Is that an Irish accent?"

"No. I'm from the Rock." Ah, Newfoundland.

"I was asking because I wondered if you knew a friend of mine, he's Irish, name of Sean. In his thirties, dark hair, blue eyes. I think he comes to the meetings here. I was hoping to see him."

"Doesn't ring any bells with me."

We chat for a while and then I wheel over to another guy who was here on Wednesday, the one who looks like he's close to homeless. He's wearing an oversize black coat and the cop part of me won-ders if he uses it for shoplifting. I ask him the same questions but get the same answers.

Noah rings a little hand bell which sits on the podium. "Starting again in five."

The bell reminds me of Rogan's call. I check. He's left a voicemail. As I listen to him I can feel the blood drain from my face. He's going after a killer without backup. Idiot! Why the *fuck* does he do things like that?

"Anyone got a copy of today's Sun?" I ask the room in general.

"Got one here." Mr. Maybe Homeless pulls a dog-eared copy out of the pocket of his oversize black coat.

I snatch it from him and look at the article about Southbrook.

The shock's so great I shout out, "Nooooo!"

That dumb-ass Rogan has got one detail wrong.

56

CAL

I hand the Healey's keys to the valet with a quick, "Take good care of her," and start toward the revolving doors. As I get inside, it hits me. How do I find out O'Day's room number? Hotels are very picky about guest privacy, they're never going to tell me what room he's in. I stop and think. Maybe I should call Steve. Get him to send a couple of detectives. Except that old need's driving me; it may be better to wait for the VPD to arrive but *I* need to be the one making the collar. Beat the VPD to the punch. But how? Without his room number I'm hooped.

I'm not thinking straight. Take a pause for the cause Cal. Three deep breaths and let it all run out of me. Drop all the tension, all the urgency, all the thoughts pinging into my brain; focus on the breath, the sensations in my body, the sounds around me; examine each thought as it arises. Then, as if by magic, the solution appears. The Hotel Vancouver is owned by the same people who own the Waterfront where I've got a friend in high places except I don't know her last name.

I scan the lobby for a courtesy phone. Only one is free and I get to it just ahead of an elderly man. I pick up the phone and a voice says, *"Good evening how may I help you?"*

"Hello, I need to speak to one of your staff urgently."

"Certainly sir, who is it you need to talk to?"

"Her name's Alexis and she's with the conferences department at the Waterfront."

"Let me call her for you." I feel my impatience ramping up as I listen to Vivaldi for a full minute. *"I'm afraid she's gone for the day sir."*

Stifling the groan which springs to my lips, I say, "It's *really* important I speak to her, it's literally a life and death emergency."

"I understand sir, please hold." More Vivaldi fails to soothe the savage beast for a full two minutes. My cell rings but I ignore it. Finally, *"I've contacted her sir. She's on her cell. I'll connect her to you.* Silence, a click and, *"Alexis here, how can I help you."* Thank heavens for five star hotels.

"Hi Alexis, this is Cal Rogan, we met last month

at the Waterfront. I was part of the security team for the debate between Larry Corliss and Edward Perot."

"Oh yes. I remember. I told you about the man in the boots having been in the corridor. You escorted him off the premises." Thank heaven for five star hotels who hire wonderful people. *"How can I help you this evening?"*

"I'm dealing with a potentially very dangerous situation. I'm at the Hotel Van and there's a guest I need to approach. His name's Sean O'Day and I need to know his room number. I know it's against hotel policy but it really is critically important."

Silence on the line. If this doesn't work I'm going to have to give up and call Steve. I relax my shoulders and take a breath. *"Just hold for a second."* It doesn't sound good; she's going to ask her boss who's going to ask more questions. I check my watch. Less than twenty minutes have elapsed since I saw the news article. Feels like a lifetime. *"I'm not really supposed to do this but Mr. O'Day is in room six-thirteen."*

"Thank you, thank you so much."

"You're very welcome. Is there anything else I can help you with this evening?"

"No you've done more than enough. I owe you a bottle of champagne. Make that two bottles."

I hang up and run for the elevator.

57

MAX

He's secured to the bed and is just starting to come round. Number three in Tallahassee was in a hotel room but that was anonymous. I'm paying for this room. When this number three is done, I'm going to have to disappear. It's a shame really; working for Southbrook has been good cover. Not too long in each city. Do three and move on. But I think a change is going to be nice. Start over in a new city with a new name and a new job. I need a new M.O. too. Pretending to be gay makes me sick to my stomach. I can't stand it when they touch me, try to kiss me. Pretending to like it is way too much work. So away I must fly.

His eyes open.

"Why hello."

He focuses in on me. At first he doesn't recognize me in the crime scene suit. Then it hits: confusion.

"Let me tell you why you're here." I've decided to tell him before I start the procedure. Number two couldn't really concentrate after I'd done the amputation, so he didn't get the full impact of why he was one of the chosen three. I was just too hasty there. This one will be just like number one. He'll know before I start.

"Let me tell you a little story," I begin. I open my backpack and take out the tailor's shears. I start to cut off his clothes. "Once upon a time," I take a leisurely cut from right wrist to collar, then left wrist to collar, "there was a very happy family." I yank the shirt off him. "There was a daddy." I cut from left ankle to waist, then from right ankle to waist. "There was a mommy." I pull off the tatters of his jeans and underwear. His disgusting thing's all shrivelled up in fear. It looks like a mushroom. I open the shears and place them on his belly one blade each side of the mushroom. "And there were two lovely little girls."

I bring the poker and blowtorch out of my backpack and rest the former on its homemade stand. "The older little girl went off to college but the younger one stayed at home." I take out the lighter and light the blowtorch. I move it into position and the flame caresses the end of the poker. "The little girl who stayed home met a boy and fell in love so she decided not to join her sister in college. Her older sister was very sad."

I look into his eyes and I can feel his terror. It starts the tingling in my belly. Oh, yes.

"When she got married the older sister was happy for her but sad for herself." I take the knife out and lay it on his chest and I shudder. Oooh. It feels nice. "But the little sister's husband was a very bad man, a degenerate man, a disgusting man. He told her he couldn't be with her. That he wanted to be with men, do things with men he said he couldn't do with her. He left her and went to live in Tallahassee."

I rotate the poker. The end's starting to take on a roseate hue.

"The younger sister was very sad but the older sister was happy because she knew that now they could go to college together. Do great things in the big wild world."

His eyes are gigantic now. Oooooh. I know what I can add. After the branding and the amputation. I can take his eyes too. No, no. Just one eye. He must watch the *coup de grâce* with the other eye. Yes, that feels right.

"But the younger sister could not live with her grief and the poor darling killed herself. All because of a degenerate like you."

I take the poker and rotate it one more time. Nice and orangey now. Almost there.

"So the older sister worked hard and made something of her life. But she was always planning to avenge her lovely sister. As luck would have it, she found herself working for a few months in Tallahassee. She tracked down her erstwhile brother-in-law and took her sweet, sweet revenge. But it just wasn't enough. She thought of all the other poor girls who were being betrayed by their degenerate husbands, so she, shall we say, killed two birds with one stone. By killing two more, it covered up the killing of the brother-in-law. And it felt so, so good. In fact it was so good, she made it her life's work to kill all those bad men who left their sweet, innocent wives to be with other degenerates."

He's shaking his head now. "I know Sean, I know. You didn't leave a wife did you?" He shakes his head faster. "But you were the one who lured Dale away from his poor Marly. You were the corrupter in their sad little story. The snake in their garden."

"You're Irish, you'll appreciate the irony here." I can't resist a little laugh. "The Friday before last, I dressed up like a man and went to that den of degenerates to find a candidate for punishment because he had broken his vows. I pulled up in my car and who should I see entering the church basement but your lover Dale. Although it wasn't my plan to kill someone I already knew, I felt that a bountiful Providence had dropped Dale into my lap. I called him and told him there was an emergency and I needed to meet him as soon as possible. He invited me over to his condo; the little love nest for his extra-curricular activities. During his punishment, I, mmm, shall we say, *persuaded* him to reveal the name of his lover and imagine my surprise when I learned it was you."

The poker's bright orange.

I pull on the insulated gloves.

"This is for my sister."

He's thrashing around on the bed. And the tingling in my belly spreads up... and down. Yes, that feels good. I think this will be the best yet. Ooooooh, yes.

58

CAL

I'm outside his room and suddenly I don't know what to do. Should I try and kick the door down or just knock? I notice the peephole in the door. If he sees me, how will he react? I put my ear to the door. It sounds like the murmur of conversation but I can't be certain; might be the television. We'll see.

I knock and resist the cliché of saying 'Room Service.' I'll leave that for the movies.

Nothing.

I wait thirty seconds or so.

I put my eye to the peephole but there is just blurry light. What I need is one of those lenses which reverses the effect of the peephole; ERT teams have them. I see movement. Then nothing. I move back and knock again. Louder. A triple knock. He can't miss that.

Nothing.

Another long thirty seconds.

He's in there I'm sure. So maybe I'll just camp out here and call Steve. He can make the arrangements for the hotel management to open the door. I squat down with my back to the wall and pull out my phone. Two missed calls from Stammo. I'll call him back after I've spoken to Steve.

I scroll through my contacts and just as I get to Steve the door opens.

I stand up.

"Why Cal Rogan, I do declare. What *are* you doing here?"

The shock of her being here morphs quickly into worry.

"Is Sean O'Day in there?" I ask.

"He surely is. Come in."

I hesitate for a moment. I put my finger to my lips, take hold of her hand and pull her gently out into the hallway.

I step past her into the room and into a small entranceway. I hear the door close behind me.

Then I see him.

"What the—"

And the world explodes.

"MMMMMGHHHH." The shock of cold water snaps me awake. I open my eyes and it all comes back. Em's dressed in a crime scene suit. She drops the ice bucket on the carpet. I try to speak. Something's in my mouth and I can't spit it out. There's a hissing in my ears. I'm tied to a hotel chair with duct tape. It's even more secure than Javier's work on Hardy Island and this time there's no RCMP ERT team waiting outside the window.

"Now don't you worry none, Cal." She says it like she's talking to a kid. "I'm not going to hurt you. It's unfortunate you showed up when you did but it won't change anything." She looks at me, thinking. "I'm wondering why you did show up here. Did you work out that it was me?" Another pause. "No. You didn't. But it was just a matter of time, I suspect." Her accent's much stronger now. "I hired you so I would know what was going on. The information you fed me was very helpful in sewing a false trail. I'm going to miss you Cal."

She played me and I'm screwed. Despite what she says, she can't just let me go. I'm a dead man.

"You can watch me work. I've become a true artisan at this. My daddy used to say, 'Max, you're too good with your hands to do a degree in business, you should be in the fine arts.' Poor daddy, he'd always wanted his first-born to be a boy. They christened me Maxine but he always called me Max. I never liked it; always told people to call me Em. Even when I was a little one. But the name *has* been useful.

"Poor, poor, Daddy blamed himself for my sister's death. He only outlived her by one year, seven months and three days. *He* deserted me too. Of course, he wasn't to blame. It was the swine she married. A filthy degenerate like this one." She inclines her head toward O'Day.

As she talks I go through a litany of everything I learned at the BC Justice Institute. We had a class on hostage negotiation but it's just a bit tricky to negotiate if you can't talk. I move in the chair. One small chance. Maybe.

"Cal you're an educated man, you must know the expression 'strike while the iron's hot.'" I nod, step one in negotiation: establish a connection. "Well did you know it dates back to the fifteen-hundreds? It was used in a play about two characters named Damon and Pithias." I did know that and I nod enthusiastically.

She gives that laugh I was starting to love. "Look at *you*," she says. "Trying to establish rapport."

She moves to the credenza and my eyes follow. I can see the source of the hissing. There's a blowtorch. It has heated the head of an old-fashioned poker to a bright orange. I shudder from the knowledge of how the digits were branded onto Dale's stomach.

"You can watch Cal. I think having you watch me will heighten my pleasure. Yes, I think it will. It will take about half an hour. Then I'll leave. By the time room service comes in the morning to make up the bed, I will be a long, long, long way away.

"But now... watch and learn." A Stammo expression. I feel the vibration of my phone. It's probably him.

She takes the poker and moves back toward the bed. She puts her head on one side and then the other as if trying to decide how best to proceed. Then she moves between me and the bed.

With every erg of energy I can summon I rock. Once. Twice. It's working. If I can just topple over onto her. Three. She turns and smiles and pushes her free hand down on top of my head, stopping the rocking instantly. "Now Cal, I promised I wouldn't hurt you because I know you're not one of *them*. Do I ever know that! But if you distract me again, there will be a punishment."

She returns to her task and I can hear O'Day's body thrashing around on the bed. His scream through his gag is a muted "Mmmmmmghhhhh."

Suddenly his volume cranks up but not enough to mask the sound of sizzling.

Then everything's overwhelmed by thunder.

The door crashes open.

"Armed police! Drop the weapon!"

She doesn't even turn. She swings the poker up over her head. I see her muscles tense as she prepares to smash it down on O'Day's skull. But the crack in my ear is the sound of the nine millimetre bullet crossing the space of ten feet in eight milliseconds.

Em's body crumples to the floor.

There is silence.

Only the ringing in my ears.

And the smell of burnt flesh.

———

"How did you know to come here?" I ask Steve. He inclines his head toward the door. Stammo's sitting in the hallway, in his wheelchair, sporting a VPD vest. He's grinning like a loon. I walk out of the room, kneel beside the chair and envelope him in a hug. He reciprocates with a man-hug: two quick slaps on the back.

"Just 'cause I came out to you," he whispers, "doesn't mean I've got the hots for you." Our excessively riotous laughter is a big reaction to the relief we both feel.

When the quasi-hysteria abates, I ask it again. "How *did* you know I'd be here?"

"When I got to your voicemail, I asked someone for a copy of the Sun. Fortunately for you someone had one. As soon as I saw the article I knew it was her."

"How did you know?"

"I saw her picture and I knew who she was. When I was at the GAMMA meeting on Wednesday there was a guy there named Max with a blond brush-cut. I remember at the time thinking he was a bit too effeminate for my taste but didn't think anything of it... until I got your voicemail and then saw his, or actually her, picture in the paper."

"But how did you know she'd be *here*?"

"I didn't at first. My first thought was to get here before you did some damage to poor old Sean O'-Day. But then I got to thinking: serial killers usually don't know their victims. She was picking them up at GAMMA meetings. But she *did* know Dale, that was a break in the pattern, a big sign she was losing it, escalating out of control. I wondered if you had told her about me being in a wheelchair and that maybe, when she saw me at the GAMMA meeting, she knew who I was. That would have made GAMMA off limits for her. But she needed another victim. Maybe she knew about Sean being Dale's lover. It made him the low hanging fruit. She killed the others in their homes so if she was going to kill Sean she'd do it in his hotel room."

"Nick you are a friggin' genius."

"Rogan, I keep telling you... Yes, I am." I grin at him and he adds, "She hired us because she wanted to keep ahead of the investigation."

He's right. I think of all the things I reported to her and everything fits. It fits like a jigsaw.

"You were right about something else too Nick; the reference to Luke Summers' church wasn't in the *twenty-thirteen.com* metadata until *after* I told her about the church on Sunday night. She was playing us."

"I was right again? Imagine that."

But his lighthearted words somehow push me in the opposite direction.

How could I not have known it was Em? As I think it over some more, I remember something she said at our dinner in Al Porto. *'Do you think she's the sort of person who could commit such a gruesome crime?'* It was to steer me away from thinking about a female killer but I missed the real importance of the question. How did she know the killing was gruesome? Up to that point I had never discussed the details with her.

I stand up and turn back toward the room.

Em's crumpled body is lying where it fell. I shake my head, hoping to wake myself up and discover it was all a dream. It's not. How could I not have known? Am I so blind I could have such strong feelings for a serial killer? Even as I look at her now, the moments of our time together flicker across the screen of my memory and I feel the tenderness I felt before.

"You couldn't'a known." Not just a genius, Stammo's a mindreader too. But he's wrong. I *should* have known. It's my *job* to know. I'm a detective for heaven's sake.

A detective!

I can't stop the tears streaming down my face.

59

CAL
SUNDAY

ere they come!" I smile at the excitement and glee in Florrie's voice and I hear a chuckle from Phil. I watch as the first two congregants push through the doors of the Church of the Pure Divine Light. As luck would have it, it's Milly and Edna. As they stop and blink in the sunlight, Florrie says, "Hello, here's a little gift from Pastor Kilman." She hands them each a thumb drive with my recording of Kilman's wife prompting him through his nasty little con game. She also gives each of them a lavender-coloured envelope.

"What's this?" asks Milly, still in her purple hat.

"Think of it as a small documentary. Put it in your computer and listen to the recording." I say.

Florrie and Phil start handing out the flash drives and envelopes to the other congregants flooding out of the 'church'. Most of the crowd know them and are happy to take the gift.

I feel a hand on my arm. "Hello Cal, did Pastor Kilman help you get in touch with Elizabeth?" There's nothing wrong with Edna's memory.

"It's all in the documentary. I hope you enjoy it Edna."

"I'm sure I will."

I can't resist giving her a little hug before joining Phil and Florrie. The three of us hand out the recordings and envelopes to any in the crowd who will take them and our activity does not go unnoticed. Before too long Kilman comes barging through the doors, anger and fear painted on his face in equal proportions. "What the hell do you think you're doing?" he asks.

"Shutting you down," I say with a grin.

His eyes narrow and he steps toward me, the violence coiled inside him about to spring out. I just smile and incline both my head and my gaze toward the two RCMP members walking up to us.

He turns and the rage washes out of his face.

"Peter Kilman?" the first officer asks.

He nods, unable to speak.

"Would you mind coming with us sir? We have some questions we'd like to ask you."

I feel myself being enveloped in a big hug from Florrie. "Thank you Detective Rogan, thank you.

Phil and I decided. We're going to get everyone together and sue Kilman for all the money he bilked from his congregation. It's all in the envelopes I'm giving to them."

Today was definitely worth getting up for.

60

CAL

TUESDAY. SIX WEEKS LATER

Before yesterday morning, I had never sat in this seat, although I've looked at it often enough. I am surrounded by bulletproof glass on three sides and have a perfect view of the courtroom. Behind the judge's bench, the oak panelling, for some reason, holds the British rather than the Canadian coat of arms.

I can only see the backs of the lawyers. They are all wearing their black gowns and from this angle they remind me of crows. There's a Crown Prosecutor and his assistant in front of me and to the left of them is Jim Garry. He rises to his feet, tugs down on his jacket, glances down at the red carpet, then looks towards Stammo sitting in his wheelchair beside the raised witness box.

Since he wheeled in, waited for the judge to be

announced and seated, and was then sworn in, Stammo has not once looked in my direction. Even now as he answers the preliminary questions he doesn't hazard a glance at me.

After the initial questions, Garry asks, "Mr. Stammo, can you tell me what you were doing on Wednesday April seventeenth?"

Stammo clears his throat and glances down at his hands for an instant. He seems to be holding something and rubbing his thumb against it.

He looks up. "Mr. Rogan and I were surveilling the residence of Carlos Santiago on Samuel Island, BC. Mr. Rogan was on the Island and I was on a boat moored off the island." He stops and cuts a quick glance at me. Why is he doing that? It makes him look guilty of something. I look towards Justice Bernice Lemay. She is watching Stammo closely.

"What was your reason for conducting this surveillance?"

"We had been hired to find a missing child and we had reason to believe she was on the island in the residence of Mr. Santiago. It turned out we were right; she was there."

Jim Garry gestures towards the other lawyers. "Although he has offered no evidence in support of it, my learned friend has suggested several times that Mr. Rogan was there for the purposes of assassinating Mr. Santiago and Mr. Edward Perot. Is that correct?"

Now's the first hurdle. Will Stammo perjure himself or will the next chapter of my life be spent behind bars?

Stammo looks towards the judge. He speaks in a clear voice. "Yes."

The shock travels through me like an electric charge. Stammo is giving me up.

"It's correct that's what the prosecution is alleging," he continues, "but it's a ridiculous suggestion. Mr. Rogan is not an assassin."

The relief washes through me and I know it must be obvious to anyone watching me. Fortunately, the judge is watching Stammo not me.

"Yet the police were unable to find any evidence that there was another person on the island who might have committed those murders." Garry is preempting the CP's likely argument.

"It's a big island and if my guess is right, they were killed by a rival gang. I understand that the police found evidence that there were explosions on the island, which I can verify because I heard them. They could have been a diversion used by the killer or killers. In addition, I saw a boat leave the island but it was shot at by some people in another boat and it sank." Thank heaven Stammo has thought this through.

"I understand that you were kidnapped by the son of Carlos Santiago. Is that correct?"

"Yes."

"Why would he do that?"

"Because the Crown Prosecutor's office rushed to charge Mr. Rogan with the murders of Santiago and Perot. Santiago's son must have learned about it and decided to seek revenge on Mr. Rogan. The CP's actions put the lives of Mr. Rogan, his family and myself in deadly danger."

Another nice point. Judge Lemay's eyes are levelled at the Crown Prosecutor.

Garry waits for a moment until the judge looks toward him. "Your son, Matthew Stammo, was a member of Carlos Santiago's gang."

Stammo's demeanour changes. It's like he has been punched. "Yes." His voice is barely above a whisper now.

"Can you tell the court the circumstances that led up to your son's death?"

This is the second hurdle. This time, if he *does* perjure himself I'll be behind bars. He's silent. He hasn't decided. The silence lengthens. You could hear a pin drop.

"Mr. Rogan killed him."

"I'm sorry for your loss Mr. Stammo. Can you tell the court why Mr. Rogan killed him?"

Another long silence.

"It was self defence" There's a catch in his throat. "He had to do it or Matt would have killed him."

Again I can't hide the relief. Garry asks for details but I don't even hear them.

———

I STAND in the doorway taking a last look at the courtroom. I look at the now-vacant judge's bench beneath the ornate coat of arms bearing the motto *Dieu et Mon Droit*. Stammo came through for me. After hearing his testimony, Justice Bernice Lemay had no hesitation in finding me not guilty in the murder of Matthew Stammo.

I turn and walk out of the courtroom a free man.

He's waiting for me in the hallway outside. As we head for the elevators I say, "Thanks man."

"S'OK," he sighs. "Y'know, sometimes water's thicker than blood."

We are silent until we get to the elevator. "D'you want to go for a beer? Celebrate?" he asks, not too enthusiastically.

"Maybe tomorrow. I've got something I need to do."

We take the elevator in silence and go our separate ways.

———

I LISTEN ENTRANCED to everything she has to say. She likes her new school, sorry she can't tell me the name but Mommy says she can't. She only went there for a week before the summer holidays started. And the new apartment's nice and she likes the boy next door; he goes to the same school as her. She chatters on about the things in her life and I long to just hold her in my arms, hug her and tell her how much I love her.

Then in typical Ellie fashion she does a rapid gear change. "Remember when we were on Grandpa's island and I stabbed that bad man with the screwdriver?" She doesn't wait for a reply before going on. "I was just like a policeman wasn't I Daddy? I made the bad man move. And that's what got him shot. Do you think I'd be a good detective because that's what I want to be? What do you think Daddy? Would I be?"

As she stops for breath I get in with, "Yes sweetie you would be a wonderful detective. But are you sure that's what you want to do? You're very good at math and science, maybe you should be a scientist."

"Well detectives use science don't they Daddy? I could be a detective and a scientist couldn't I?"

"Yes sweetie, you could."

She does another gear change. "Ooo, ooo, I forgot to tell you, Mommy said we can have a kitten..."

As her enthusiasm spills out of the phone, I try and join her in it but there's still a great weight on my shoulders. I look toward the kitchen. "El," I say as she pauses for breath again, "can I speak to Mommy please?"

She goes silent. "Uh, Mommy said she wouldn't be able to speak to you right now. She said the call was just for you and me."

I've had no contact with Sam since Hardy Island. Ellie calls every week from a number with a blocked caller ID but Sam always refuses to speak to me. I want to tell her I was found not guilty. Not that it would make a difference. She knows what I've done and it's the wedge that will forever keep us apart.

"Anyway Daddy, Mommy's making that sign that means it's my bedtime, so I have to go."

We say our goodnights and she hangs up. It's five in the afternoon. If it's Ellie's bedtime it must be eight or nine o'clock where she is. That's three or maybe four timezones east. I was hoping...

I feel the loss deeply. Not just of Ellie and Sam but also of Em. I can't get her out of my mind.

Only work pushes down the memories. Most of the time anyway.

Right now... there is only one thing that will do the trick.

I walk into the kitchen and look at the eight

items laid out on the countertop: spoon, sterile water, lighter, cotton ball, needle, elastic strip, syringe and a tiny baggy of what I hope is just heroin.

Time to give in to the Beast and embrace the solace of Morpheus.

AFTERWORD

Thank you for reading *Three*. Reviews are the life blood of an independent author. If you have a minute to do a review on Amazon, it would be *really* appreciated. Also, a review at Goodreads or Bookbub is always appreciated.

I invite you to read the other books in the series: *Junkie, Oboe, Lockstep, Cabal, Captive* and *Jailed*. All are available in large print paperback from Amazon.

ABOUT THE AUTHOR

Hi. I am a former software developer, turned actor, turned author. The Cal Rogan mysteries are set in Vancouver Canada and, I hope, reflect the best and worst of the city. If you would like to know more about my views on the drug scene, publishing and writing, or would like to contact me:

My website: robertpfrench.com.

Facebook: facebook.com/robertpfrenchauthor

www.ingramcontent.com/pod-product-compliance
Lightning Source LLC
Chambersburg PA
CBHW072301020726
47501CB00002B/336